"I vowed never to get involved with a man who worked in a dangerous job."

"Like cops...and firemen?"

"Exactly like cops and firemen." His handsome face was heartbreakingly compassionate at that moment, but she'd struck him down again.

"Listen, Beatrice. I'm a highly trained and skilled fire jumper. I'm certainly more careful going into a fire than you were. I know what I'm doing. Seriously."

"It's still dangerous. You're not an accountant who sits in an office behind a computer all day. You risk your life for others!"

"I certainly do," he replied proudly.

This had to stop. With each moment she spent with Rand, their attraction grew. That kiss... No. It was more than attraction. Her heart was opening to him, and she couldn't let that continue.

But another part of her grew queasy with uncertainty, as if warning her that she was making the wrong decision...

Dear Reader,

I'm thrilled and humbled that you are reading my newest story in the Shores of Indian Lake series. Earlier this year, Hallmark Channel aired the movie *The Sweetest Heart*, which is based on book two of the series, *Heart's Desire*, now also available under the same title as the movie at Harlequin.com and on Amazon.

As I moved into writing Beatrice Wilcox's story, I was aware of one of the aspects that make our Harlequin Heartwarming stories so poignant: not only do our heroines and heroes find their happy-ever-after, but their dreams really do come true. Beatrice is hardworking and has put everything on the line for her children's camp. Of all my heroines, Beatrice has the biggest heart. She is all love. She's who I strive to be.

The kids in the story, little Eli and Chris, have been abandoned by their parents. When Chris accidentally sets the nearby forest on fire, Beatrice runs into the fire to save the boys, never thinking of her own safety.

Rand Nelson, firefighter, comes to the rescue. Spellbound by Beatrice's courage and love, Rand can't help but fall for her. However, Rand works in a dangerous job and Beatrice has sworn she will never be with a man who takes such risks.

I hope you enjoy this and all the Indian Lake stories. Believe me when I say I can't write the next half dozen fast enough!

God bless and happy reading,

Catherine

HEARTWARMING

Rescued by the Firefighter

—

Catherine Lanigan

❖ HARLEQUIN® HEARTWARMING™

Recycling programs
for this product may
not exist in your area.

ISBN-13: 978-1-335-63388-0

Rescued by the Firefighter

Copyright © 2018 by Catherine Lanigan

This edition published by arrangement with Harlequin Books S.A.

For questions and comments about the quality of this book, please contact us at CustomerService@Harlequin.com.

® and TM are trademarks of Harlequin Enterprises Limited or its corporate affiliates. Trademarks indicated with ® are registered in the United States Patent and Trademark Office, the Canadian Intellectual Property Office and in other countries.

Printed in U.S.A.

Catherine Lanigan knew she was born to storytelling at a very young age when she told stories to her younger brothers and sister to entertain them. After years of encouragement from family and high school teachers, Catherine was shocked and brokenhearted when her freshman college creative-writing professor told her that she had "no writing talent whatsoever" and that she would never earn a dime as a writer.

For fourteen years she did not write until she was encouraged by a television journalist to give her dream a shot. That was nearly forty published novels, nonfiction books and anthologies ago. To add to the dream, Hallmark Channel has recently released *The Sweetest Heart*, based on the second book in her Harlequin Heartwarming series, Shores of Indian Lake. With more books in the series and more movies to come, Catherine makes her home in La Porte, Indiana, the inspiration for Indian Lake.

Books by Catherine Lanigan

Harlequin Heartwarming

Shores of Indian Lake

Family of His Own
His Baby Dilemma

Visit the Author Profile page
at Harlequin.com for more titles.

This book is dedicated to my husband, Jed Nolan, who was my hero on earth and is now my protector on The Other Side. It is love that brings heaven and earth together. You prove that to me every day. I love you to the moon and back and all the universes and galaxies between and beyond.

ACKNOWLEDGMENTS

My sincere thanks to my agent, Lissy Peace, who said, "Why don't you write about a Youth Camp and a smoke jumper?" Little did I know that this story would take on a life of its own—like a raging fire—so quickly. Thank you to Claire Caldwell, my former editor, who worked on the initial story line with me. And a big hug to my editor, Adrienne Macintosh, who took over after Claire's departure and jumped into the story with me. I'm looking forward to the next books with you, Adrienne.

To Kathleen Scheibling, Heartwarming's executive editor, and always to Dianne Moggy for over two decades of working together. The next twenty years won't be enough.

CHAPTER ONE

Indian Lake, Indiana
July

THE SUMMER NIGHT sounds of chirping tree frogs and cicadas drifted through the open screen window of Beatrice Wilcox's sixty-year-old log cabin. Loving the wildlife melodies, she closed her eyes, her weary body spent from a long day with ten rowdy, sometimes frustratingly taciturn children and preteens.

But running this camp was her dream. She wanted to create a summer idyll for kids who faced challenges in their young lives, as she had when she'd been a camper herself as a child.

But how to pay for it? Worrying over money often kept her awake at night. Tonight being no exception.

She kicked the old patchwork quilt off her body. Then she flung her forearm over her brow. She was still wide awake.

Breathing a sigh, she sniffed the air. And froze. Then sniffed again.

"It...can't be."

Curling through the screen was pungent smoke. Not the smoke from a cigarette or cigar, or the acrid, bitter smoke from a country farmer burning garbage. This was clean smoke. The kind from burning vegetation.

Beatrice bolted upright in her bed, her eyes wide. She tossed aside the sheets and swung her legs to the rag rug she'd made herself that covered the painted concrete floor.

"No!"

Going to the window, she cranked the casement window open wide. The smell of smoke was unmistakable. "Not a fire. Not now. Not ever!"

Spinning around, she shoved her feet into her sneakers and grabbed her cell phone off the varnished tree-stump table.

"Please don't let it be one of the cabins. Or the kitchen!" She raced out to her front porch, the wood screen door banging behind her. The yellow "bug" light on the front porch did a good job of keeping the mosquitoes and flies away, but unfortuntely gave little illumination. She leaned over the wide log railing that extended down the four steps to the gravel path that served as her sidewalk.

The camp consisted of ten sturdy small log cabins, with five on either side of the main dining hall and activities center. Up the hill at the end of the five cabins was a larger cabin that housed the male counselors, though right now there was only the one. Beatrice's cabin was on the left side after the five girls' cabins and a larger cabin for the female counselors.

Her eyes scoured the little cabins and the main hall. She saw nothing amiss.

Walking farther down the path, she stopped abruptly as a crimson glow illuminated the side of her face. She turned toward the forest that stretched for acres across the country road. "Oh, no!"

Forest fire.

The summer had been hot and dry with barely a sprinkle of rain in the past month. The Weather Channel had said it was the driest summer in Indian Lake history. This was Southern California weather, not northern Indiana weather. July was known for heat in Indiana, and even soared over one hundred degrees, but seldom did the region get this dry. In recent weeks, the corn was withering on the stalks. The leaves of the soybean crops were already turning golden six weeks ahead of normal.

She punched in 911 on her phone.

"What is your emergency?" the dispatcher asked.

"Fire! I'm at Indian Lake Youth Camp. Up Highway Thirty-Five. There's fire in the woods across the road. It's been so dry, I'm afraid the fire could move fast and head right for us."

She looked around and saw the light in Maisie and Cindy's cabin switch on. Cindy had just turned twenty-two, and though a year younger than Maisie, she possessed a child's boundless energy. She was pulling a light sweatshirt over her head as she rushed out onto her porch.

Beatrice beckoned to Cindy, who started running toward her, her sneakers digging into the gravel with purpose.

Cindy's streaked blond hair was clipped up on her head into a thick spike, making her look just like Cindy Lou Who from the Grinch cartoon. There was nothing comical about the fear in Cindy's face, however. She pointed to the fire. "This is a nightmare."

"It is," Beatrice replied, still listening to the dispatcher.

"The units have been sent. They're on their way," the dispatcher said.

"Thank you," Beatrice said and hung up

while simultaneously grabbing Cindy's arm. Cindy was shaking.

"Cindy, look at me. This is no time to panic. We have to get the kids up and dressed. Then you and Bruce need to take them to St. Mark's."

"St. Mark's?" Cindy's voice cracked.

"Yes. You remember, right?" Beatrice asked firmly. Beatrice knew she could do this.

But Beatrice was their leader. She was responsible for these children. Their lives might depend on her tonight.

More than the danger the fire posed to her beloved camp, it was the children she cared about. Each child was a gift to her. She took special care to learn their needs and idiosyncrasies, their fears and their delights.

When misgivings about money turned to dark moments, when she wondered why she'd placed all her dreams into this black hole of continual and costly restoration, she reminded herself it was for the kids, whom she cared about as if they were family.

"Cindy…"

"St. Mark's! I remember. Father Michael offered his activity hall in case of any emergency." Cindy brushed a lock of her hair away from her cheek. "This definitely qualifies."

"Yes, it does, Cindy. Wake up Bruce. Believe me, it takes a bomb to get that guy up. You and Bruce wake up the boys. Maisie and I will take the girls' cabins. Get everyone to the dining hall first, then hustle them into the SUVs and drive them into town."

"What about you?"

"I have to stay here. It's my camp. Now, go!"

As Cindy raced off to Bruce's cabin, Beatrice waved to Maisie.

Maisie had put on jeans, sneakers and a light hooded pullover. She held up her cell phone as she ran toward Beatrice. "I'll get the girls."

While Cindy was all emotion, hugging the kids, giving them encouragement, Maisie was the organized, Excel-sheet-minded counselor who kept the kids in line. She also helped order the food and had their consumption quantities down to the number of tiny boxes of raisins and bars of soap they would need each month.

"Yes. Good thing I filled up the SUVs' gas tanks yesterday. We are good to go," Beatrice replied as they went to the first girls' cabin.

Jessica and Susan Kettering were two sisters from Chicago whose parents were in Europe for work. The girls were living at the camp for a month, and Beatrice had gotten to know them well.

The girls, ages six and eight, both had amblyopia, or lazy eye. They refused to wear their eye patches on corresponding eyes at the same time. Thus, Jessica's patch was on her right eye for six months, and Susan's patch was on her left eye. In addition, they both had myopia and couldn't read or see objects up close. Their glasses were thick and cumbersome for many of the sports, but their lighthearted attitudes overcame their personal struggles. Beatrice admired their closeness; they were always holding hands and helping each other.

Jessica awoke first. "What is it, Miss Beatrice?" She rubbed her eyes.

Jessica was thin and short, and had cropped auburn hair. She looked like a little ladybug to Beatrice, because she had a smattering of freckles across her nose. "Bruce and Cindy are going to drive you kids into town."

"But why?" Susan asked, putting her glasses on before she sat up in bed. She lifted her little arms to Maisie.

Maisie leaned down to the girl. Beatrice didn't know what it was about Susan, but she had a way of melting Maisie's analytical heart.

As Maisie whisked the child out of bed and to the floor, Beatrice pulled a long-sleeved T-shirt over Jessica's head. She held out a pair of pull-on pants.

"Once these two are dressed, Maisie, take them to the SUVs. I'm going to the next cabin. Belinda and Sherry are older. They can meet you at the SUVs. Then I'll get Aubrey and Anna."

"Got it," Maisie said, tying Susan's shoes. "In fact, you should go now. I'll help Jessica with her shoes."

"I can tie my own," Jessica said proudly. "It's okay, Miss Beatrice. I can help Maisie with Susan," Jessica insisted. "She's my sister."

Beatrice felt her eyes sting with tears and a lump invade her throat. Jessica was so precious to her—if those flames came anywhere near…

"You're such a help, Jessica." Beatrice leaned down and kissed the top of her head.

Maisie stood upright, her eyes darting to Beatrice. "You did call Father Michael, right?"

Sucking in a deep breath, Beatrice halted. She'd been so concerned about getting the kids out of danger, that she'd skipped a step. "I—I…"

"It's understandable," Maisie said, her eyes going to Beatrice's back pocket, where she kept her phone.

Beatrice yanked the cell out of her pocket and found Father Michael's number.

He picked up on the first ring.

"Bless you for answering so quickly, Father Michael. It's Beatrice Wilcox at the youth camp. I need your help."

"Name it," he replied.

Beatrice had only just started her explanation when Father Michael stopped her. He was already on his way to the church's activity hall to turn on the lights and fans. "I'll have everything ready."

He hung up.

"Maisie, are you sure you're all right here?" Beatrice asked, knowing that the girls' eye conditions caused them to stumble and trip a great deal in addition to their having trouble dressing.

"I'm fine. We're fine," Maisie assured her.

Beatrice shot out the cabin door and paused for a moment to see Bruce taking two of the younger boys to the large black SUV. "Bruce!" she shouted.

"It's A-OK! Cindy is checking the last cabin."

"Good…" Beatrice's voice trailed off as she glanced across the road. Flames snaked along the ground. The mounds of dry pine nettles around the trees sparked like tiny fireworks as they ignited. Then the tongues of fire wove up and around the tree trunks, following the growth of poison ivy and clinging vines.

In the distance she heard sirens pierce the summer night. At the sound, she felt the first burst of hope since she'd breathed in the smell of smoke. "Hurry," she breathed.

Racing to the SUV, she found Bruce belting in nine-year-old Joshua Langsford. Joshua had tears in his eyes.

"Are we going to be all right, Miss Beatrice?" the dark-haired boy with the leg brace asked.

She ruffled his hair and wiped his tears away with her fingertip. "Yes, sweetie. Bruce is taking you all to Father Michael's church hall. You'll stay there until the firemen put the fire out. He and Cindy will stay with you all night. Maisie will drive in later and help bring you back when it's safe. Don't you be afraid. You're a brave boy, Joshua. If you can survive all the pain from your leg surgeries, you can do this. You help Bruce with the younger boys, okay?"

"Okay," Joshua replied, pursing his lips and slamming his back against the seat.

Cindy came rushing up with five-year-old Ricky Sanders, the youngest child at the camp that week. He was a foster child, hoping to be legally adopted by his new foster parents, and was Cindy's personal favorite. "Did one of you get the Dunning boys?"

"Eli and Chris are in the last cabin," Beatrice replied. "I thought you were getting them."

"I was…" Cindy hesitated, looking at Ricky. She put Ricky in his child's seat and belted him in. She turned away from the boy so that only Beatrice could hear her. Nearly in a whisper Cindy said, "They weren't there. That's why I thought one of you might have gotten to them already."

"What?" Chills spread over Beatrice's body faster than any fire could eat a dried leaf.

"Tell Maisie to check the common areas. I'll do a sweep of their cabin."

Beatrice had been a runner all her life. Track. Five-k races. She'd won them all, but never in her life had she run as fast as she did now toward the last boys' cabin. She flung open the door.

"Eli? Chris?" she shouted. Their bedcovers were pulled back, but the boys clearly hadn't been in bed for a while. She ran to the small bathroom, which had been the most recent one to be modernized. Right now, though, the last things on her mind were tile, plumbing or the new toilet she'd found on sale. The bathroom was empty.

"Eli! Chris!" she shouted, going around to the back of the cabin. Thinking the boys might have gone down to the lake past their curfew, she ran down the grassy slope. The cabins were outfitted with motion lights that illuminated the area like daylight for her.

The little lake was placid with a ribbon of silver moonlight gleaming across the surface. No one was on the diving raft. No one on the short pier. No one hid near the kayak rack or the beached canoes.

She ran back to the driveway.

She whispered to Bruce, "They weren't there. Take these kids to Father Michael's. Cindy will drive the other SUV. I'll keep Maisie here with me while we keep looking for Eli and Chris."

"You're sure?"

She nodded. "Call me when you get there. I have to know the kids are safe."

The screams of the sirens grew louder.

Bruce climbed in the SUV and started the engine. Beatrice walked back to the second one and gave Cindy a thumbs-up.

As they drove away, Maisie jogged up to Beatrice. "I've just checked the kitchen and the activity room. I can't find Eli or Chris anywhere. Where on earth could they be?" she asked.

Beatrice heard fear trembling in the raven-haired girl's voice.

"I don't know."

The sirens wailed to an earsplitting level as they barreled down the country road.

Beatrice looked at the fire. It was clearly raging now. She was glad the gravel road put distance and a natural fire barrier between her camp and the fire.

Then her mind recognized a figure standing behind a wall of flame on the other side of the road.

"Eli! Eli!"

Beatrice ran into the fire.

CHAPTER TWO

BEATRICE HEARD MAISIE scream for her to come back. But if anything happened to Eli or Chris, Beatrice's life would be over. She'd never handle the guilt or the sorrow.

Smoke filled the air, but the heat was so intense, Beatrice couldn't smell it. For that she was thankful, because she hadn't thought to cover her nose and mouth. She hadn't thought about protective clothing, either. Not even a long-sleeved shirt. She still wore one of her lake-water-blue youth camp T-shirts and the navy shorts that she slept in every night. She was ill-prepared for saving anyone.

"Eli!" she called.

From between a curtain of flames on either side of him, little six-year-old Eli stood frozen to the spot, tears spilling down his cheeks.

"Miss Beatrice!"

"Don't move, Eli! I'm coming to get you!"

"I'm scared!" He started to take a step.

She kept running, dodging puddles of

smoldering pine nettles, hoping her sneakers didn't melt from the heat. Even if they had, she wouldn't have stopped. Nothing would stop her. She had to save Eli.

Fortunately, Eli was wearing a long-sleeved sweatshirt. Even in the heat of the day, Eli always claimed he was cold. She didn't doubt it. He was so thin. The kind of thin that broke her heart and made her want to cook his favorite dish, spaghetti, for him—at every meal.

He also wore jeans and high-top sneakers. Eli never went anywhere without his high-top sneakers. He was determined to become a basketball player in the NBA someday, and though he was of average height for his years, he was the kind of kid who would "think" himself tall.

This was Eli's third week at camp, which was due to the good graces and hard efforts of Zoey Phillips, the director of Indian Lake Child Services.

Eli and his brother, Chris, who was ten, were new to foster care. Their father had recently been sent to prison for drug dealing. Their mother had simply abandoned them in an upstairs apartment over an antiques store on Main Street. She'd told the boys she was going out for groceries, but three days later, she hadn't come back. It was Eli who had called the police, hoping they could find his mother.

His brother's call had angered an already resentful Chris. Chris had an iceberg-sized chip on his shoulder. He'd worshipped his father and copied his arrogance and cocky attitude.

From their first day in camp, Chris had posed one problem after another to Beatrice and her counselors. Beatrice believed the boys needed—*craved*—attention and caring. Eli was bright and genuinely a good kid. Chris rattled her nerves from breakfast to lights out. She was amazed the two were genetically linked. Bruce had tried to get through to Chris, but Chris had so far only stonewalled him. Beatrice believed Chris's heart was broken, but she hadn't the first idea what kind of glue would mend him.

Once the boys left her camp, Beatrice feared she would never see Eli or Chris again once the system sent them to a proper foster home. They'd likely be split up and sent out of the county.

As the flames jumped from tree to tree, Beatrice kept her eyes on Eli and his outstretched arms. She leaped expertly over a burning log, miraculously evading the flames. She kept running.

"Stay still," she warned as she drew closer to Eli.

The fire had made daylight of the forest. It was hard to imagine that it was night. Flames shot out of forty-foot-tall dead pine trees that should have been felled years ago.

A pine tree about seventy yards away exploded like a cannon. The sound frightened Eli so much that his feet left the ground when he jumped.

"Miss Beatrice! Help me!"

She continued toward him but an enormous branch swooped through the air with a hissing sound and thudded in front of Beatrice.

She slammed to a stop before falling over the branch. The smell of it was pungent. The odors of pine, flame and smoke mingled to form a forbidding fragrance.

Like flaming needles, the sparks from the logs shot into the air and seared the skin on her arms.

She simply brushed them off, not feeling a thing.

Everything about her had turned to ice, except her heart. It was beating through her chest as if it knew she was going to die this night, and had to beat its last moments as hard and powerfully as it could to make up for all the years she would lose.

Eli's face was covered in tears and snot when she finally reached him. She scooped him into her arms and crushed his face into the crook of her neck. "I've got you now," she said comfortingly. "Nothing bad will happen to you."

"You promise?" His voice was muffled as he burrowed his head into her throat.

"I do."

"How can you promise? We're both going to die."

"No, we won't," she said sternly. "Didn't you just see me jump?"

"Huh?"

"I was state champion in high hurdles for my girls' team in high school."

He hugged her tightly. "I'm sorry for this."

"It's not your fault, Eli," she said. "But you shouldn't have been out here. That's why we tell you to stay in your cabins at night. The forest can be dangerous."

He lifted his face from the shelter of her neck. "I'm sorry," he repeated.

She looked around. "The fire is getting stronger. You hang on to me and I'll get us back."

"I can walk," he protested.

"*No*. And I mean it. You stay with me. Understand?" She had him in her arms. There was no way she would let him go. For this moment, she felt in control, though her brain told her that she had just done about the most unthinkable act of her life.

The heat of the flames had increased, and perhaps she was allowing her senses to register something beyond her fears for Eli. She finally felt the burns on her arms, but she willed away the pain. She lifted her foot to start back to the camp when a second tree blew up.

This time she was the one to jump. She rocked back on her heels. Cinders filled the air. Branches flew overhead and landed behind her. When the pieces hit the ground, the earth shook beneath her feet like an earthquake.

Eli screamed. The sound of his terror clanged in her head like discordant and mournful bells.

She realized that she didn't hear the sirens any longer. Had the trucks arrived? Or had it been her imagination all along that they were on their way? Had she imagined the dispatcher's words? What other mistakes had she made in this nightmare? Would she be Eli's hero or the cause of his death?

From somewhere, she found a thread of solid strength that bolted up her spine and empowered her arms. She pulled Eli close to her chest. "We're going to make a run for it," she said decisively.

"We can't leave..."

"What? Why?"

"We have to find Chris."

CHAPTER THREE

RAND NELSON PULLED his fire engine to a stop in front of the camp and stared over the steering wheel in disbelief at what he was seeing: a woman running *toward* the fire.

"No way in..."

He jumped out the driver's door, his heavy leather-booted feet hitting the ground with a thud. He grabbed his thermoplastic helmet off the console, then his goggles and pigskin gloves.

The massive Indian Lake fire engine pulled up behind him, Captain Bolton quickly exiting the truck and assessing the situation.

Bolton quickly dispensed orders to the team, though every man knew their tasks. Extensive, in-depth training and experience had taught the Indian Lake crew how to manage and overpower forest fires big and small.

"Was that a woman? Running *into* the fire?" Rand asked Captain Bolton.

"You've got to be kidding. Where?" Captain Bolton spun around to follow Rand's extended arm as he pointed into the worst section of burning trees and brush.

"That blonde woman. Right there." Rand put on his goggles. "I'm going in after her."

Captain Bolton waved Rand on. Then he quickly went to the large hose lays on the wildland fire engine.

Rand had seen some crazy, reckless acts in his years as a smoke jumper in California, then as a trainer in Boise, Idaho, and now, as a part-time firefighter at Indian Lake Engine #2, but this was a first. He'd heard about people who went back into burning houses to save a family member or a pet. But he'd never seen anyone run into a forest fire.

And why?

Was there someone else out there? Even if there was, the long-haired blonde should have left the rescue to the professionals. She wasn't wearing a Nomex suit like he was. Or a helmet, boots and gloves. Didn't she know that the heat alone could boil her skin? Set her hair on fire? And why wouldn't she at least tie that long hair up?

Should he use the hose to try and contain the fire around the woman? Their truck could pump five hundred gallons of water on the flames. As long as the wind didn't change direction, they'd be able to keep the fire to the forest, and the kids and the camp property would be safe. Then the situation would be safer for both him and the woman.

"Sir! Sir!" He heard a female voice behind him. Then a tug on his arm.

A young woman with chin-length black hair pointed to the fire. "She's in there. She went after him. You have to help her!"

"Who is she?"

"Beatrice Wilcox. My boss. She owns the camp." The woman struggled for breath, coughing on the rising smoke. "I'm Maisie. A counselor. We evacuated the children. She and I are the only ones left. Except for Eli and Chris—they're missing."

"Missing?" His jaw dropped as he looked back at the fire. "How old?"

"Eli is six. Chris just turned ten. They're brothers. Beatrice thought she spotted Eli. But now I can't see her." Maisie's eyes filled with tears. She put her palms to her cheeks. "She's not like this. Daredevil things are not her deal, you know?" Her eyes shot back to his face. "Please, sir. Help her. She's in there…somewhere."

He put his hand reassuringly on her shoulder. "I'll find her. And the kids."

Maisie held her breath and nodded.

The familiar sweetness of adrenaline shot

through his body as he entered the fire. He was on high alert. The perimeter of the fire was already losing energy as it neared the road. However, the farther he went into the forest, the mightier the flames.

An explosion shook the air and the ground as Rand stepped over a burning log. He lifted his head to see a flaming branch head straight for him. Backing out of the path of the falling log, he reached into the tool belt around his waist and grabbed his hatchet, ready to attack any errant shrapnel that often erupted from dry branches as they crashed to the ground.

Only inches from his boot, the log landed with a thud, the flames smothering themselves on the ground.

He stepped over the log and scanned the area.

Then he saw her.

Remarkably, she was standing in a tiny space that was untouched by the fire, though flames created a curtain on either side of her. She held a child close to her chest, the burning forest giving them a crimson outline. She almost didn't look real. The heat from the fire lifted her hair from her shoulders. He could almost feel her eyes on him, as if they had a force of their own, drawing him in.

Terror was powerful like that. The little boy was crying as he clutched Beatrice's neck. "Chris!" she called.

Rand assumed that the child in her arms was Eli, the younger of the two brothers. Chris, evidently, was still missing.

Not good.

"Beatrice?" Rand called as he moved quickly toward her.

"Yes! Yes!"

"Don't move. I'm coming in to get you," he said, just as a sharp crack sounded. He glanced up.

An enormous limb from a forty-foot syca-more tree broke off. Flames waved long and wide from the limb, looking like amber silk scarves as it sailed straight for Beatrice and the little boy.

She dashed toward Rand, but her foot caught on an exposed tree root. She fell to the ground, still holding the crying little boy.

"Bee—!" Rand never got out the rest of her name as he bolted forward. In three long strides he was at her side. "Beatrice. I'm here," he said. Then he looked at the boy. "Eli, don't be afraid. I have you now."

"It's okay, Eli," she said softly as she lifted her face from Eli to Rand.

He gazed into the bluest eyes he'd ever seen. "I can take the boy."

"No!" Eli cried. "I want to stay with Miss Beatrice."

"It's okay, Eli. He's come to save us. You'll be fine," she said, massaging Eli's back. Then she handed Eli to Rand. "Thank you," she said as she put her hand on her ankle, which was swelling before his eyes.

"Can you walk?"

"I don't know."

"Here. Take my hand. I'll help you up."

Rand eased her to a standing position. "Put your weight on it. Test it."

Gingerly, she stood. "Agh!" She flung back her head. "I think I'm going to throw up. The pain…"

"It's probably broken," he assessed. "Just lean on me."

"Okay." She nodded. He could tell she was bravely fighting tears.

Finally getting her steady and with Eli in his arms, he turned just as another large tree limb fell from above.

Rand instantly chided himself. He hadn't heard the crack. His instinctual "alert" system had faltered for a fraction of a second while he'd focused on Beatrice. He shouldn't have done that. He should have kept all his senses amped.

The limb fell behind them.

He checked Beatrice and he realized that the limb had skimmed her back. Her hair and the back of her T-shirt were on fire.

"Help! Help me!" she screamed and grabbed her hair. She hobbled and nearly fell again.

Rand instantly put Eli on the ground.

"Stay!" he said roughly and firmly.

Eli stopped crying as terror and submission rooted him to the spot.

With lightning speed, Rand grabbed Beatrice and pushed her to the ground. He batted her hair and put out the flames. He rolled on top of her back and extinguished her burning shirt. Once she was safe, he examined her quickly and decided she would have some burns but the skin was not charred. He'd gotten to her soon enough.

Quickly, he stood, reached down and pulled her to her feet. "My ankle…it's worse," she groaned painfully, her face contorted.

He swooped Eli off the ground and handed him to Beatrice. "Hold him close." Then Rand lifted her left arm. "Put your arm around my neck."

"But…"

"Now! We have to go!" he ordered.

He hoisted them both firmly against his chest. He was surprised how light they seemed. He'd never carried two people at once. She was tall, though quite slim. The boy was very thin. Still, his best guess was that his adrenaline was working overtime. Again. It was a rush.

Beatrice's arm clutched his neck as she cradled Eli between them both. The boy had stopped screaming.

Just as they walked out of the tiny clearing, a massive pine fell with an earthshaking thud, covering the oasis they'd found for the brief moment they'd needed it.

He walked as quickly as he could over burning tree limbs and smoldering brush.

One more second in that clearing and they all would have been hit. They might never have made it out. The kid would have been crushed if the pine fell on him.

But they had made it. Rand's mother would have said it was a miracle.

Rand would have to agree with her.

Still, he was just doing his job.

This kind of extraction was not new for him. But it was never routine. The circumstances were always different, but the pounding, throttling sense of triumph that shot through his veins was always the same. This was why he did what he did. This was why he chose to risk his life. He was saving lives.

Someone would live—perhaps live better than they had before—because he'd been there at the instant between life and death.

Rand walked through the last of the flames and felt the spray of water from the hose lines. As if walking out of another dimension, he heard Captain Bolton shouting orders to the team over the deafening sound of gushing water.

Two of the team had moved one hose to the far right of the fire and were advancing toward the center from the west, where a slight night breeze had originated.

Two others were hosing from the opposite direction.

An EMT crew and their ambulance had arrived. He spotted Maisie off to the side and behind the wildfire engine.

Joy leaped into her face as she saw them. She threw her hands in the air and then clamped them down on top of her head. "Beatrice! Eli!"

Maisie raced toward them.

The EMT crew got there first with a stretcher and oxygen.

"Thanks, guys," Rand said to the EMT crew as he lowered both Beatrice and Eli onto the stretcher. He looked down at Beatrice. "You'll be okay now. These guys are the top gun."

He noticed that she never let go of Eli, and the little boy clung to her like a monkey.

To the EMT, he said, "Possible broken ankle or foot. Burns on her back."

"We'll check it out," the taller of the EMTs said and immediately started to take off Beatrice's shoe.

"You'll be fine," Rand assured her again.

Her blue eyes were wide as she looked up at him pleadingly.

"What is it?"

"Chris. He's still in there."

Rand nodded, taking off his glove. "I know, Bee." He touched her face where a black mark slashed her cheek. The black soot smeared his fingertips.

Rand stood, and as he did she reached out and took his hand. She had a surprisingly strong grip. "What?" he asked.

"Just…thank you. Now, go."

Rand dropped her hand and raced away, wondering if the tear he'd seen was gratitude or smoke in Beatrice's eye.

CHAPTER FOUR

"CHRIS!"

Rand ran into the forest, the flames dying around him as the fire crew blasted water through the trees. He pushed through the piles of smoldering pine nettles and over the downed limb that had almost killed Beatrice, Eli and him.

As a firefighter the smell of wet earth always gave Rand hope. But would he find the boy in time? Did he even want to be found?

"Chris!" he yelled into the shock of burned and blackened trees, denuded of foliage and standing like spikes against the night sky. "Chris!"

Kids were strange ducks in Rand's book. Most of them could outsmart the majority of adults. Granted, he didn't hang with philosophers and academics, but his family and friends were no dummies. Kids, however, were open to all possibilities and concepts. That's why a lost kid was so hard to find. They didn't sit still. They didn't follow patterns that "thinking" adults would take. They relied on base animal instincts. When trapped, they bolted for freedom. When cornered, they would outsmart their prey or vanish. They bucked rules, ignored safety measures and took risks.

He guessed that Chris had used plenty of animal instincts to avoid Rand's search thus far. With the blaze petering out, Chris could circle around, exit through an unburned area and get back to camp. Of course, that scenario assumed Chris wanted to return to camp. But what if he didn't? What if he was a runner? A kid who felt so displaced in his life that all he wanted was to skip over these tough years and wake up when he was much older. Rand had seen that kind of kid.

Sometimes they were arsonists.

Rand had fought fires from the Upper Peninsula of Michigan to Idaho to California. He knew exactly the kind of conditions that it took for Mother Nature to burn. But there had been no thunderstorms here in Indian Lake. No lightning bolts. And not quite enough heat to spark spontaneous combustion. No, this was a fire started by human hands. Rand would bet his reputation on it.

And if he was right, Chris had all the more reason to stay clear.

Rand had one shot at bringing out Chris. He had to take it.

"Chris! I know you can hear me. It's safe now. Eli is safe."

Rand kept going, toward the most burned section of forest. It was his guess that it had been near here where the fire started.

"Chris!"

"Do—do you promise?" The young voice traveled down from the sky to Rand.

Rand turned on his boot and looked up. To his right was a tall, wide pine tree that had been burned on the bottom, but halfway up the tree, the limbs were unscathed. Huddled between two enormous lush pine limbs was a boy. Rand couldn't see his face in the dark. But he could feel his fear.

"Yes, I promise your brother is safe with Miss Beatrice at the camp."

"I don't believe you," he sniffed.

"It's true."

"How did they get out? I barely got up here myself before it all exploded."

Now the boy was crying and the sobs caught in his throat, restricting his words.

"The trees did explode," Rand said, careful to keep his words calm.

"It was scary. Really bad."

"But you were brave. You climbed that tree all by yourself."

"I've been climbing stuff all my life."

"I'll bet you have. Let me guess. Windows? Fire escapes? Rooftops, maybe?"

"Yeah."

"I was kinda like that, too. I'm still climbing ladders. Ropes. That kind of stuff." Rand paused as he heard the dissipating sound of the hoses. The crew was winding down. "The fire is under control. You come down."

Silence.

Chris coughed and then hacked. Rand guessed the kid had inhaled his share of smoke tonight.

"There are paramedics here who need to help you. The smoke—"

"I know all about smoke," Chris interrupted. "Okay?"

Rand felt impatience kindle in his belly. "Chris. You have to come down, son."

"I'm not your son."

"No kidding." Rand ground his teeth. This was no place for attitude. A burned limb could fall at any moment and crash into them both. But while he could think of a dozen retorts to Chris at the moment, not one of them would get the kid to climb to the ground. "If you don't come down, I'll come up and get you."

"How?"

"Just like you did. Climb. Then I'll tie a rope to you and lower you to the ground. Or you can stay there, where the burned bark will skin you alive. Your choice. But I'm not leaving here without you."

"Why?"

"It's my job."

"Oh." Chris started coughing. He cleared his throat. He coughed again. "I'm coming down."

Rand knew that once Chris got past the living foliage and sturdy limbs, his descent was going to get rough. There was a good twenty feet of burned bark and sharp splinters on that half-denuded trunk. Rand could see jagged stubs of limbs on the trunk, but could Chris? Were they strong enough for him to get a foothold? Or would they break under his weight? Worse, would the kid make a jump for it and risk breaking a leg or ankle in his drop?

"Once you get to the last limb, Chris, I want you to take it slow. I'll guide you down."

"I don't need your help, okay? I made it up here and I can make it down on my own."

Rand heaved a frustrated sigh and put his

hands on his hips. Beatrice certainly had her hands full with this one.

"You're doing great," Rand encouraged the boy as Chris moved down through the limbs and came to the burned part of the trunk.

Chris toed the trunk with his sneaker, searching for a foothold, but he found none. The boy grabbed the limb with both hands and lowered his feet farther down the tree, still looking for a brace.

"The trunk is too wide for you to hug and slide down. Plus, you'll scrape your skin in the process," Rand said. "Or..."

"Or?" Chris asked with just enough trepidation that Rand thought he might have made an impression on the kid.

"You can drop and I'll catch you."

"No way."

"It's okay, my body will cushion your fall."

Chris peered down at Rand, his arms stretched over his head as he hung on to the limb. His knuckles had gone white and his fingers were starting to slip. The kid wouldn't last much longer.

"Why?"

"There ya go with the questions again. Just drop."

"You're angry at me."

"I'm getting there, yeah."

Rand heard the hoses stop, then he looked up. The wind had died completely. Tiny pellets of long-overdue rain had started to sprinkle from the sky. A mist of droplets hit his face. It certainly wasn't a downpour—only a gentle rain—but it was wet, nonetheless, and would ensure the fire was completely extinquished.

Rand heard one of the other firefighters shouting his name. He heard boots stomping over brush and smoldering leaves and nettles.

"My friends are coming."

Chris coughed and that led to another cough. "I can't breathe so good."

"I can imagine," Rand replied. Another minute of hanging from the limb and Chris would be in trouble. Rand needed the boy to try to aim for his outstretched arms.

"Chris, let go, and when you do, pretend you're lying down horizontally. It'll be like skydiving."

"Rand!" a man's voice shouted.

"Over here!" Rand replied as loudly as he could.

"You skydive?" Chris coughed out the words.

"Yes, Chris. Now, let go and do it!"

"Okay!"

Chris let go of the limb, flattened his back and closed his eyes.

Rand dug his heels into the ground, bent his knees to keep his back solid and reached out to catch the boy. Chris landed in Rand's arms with a wallop. Rand had expected his biceps to sting with the sudden impact, but, like his brother, Chris was much lighter than he'd braced for.

Chris popped his eyes open, blinked and squirmed out of Rand's arms.

"You're safe," Rand said. "Here, put this oxygen mask on. It will help you with the smoke inhalation."

"I'm fine." Chris pushed Rand's hand away.

"Wear it!" Rand ordered and then clamped the mask over Chris's face and put the elastic strap over his head, making sure the back was secure.

"Rand!" Another shout came toward him along with the sound of many boots crunching over the burned ground. Ted McIntyre and Manny Quale stood shoulder to Nomex-suited-shoulder in front of them.

"You found him," Ted said, pointing with his gloved hand to Chris.

"He was up that tree." Rand looked at

Chris, who was staring at the smoking forest floor.

"I'll go back for the paramedics," Manny said.

"I'm fine," Chris said sternly as he ripped off the mask, shoved it back to Rand, and marched away from Rand, Ted and Manny. "See?" He swung his arms as he walked away from them.

Both Ted and Manny looked back at Rand.

"What? No 'thanks'?" Ted asked.

Rand shrugged his shoulders. "Apparently, he didn't want to be rescued."

"Oh," Manny said. "One of those."

"Afraid so," Rand answered.

They walked out of the smoking forest after Chris.

BEATRICE LOOKED DOWN at her right ankle as she sat on the gurney in the ER. "Acute metatarsal fracture?" she repeated to Dr. Eric Hill, the ER doctor who was documenting her injury into a laptop computer on the counter to her right. A nurse with streaks of purple and pink in her midlength hair was inputting more information into another computer with a larger screen on a wheeled cart.

"Correct," Dr. Hill replied. "Which means you broke the long bone in your foot. The one that attaches the ankle to the toes. Luckily the bones are aligned and don't need surgery."

"Will I have to wear a cast and use crutches?" Beatrice swallowed hard, thinking of all the camp chores, the climb to her cabin and supposedly easy things like helping the kids dress in the mornings. Such simple chores, these daily bits of her life, but they made her days rewarding. She'd have to put the crutches down each time she wanted to hug a child.

Tears stung her eyes but she blinked them back.

"I'd rather not go that route," he said.

"Seriously?" She brightened. "But you said the recovery time is six to eight weeks."

"It is. But we can outfit you for an air boot. I prefer it to a cast because it has a reservoir that can hold ice-cold water around the injury for as much as six hours. Right now, I want the swelling to go down and ice is the answer. More than any medication. And over-medicating can lead to bleeding and that's not good, either. In a week, I'll start you on some exercises with that foot."

"Exercises?"

"Easy things at first. Well, they sound easy to the uninjured. And make sure to keep the foot elevated as much as you can. Keep your weight off of it. The air boot will help a lot with redistribution of weight."

"Good."

He rose and looked at her with more empathy than she'd seen in anyone's eyes in a long time. "Those burns on your back are going to sting for a few days, but could be worse. You'll need to apply aloe vera and an antibiotic cream for a week to ten days. Take two Tylenol and three Ibuprofen for pain. And you'll probably want to get a haircut."

"Smells pretty bad, doesn't it?"

"Like burned hair." He gave her a faint smile and continued. "We've put loose gauze over the burns for now. Do you have someone who can change the bandages for you every day?"

"Uh, sure. Cindy or Maisie at the camp…"

"Great. I want to see you in my office a week from today. I'll have the nurse here set up an appointment for you."

"Thank you, Doctor."

"You take care, Beatrice. I'm glad the camp is unharmed."

After setting up the appointment, the nurse wheeled the trolley with the computer out of the ER bay, giving Beatrice a wide smile as she said goodbye.

"Dr. Hill, before you go. Could you tell me more about Eli and Chris?"

"They're both fine. Eli was more frightened than injured. Chris is suffering from mild smoke inhalation. The firefighter who found him administered oxygen. He's got a cough, but frankly, considering all he's been through, he's done remarkably well."

"It's a miracle," she said, more to herself than to the doctor.

"The fact that he climbed a very tall tree and stayed far above the fire and smoke helped. He was high enough that the air was at least somewhat clearer. That was smart thinking on his part."

Given his past, it didn't surprise her that Chris was resourceful. His intelligence wasn't the issue, however. He'd been closed-off, quiet and seemingly resentful at camp. She was sure he just needed to be loved. But he'd be gone from camp soon, and she couldn't guarantee he'd get the care he so desperately craved.

"It'll be a few minutes for the nurse to get all the release papers and instructions. You just rest for a bit." He patted her shoulder, pulled back the curtain that hung over the sliding glass door and walked away.

As Dr. Hill left, a sandy-haired young man

in surgical garb and a white lab coat entered the room. He carried a drawstring bag that looked almost as big as Santa's sack. "I'm here to fit this boot on you," he said.

"Of course." Beatrice smiled, and the man went quickly to work.

The black-and-gray air boot looked like something an astronaut would wear to walk on the moon, Beatrice thought, as the man very gently lifted her injured foot and slid the boot into place. His fingers flew over the straps, making certain the boot fit comfortably. Beatrice eased herself off the gurney to try the rocker bottom of the boot, which was supposed to improve her gait. He explained how to use the ice-water feature, then instructed her about donning and doffing the boot and how to clean and maintain her new "friend."

"This boot is my favorite," he said. "I used it when I broke my ankle. I was back to fast walking in three weeks."

"Three weeks? The doctor said six to eight weeks for me."

"Oh, sure. That's *total* healing time. But I can't live without running. The docs let us ease back into our normal exercise fairly quickly."

"Well," she said, grinning, "then this is exactly the boot I want."

"Great," he said and handed her a card. "Here's the number to the ortho department. Call us if you need."

The young man left and Beatrice leaned her hip against the gurney as she rocked her foot back and forth in the boot. She lifted her knee, but felt a stabbing pain when she did.

Wincing, she glanced up and saw him.

He was leaning against the doorjamb. Gone were the Nomex suit, goggles and gloves. The helmet. She noticed his thick, dark, nearly black hair first. A hunk of shining, slightly damp hair hung over his strong forehead. His jawline looked like it had been carved from granite. In fact, everything about him was strong. He didn't need a firefighter's suit to make his shoulders wide; his presence filled the doorway, the room, the expanse between them. He wore a black short-sleeved T-shirt that stretched over biceps that could only have been built by hours in a gym. His black jeans fitted close to his narrow hips and muscular thighs. He wore no jewelry. No watch, no wedding ring, no tats. There was nothing extraneous or ornamental about this man. It wasn't necessary—his whole being shouted, "I'm a man."

He pushed himself off the door and took a short step inside. "You okay?"

That was all he said, yet his words caused her to be tongue-tied.

"You saved my life," she croaked over a tangle of emotions that had yet to be released from the night's ordeal. Fear that Eli and Chris would be burned alive. Shock that her dream camp could be swept away by fiery fingers. Despair that she would disappoint her employees. Anger that she'd failed herself. And utter sadness that the children would lose their idyll.

And then this man had walked through fire and carried her and Eli to safety, before entering the inferno again in search of Chris.

She couldn't help the hero she saw in him.

"Just doing my job," he replied flatly as if he did this every day.

Of course he did. She was just another of his tasks to be accomplished. Most people didn't think twice about firefighters, police or prison guards until their circumstances collided. They were the protectors, sworn to their duty, and she didn't know his name. "Thank you," she replied simply. "Mr...."

"Nelson."

He still didn't move any closer, but his eyes examined her more closely than Dr.

Hill had. By the troubled expression on his face, she got the sense he wasn't pleased with what he saw.

She fingered her singed hair. She hadn't felt so self-conscious since middle school. Her mother, Jenny, had been acting as a fill-in host on a local Chicago PBS talk show. The show was a favorite among Beatrice's schoolmates' parents. They were vocal with their opinions that Jenny was a joke—and their kids echoed their parents by taunting Beatrice. Beatrice's shame and embarrass-ment lasted the six months until the regu-lar show host returned from maternity leave.

But those months had taught her a lesson. She learned that kids can be placid, lonely, mean, arrogant, spiteful and defiant—but be-neath it all, kids were afraid. Life came at children at jet speed or faster, and they were vulnerable to its whims.

That insight had led her to found her camp, and to try to go that one step further for kids like Chris and Eli.

What drove this fireman to do his job?

She was aware she hadn't taken her eyes away from the velvet brown pools that were locked on her. She wondered if he was un-comfortable under her gaze. Probably not.

He was too self-assured. She would be, too, if she'd just saved three lives that night.

"Rand Nelson," he said. "Short for Randall."

"I'm Beatrice. I don't have a short." She smiled and extended her hand.

"Sure you do, Bee."

"That's...what you called me in the forest."

He walked to her, which only took three long steps. His thigh muscles flexed beneath his jeans. His movements were fluid, as if he was the most perfect human ever sculpted. She wanted to rub her eyes to make sure he wasn't a dream. Then she felt his hand in hers. Flesh against warm flesh.

"Your hand is cold. You've been through a lot." He withdrew his hand from hers and pushed back his hair. "I came as soon as I got cleaned up. I wanted you to know the fire is out. The wind died completely, which left nothing to fan the flames. That brief sprinkle of rain wasn't much, but it helped. And the crew did their job well."

"Masterfully done, I'd say."

"The fire poses no more danger, so you can bring the other kids back to camp anytime."

"That's great," she replied, amazed she'd managed a full sentence. That was a full sentence, right? Most likely she was still in shock. She did feel cold. But she'd bet her last dollar that her cheeks were hot—a heat caused by being this close to Rand. The hero who had saved her, two children and, along with his team, her entire youth camp.

He clasped his hands behind his back. "I don't usually make hospital visits," he said, clearing his throat as if he was uncomfortable.

"No?"

"Officially, you're the victim. The regulations stipulate that what you tell me should be recorded." He glanced away and back. "But I, well, wanted to see you. Er, to make sure you're okay."

"I'm fine. Except for my broken foot."

"You were lucky. You could have died out there."

"I know I said it before, but thank you, Rand. Thank you for everything. And please tell your men how deeply grateful I am to you all for everything..."

He put his hand over hers, which was grasping the edge of the gurney for support. "It's what we do, Bee."

He'd leaned his face closer to hers and she smelled peppermint on his breath and something spicy on his recently shaven cheeks.

She was bombarded by a storm of sensations that already screamed "Rand" to her. She swayed.

"Beatrice! Thank God!" Maisie burst into the ER bay, shoving the curtain back even farther. She glanced up at Rand and then ignored him as she nearly flew to Beatrice's side.

"Oh, my God, I was so worried when they took you and Eli away. I thought I'd lose my mind until that man came out of the woods with Chris. I've never been through anything remotely like this, Beatrice." Maisie stopped abruptly, her eyes shooting from Beatrice to Rand. "Wait, *you're* that guy!"

Rand's face was implacable, as Maisie's gratitude and dawning hero worship bounced off him like he was made of Teflon. "Yes, we met at the camp earlier."

Though Maisie was taking huge deep breaths like a track runner at the finish line, she calmed instantly, offered her hand and said, "Thank you for your service."

Rand gave her hand a quick shake and stepped back a pace. "You're welcome." He looked at Beatrice. "I'm glad you're okay."

"I'm fine."

"Okay...well, um, then I'll be out to your

camp in the morning. With the forensic team. What time would be good for you?"

"Forensics?" Beatrice's heart thudded to a halt.

"By law we have to assess the origin of the fire."

"Of course." Her mind scrambled for logic. "Nine a.m. would be good."

"See you then."

He turned and left. The room was instantly less vibrant.

Beatrice's booted foot slipped as she watched Rand walk through the bay door. It was as if Rand's presence had provided an extra measure of stability, something she'd never needed before.

She looked down at the boot. It was only the bone that was broken. Nothing else. She was fine.

But an investigation…? Her hero apparently came with a double-edged sword. When he wielded it on the side of the law, would she and her camp survive the blow?

CHAPTER FIVE

BY THE TIME Beatrice returned to camp at dawn, reality was crashing down on her. Pain was the first of her comprehensions of change. The ice water in the boot was warmer than her body temperature now. Dressing, bathing and asking Maisie to come to her cabin to redress her burns added another twenty minutes to her morning routine. Pain accompanied all these tasks that just yesterday she'd taken for granted.

Just yesterday, I wasn't under investigation, either, she thought.

But after agonizing about it for the last couple of hours, she'd steeled herself for whatever Rand could bring. She tried not to think that an investigation could be the worst thing that could happen to her. The camp was old, and when she'd bought it, the list of repairs and necessary maintenance had been three sheets long. Two sheets longer than she could afford to fix, even with a small inheritance she'd received from her aunt Elizabeth.

She'd done much of the work herself. The repainting, the gravel for the driveway. She'd pulled every weed, and torn out the unproductive old rosebushes. She'd relaid the heavy stones around the gravel driveway. She'd hauled 52 tons of rock that first spring to create pretty flower beds and garden "islands," where yard-sale benches mingled with Victorian iron arches that she'd also found at junk shops along Red Arrow Highway. She'd begged and bartered for all the used commercial kitchen appliances that their cook, Amanda, made the meals on.

Beatrice had suffered through one building inspection after another as she readied the camp for opening. She'd bought twice the liability insurance required. She and the camp had passed every building, plumbing and electrical wiring inspection required. Even her little lake was considered safe for all activities because it was only three to four feet deep. Safer than a swimming pool.

She'd obtained her state license as a caregiver. She limited the number of campers to ten and hired three counselors so that her counselor-to-child ratio was better than the one required by the state, which was four to one. She knew children with special needs required one-on-one care, and Beatrice, with sixty clocked hours of training and a child-development-associate credential, took care of those children herself.

The camp and the positive influence she had on the kids' lives was more than just rewarding for Beatrice. It was her reason for living.

So if Rand came at her with his sword clashing, she'd strike back with a blade just as mighty.

She stood, then winced as pain shot up her leg.

"You okay?" Maisie asked as Beatrice eased her way on her crutches out the door and to the front porch.

"Fine."

"Yeah, sure. I'm not buyin' that one."

They gazed out at the scorched woods, the felled trees and the blackened ground.

"It looks as bad as your hair," Maisie mused.

"My hair? I just washed it."

"Okay, but those burned chunks still look bad. Cindy is good with scissors. Maybe she can whack it off."

"Yeah." Beatrice closed her eyes. Her long, natural-blond hair had always been a source of pride for her. Pride before the fall, she couldn't help thinking. "I figure six inches will need to come off."

"And that would just make it even."

Beatrice gasped. "And it would be shoulder-length."

"An improvement." Maisie grinned, touching her chin-length cut. "Cindy cuts mine. Saves me lots of money compared to what I paid my stylist in Chicago."

"I'll ask her to do it this morning."

"Good," Maisie replied. "So, look, the kids are at breakfast. I'll meet you over there." Maisie started running backward, then twirled and took off toward the dining hall.

Beatrice was nowhere near close to being able to twirl. She was still navigating her new life with the awkward contraption on her foot. She'd come home with a pair of crutches, which were a hindrance inside her little cabin. She'd knocked books off her small, rickety bookshelf and nearly tripped on the rag rug next to her bed when the crutch caught on an edge. That was when she tossed the crutches down and decided to wing it without them. Fortunately, she'd been told she only needed the crutches for this first week. Then she would start rehabilitation. Exercises. Writing the alphabet with her toes.

The very idea made her wince.

Right now, she needed ice water for the interior of the boot to keep the swelling down. She grabbed the crutches and slowly made her way down the three steps of her porch and onto the gravel path that led to the kitchen.

In the kitchen she greeted the cook, Amanda Reynolds, who was turning Mickey Mouse–shaped pancakes on the griddle. Amanda was sixty-five years old, and had recently been forced to retire as a paralegal from a large law firm in Chicago. Amanda had been nowhere near ready to retire. She had enough energy to run rings around both Maisie and Cindy, from what Beatrice had observed. A widow whose only daughter lived in London, Amanda had always loved to cook. Though she preferred gourmet fare for herself and her guests, what she served for the kids was pure home-style family food at its all-American best. The kids loved it and, better still, they ate it.

"Pancakes? It's not Sunday," Beatrice said as she entered the kitchen by the screen door.

Amanda jumped. "Good heavenly days! You scared me to death! Don't do that!" She flipped a mouse head. "I thought you'd take the day to rest." Amanda walked over and gave Beatrice a big hug. Amanda was tall and slender, and wore very tight jeans, expensive running shoes and a camp T-shirt. Her dyed chestnut hair was clipped up on her head, and her makeup was immaculate, all of which confirmed her stylish Chicago career days. There was nothing "down home" about Amanda.

"After that ordeal last night, I thought the kids and the counselors needed something happy. I've got blueberries for the eyes, cherries for the nose and whipped cream smiles."

Beatrice gave Amanda a smile of her own, the first one that had creased her face since she'd whiffed smoke. "You're an angel."

"No. I'm a cook, honey. You're the angel for going in after those boys."

Beatrice drained the warm water from the boot, went to the freezer and scooped ice cubes from the bin. She filled the boot resevoir. "Ah. Better already."

Amanda scooped the pancakes off the griddle, placed them on plates and started decorating.

Cindy came through the swinging kitchen door. "Beatrice! You're up!"

"Wobbling, but upright, yes."

"Good. I could use you out here."

"How so?"

"Would you talk to the kids? They're upset, and Bruce and I are at our wits' end. They need—"

"Leadership," Amanda interjected. "Like the kind most of them don't get from their parents."

Beatrice stared at Amanda, who always spoke the truth sans varnish. And didn't care when she said it or to whom. Sometimes, Beatrice wondered if that was the real reason she'd been pushed into retirement.

Cindy glanced at Beatrice's air boot. "That's just so intimidating. To a kid, I mean. Possibly scary. But hey, if anyone can pull this off, you can."

"It can't be that bad," Beatrice replied and hobbled past Cindy and out the kitchen door into the large, vaulted-and-beamed dining hall. The long wall of windows at one end overlooked the little man-made lake at the back of the property, and the morning sun glinted off its surface. The opposite wall of windows looked out over the burned trees. Cindy was right. The atmosphere was already daunting to her camp kids.

She gazed around the room at the fear-filled wide eyes. No one said a word. No one was eating, pinching their neighbor, arguing or joking. They weren't camp kids now; they were children floating through insecurity's seas. The Kettering sisters held hands as Beatrice walked into the hall. Little Ricky stared blankly at his full glass of orange juice, though Beatrice perceived the tiny movements in his shoulders to be quiet sobs.

Eli wore a gauze patch over half of his left cheek, but he was the only child who ventured to smile at her. To his right was Chris, whose eyes were focused on the wall above Beatrice's head. Eli reached for Chris's hand, but Chris brushed him away and leaned back against his chair, folding his arms defensively over his chest.

Joshua Langsford was the only one who spoke, as he asked, "Does it hurt, Miss Beatrice?"

"A little bit, but nothing like what you've had to go through, Joshua." She smiled. He didn't smile back.

Every one of the kids clamped their eyes on Beatrice's air boot. "So, here's the scoop, guys. I broke a bone in my foot. I'm going to be fine. But for now, I have to wear this boot and use crutches when I'm outside or going up stairs to my cabin. I'm hoping the doctor lets me toss the crutches in a week."

"Yeah, crutches help, but they're a pain after a while," Joshua said.

Beatrice's cell rang. She looked at the caller ID and didn't recognize the number, but it was local. She hit the decline button. "I'll get it later. So, this is what I want you all to know. Last night was an accident and luckily no one was seriously hurt. What we need to focus on is the loss of trees."

"The trees?" the kids said in unison.

"That's right. Those trees were here when I was your age. I loved those trees. They were my friends when I didn't have friends."

Amazement and incredulity hung in the air as the kids leaned a bit closer, propped a chin on a palm or cocked their heads.

An adult revelation was rare to them, which made this moment all the more precious. Their hearts and heads were open to her and she hoped they felt her sincere caring.

"The Indian Lake Nursery has agreed to deliver over a hundred baby trees to us tomorrow. We're all going to work together and plant these new trees to rebuild the forest."

"But the ground is burned," Ricky said.

"That's the interesting thing. Did you know that ancient tribes used to purposefully burn the land in order to start new growth?

The trees have cones filled with seeds that start new trees, but the cones only open with great heat. In one month, we may see little trees peeking up through the ground. It's new life. A new beginning." She paused to let the children absorb what she was saying. "We aren't required to plant new trees, but I wanted you all to be part of helping to rebuild the forest. It's sort of our way to put the past behind us, and to learn that out of every sorrow, every pain, there is something good and wonderful to be found. But you have to look for it. Work for it."

The errant tear that rolled down Beatrice's cheek didn't let its presence be known until it hit the edge of her jaw. Only then, when she stopped talking, did she lift her fingertips to whisk it away. She'd never cried in front of camp children before. This was a first.

Then again, she'd never run headlong into a blazing fire to save one of her kids, either.

"For all of you who went to St. Mark's last night, Father Michael phoned me early this morning and told me that you were the best group of kids he's ever seen. You made me proud. Bruce and Cindy didn't have to worry about any of you. You took an emergency situation and dealt with it calmly and respected those in authority. I couldn't ask for more. Thank you to the older kids who helped the younger ones. Everybody pitched in. You're all—" she looked directly at Chris and Eli "—the best group of campers who've come to stay with me. I hope you all come back next year and stay for a whole month!"

The room erupted in cheers and clapping. Beatrice's heart swelled and she breathed in their affection.

They were so young, and though the night had been fraught with terror, they'd all grown from the experience.

"So, listen up, guys. Amanda has made a special breakfast for you all. Pancakes, bacon and baked cinnamon apples with oatmeal crunch. We have lots of homemade syrup from the Indian Lake Boy Scouts and plenty of butter. After breakfast, Cindy is taking those who signed up for kayak lessons to the lake. Bruce and Maisie are heading up baseball practice. Joshua? How's the leg? You think you want to try some batting practice?"

"You bet, Miss Beatrice," Joshua replied happily.

"Great!"

Amanda, Bruce, Maisie and Cindy entered the dining hall with trays filled with special breakfast plates. While the kids cheered, Beatrice's cell phone rang again.

This time, she turned away from the dining tables and headed toward the door. Walking in her boot slowed her down enough that she could read the caller ID.

It was the same number that had tried to reach her previously.

Still looking down at her phone, she reached for the screen door to the outside porch. "Who in the heck is calling me?"

Then she ran smack-dab into a broad, rock-hard human chest. Beatrice wondered if she'd suffered a concussion. Not another trip to the ER! And what would that cost? "What?"

"I called," Rand said. "You didn't pick up."

"I didn't know it was you."

"I gave you my card."

"When?"

"Last night. Er, this morning. In the hospital."

"Sorry. I was drugged. I mean, medicated."

"I see that. We're here about the investigation."

Beatrice's skin iced over as if the contents of her boot had thrown over her whole body.

She tried to remember that he was responsible for saving her, and Eli and Chris. He was handsome. And strong and heroic.

But Rand stood like a colossus in front of

her, and at this moment he represented every fear that had festered in her head from the instant she'd smelled smoke. Her earlier resolve to go toe-to-toe with him faltered.

Ultimately, she was responsible for Eli and Chris being in that fire last night. Their safety was her obligation. She'd put them in harm's way. Would Rand report to his superiors that the camp was unsafe? That she, personally, was at fault for the kids being out by themselves?

If Rand found one fault and declared her camp unsafe, the sheriff could shut her down, send the kids away and force her to make improvements. Not until a city inspector deemed the camp safe again, could she open. If Rand or his superiors declared her negligent, her state license could be revoked. She would lose more money than she could ever recoup.

And Beatrice's dreams would be lost, too.

The fact that everyone was safe and alive didn't matter, she realized. Rand was here to find fault. From the dour look on his face, she guessed that he believed she should be toe-tagged with the blame card.

CHAPTER SIX

"YOU'RE READY TO START?" she asked, her mouth suddenly dry. She forced a smile that she was sure would crack her lips. She just hoped she didn't bleed in front of him.

"Yes. The forensic team is already on the job."

She tried to peer around him, but his shoulders nearly blocked the entire entrance and all of her view of the outside. "Okay—"

He didn't let her finish. "Since that—" he tilted his head to indicate the fire site across the street "—is county property, this is just a courtesy to let you know we're here."

Her sigh of relief was instantaneous. He wouldn't be investigating the camp. She was off the hook.

"However…"

She held her breath. She should have known she wouldn't escape this man's scrupulous and discerning eye. "Yes?" She lifted her chin defensively. She was ready for him. She had nothing to hide.

That I know about.

She thought of the previous night with Eli and Chris, all their infractions and possible broken laws huddled together like balls inside a pool-table rack, waiting to be broken apart. Dispelled. And sunk.

Beatrice's best defense was honesty. "I intend to cooperate in any way I can."

"I should hope so," he said brusquely. "After all, we're here to ascertain if a crime has been committed."

"A crime?" Beatrice nearly lost her balance. She slammed her palm against the wall for support. "Sorry. I'm not used to the air boot."

His eyes flitted down to her foot and then back up.

Oddly, she didn't recoil from his glance at her camp shorts and T-shirt. When his eyes met hers, she could have sworn she saw empathy in them.

"I'll need to interview you, your staff, the two kids…" He lifted a notebook. "Chris and Eli." He lowered his hand. "I trust they're all here now?"

"They are. And Officer Nelson, I'd rather you didn't talk to Chris or Eli in the dining hall. I don't want to disturb the other kids. You can use my office."

"That would be good." He stepped back from the entrance, put the slim notebook in the back pocket of his jeans and smiled at her with a quirk of his lips. "Uh, and Bee. I'm not an officer. My father was a navy officer, an admiral, actually. I'm a firefighter. You can call me Rand."

Beatrice's head hitched back as if she'd been doused with a bucketful of water. She wished he wouldn't call her that. No one had called her "Bee" since she was little. Coming from Rand, she'd never heard it said with so much velvety charm.

And where had that come from? Rand had been stoic and strong and purposeful during the fire, when he'd saved her and the boys. His gruff exterior only a second ago had caused her to believe he was as rough as sandpaper on the inside as well. But this sudden glimpse of something else—someone else—was unexpected.

But was it real?

He stepped outside. "I'll get my recorder and be right back."

"Recorder?"

"Yeah. I tape the interviews for the captain's records. It will go with all the other forensic samples."

Beatrice wrung her hands as the depth of

his investigation hit her. She looked at her hands and shoved them to her sides. She wasn't the hand-wringing type. She'd just risked her life for her camper kids. She'd do it again. No second thoughts.

But what if Rand's investigation exposed some nuance of neglect? Just how far would he go to fulfill his duties as a firefighter?

"Maybe you should tell me what exactly you're looking for?" she challenged, raising her arms to cross over her chest. Armor to deflect the threat he posed.

"Noncompliance with safety regulations." He raised an eyebrow. "Unfortunately, it's all too common. I've even seen day-care owners who posed as caretakers but in truth were anything but."

"And you think I'm capable of such behavior?"

He stared at her.

"Why would I—or anyone—do such a thing? They're…children, for goodness sake."

"Money. Government funds. Grants."

She held up her palms. "Stop right there. I would never do anything to harm these kids. And what on earth would I gain by starting a fire?"

He shrugged his shoulders. "Insurance

money? I've seen that before, too. Insurance money is a quick way out for people who get into debt."

She narrowed her eyes to slits to filter out his accusations. He probably had seen that kind of person a dozen times over in his line of work. Maybe worse. Pyromaniacs. People whose euphoria escalated with the sound of sirens.

And even though that was nowhere near the kind of person she was, Rand was the kind of by-the-book official who would shut down her camp if he found the tiniest infraction.

Had she caused herself great harm by running into that fire to save Eli and Chris?

And what of the boys themselves? The boys might have had something to do with the fire, but she would not let herself think that either of them had done anything intentional. It all had to be an accident. But even if it was, would the fact that the boys were in her care still be enough to bring charges against her?

She could see the case Rand could make. That accusatory finger of the law was itching to point at her.

Beatrice sensed that if she let her growing sense of guilt show on her face or in her tone of voice, he would suspect her of crimes she hadn't even thought of. That was the problem with being a cop's kid. You could always see the dark side of a situation before you saw the light.

She cocked her chin and pursed her lips. "Well, Mr. Nelson, I can tell you one thing—you're never going to get the truth out of a kid acting like this."

"Me? What are you talking about?"

"None of your questions and interrogations will be easy for a kid. I know you're doing what's necessary and all this is required by the law, but these kids—" she turned her head toward the dining room and then, after a thoughtful pause, back to him "—they're good kids. *All of them.*"

Ouch. Even she thought her defensive tone was sharp enough to pierce granite.

"Look," she said sweetly, changing tack. "Some of them have had a rough life. A couple have had a *very* tough life. Could you be a little…well, softer in your delivery?"

"Softer?"

"Yeah. Not so gruff."

His biceps flexed, bulged and relaxed as he folded his arms over his chest. "You think I sound harsh?" He leaned forward a few inches, but instead of seeming threatening,

his closeness reminded her of the other re-
actions she had to him. The ones that made
her wish they were not in this antagonistic
situation. The ones that flashed visions of
being held in his arms.

"To a kid. Yes."

She peeled her eyes off his arms and
hauled them up to his face. She met his gaze
dead-on.

"I'll take that into consideration. Thanks
for the advice. I'll be right back."

He walked toward the huge fire truck.

His heavy black boots left shallow im-
prints in the dry dirt as he headed across
the summer-bleached grass that in spring had
been dark green velvet. Their indentations
left proof that he was on the job, perform-
ing his duty. Beatrice inhaled deeply as the
space between the two of them lengthened.
She realized that when she was near him, he
didn't just fill the inches and feet between
them, but he overtook her thoughts as well.

He wore regulation black jeans and a short-
sleeved knit shirt, which had the ILFD logo
over the breast pocket. Beatrice had never
been the type to linger long over any male's
physique, but Rand was so perfectly sculp-
tured, it was impossible not to conjure vi-

sions of ancient Greek Olympians and the mighty feats they accomplished.

But then, Rand had carried her and Eli out of a blazing inferno. What was more Herculean than that?

Beatrice was so immersed in her fantasies about Rand, that she didn't notice that he'd walked back to her and had started talking to her.

"Sorry, what?"

He sighed, and started over. "I need to talk to all the kids about fire safety before I have the private, er, interviews."

She had to give him points for carefully choosing his words. Maybe he'd listened to her.

She turned her boot around and let her body follow, using the wall for momentary security. "This way."

The kids were nearly back to normal, Beatrice realized as she entered the dining hall. Their voices were sprinkled with chuckles and had returned to the loud, happy tones she'd heard before the fire.

She clapped her hands three times, the signal for their attention. Usually, it took them a few moments to stop joking with one another. This time they came to abrupt attention.

"Guys. This is Firefighter Rand Nelson.

Some of you met him last night during the fire." She looked pointedly at Eli and Chris. Eli smiled at Rand. Chris scooted back on his chair. He clutched either side of his seat with his hands. Little Ricky's eyes were filled with adoration.

Cindy stared blatantly at Rand's chest. Maisie's cheeks were pink.

Beatrice continued. "Mr. Nelson wants to talk to you all about fire safety."

Beatrice took a step back and nearly toppled over. Quick reflexes on Rand's part saved her from the fall. "Thanks," she said, feeling both clumsy and embarrassed.

"You're welcome," he whispered but didn't give her a second glance.

He turned his attention to the children. His "official" hat was back on.

"The first thing I want to assure you kids is that the fire has been extinguished. To make doubly certain, later this afternoon, our crew will be out here to cut down any remaining trees that appear to be a hazard. At this moment, our forensic team is in the forest to ascertain the origin of the fire."

Little Jessica Kettering raised her hand high above her cropped carrot-red hair. "Sir! Sir!"

Rand looked at Beatrice.

"Her name is Jessica." Beatrice smiled. "Yes, Jessica. What's your question?"

Jessica shoved her thick glasses back up her nose, and angled her unpatched eye directly at Rand. "Do you think someone started it?"

"We can never be sure until our investigation is complete. But since there were no thunderstorms or lightning strikes anywhere in our area last night, we felt we needed some expert eyes on the situation."

"Sir!" Little Ricky threw his hand up. "I think it was gangs."

"Gangs?" Rand questioned. "What's your name, son?"

"Ricky. I've seen all kinds of things on the news about the gangs near Indian Lake. We have to be careful because they try to give drugs to little kids."

Beatrice realized there were more fears buzzing in her camp kids' heads than hornets in a nest. Camp was supposed to be an oasis for children. Their summer idyll. "Ricky, you are right. We all have to be very careful. That's why we have camp rules about lights out and being in your cabin at sundown. We take special care to make sure all you kids are safe. That's why Miss Cindy, Miss Maisie and Mr. Bruce are always close to you. We don't ever want you to feel that you are alone."

"We don't feel alone, Miss Beatrice," Susan Kettering said, grasping Jessica's hand. "This is the best place. You make it the best for us."

"Thank you, Susan."

Beatrice felt yet another tiny tear fall from her eye. She blamed the fire for her highly charged emotional state this morning. As she lifted her finger to slide it off her cheek, she noticed Rand watching her. His face was expressionless. Part of his stoic on-the-job mask, she guessed. But his eyes probed her more deeply than she ever remembered a man doing. She felt her knees weaken, but this time she was glad she had the air boot, because it helped her maintain her balance.

"And thank you for listening, kids. Finish your breakfast and take your dishes to the kitchen for Miss Amanda. You all know your next activities." She nodded for Bruce, Maisie and Cindy to gather their groups.

"Except for Chris and Eli," Rand said in a loud tone that caused both boys to stop in their tracks. "I need to talk to both of you. Miss Beatrice has said that I can use her office." Rand walked over and put strong hands on each boy's shoulder. "Where is it?"

"This way," Eli replied, looking up at Rand.

Beatrice held her breath as she watched Chris blanch to a ghostly white.

"Um, Mr. Nelson, didn't you say you needed to speak with me, first?" she asked.

He glanced at Chris and then raised his eyes to Beatrice. He dropped his hands off their shoulders. "I did."

"Okay, boys. You go out and join Mr. Bruce. I'll call you later if we need you."

Chris nearly shot to the dining hall's back screen door. Eli raced after him.

Beatrice hobbled over to Rand, one hand on her hip. "I know what you're thinking."

"Do you, now?"

"I do. But until I get a formal forensic report from your guys out there in that forest, I'd rather you didn't upset the children."

"Fair enough."

"If there's any hot seat you're cooking up, I'll be the only one occupying it."

"Look, Bee—"

"The name's Beatrice."

He frowned. "All right. I'll focus the questions on you. For now."

Questions that can trip me up, she thought. Her dad had been a cop. He'd always said that anyone who disclosed personal information was at risk. People didn't understand how ordinary actions in one's life could be twisted by a prosecutor against them. He'd told her he'd seen innocent men sent to prison and murderers set free. She didn't have anything to hide from Rand, or anyone, but an investigation of any kind made her nervous. It rattled the bars of her carefully built security gates.

Curiously, trepidation filled his face and he shifted his weight from one foot to the other as if he didn't want to go through this any more than she did. But how could that be? He was so formal. So official.

She knew he had a job to do, but could she trust this feeling of hers that he was uncomfortable enforcing codes and regulations? Did he always feel this way about this part of his job, or was it just her camp and this particular fire that bothered him? And if it was, could she trust that he might be lenient with her if he did find her culpable?

"Let's go to my office," she said, then led the way down a wood-paneled hallway.

Her office was quaint and situated in the southwest corner of the building with casement windows on two sides of the room, which allowed dappled light and patterns of maple leaves to splay across the plaster walls.

There were no drapes or blinds on the windows, as Beatrice wanted as much sunlight to enter the room as possible.

Her desk was like most of her personal furniture—old, distressed, battered, in need of reupholstering and bought at yard sales, though loved and adored by her. The lamps were another thing altogether. They were true antiques. Most were Frank Lloyd Wright designs in stained glass and she'd sat in the rain for hours at area estate sales to win them. Luckily, she'd never paid more than a hundred dollars for any of them, but they were her treasures. Where other women fancied jewelry or leather handbags, for Beatrice, her Achilles' heel was the lamps—these illuminations that glowed with colored lights through dark nights or gloomy days. They made her smile and gave her hope when she banged away at her electric calculator and pulled up a white tape with globs of red ink.

"Please, have a seat," she said, motioning to a rumpled linen-slip-covered club chair that sagged, but whose bones were pure 1940s craftsman-designed hardwood.

Rand lowered himself into the chair. It groaned with his solid weight. He laid his hands on the rounded arms. "I like this chair. A family heirloom?"

"Not quite. There's nothing heirloom about my family," she said, sitting in the swiveling wooden desk chair.

Though the desk chair was circa 1930 and she'd seen replicas in box stores selling for hundreds of dollars, she'd snagged hers on Maple Avenue in Indian Lake during the spring cleanup days—an event in April where residents put out unwanted furniture and the city garbage trucks picked them up for free. Mrs. Beabots, whom she'd known since she bought the camp and was a true believer in her mission, had phoned her to tip her off to some special finds down the boulevard, at Katia and Austin McCreary's house.

Beatrice hadn't wasted a minute. A call from Mrs. Beabots, who'd obviously prescouted Maple Boulevard for her, was never taken lightly by anyone in town. That day, Beatrice came back to camp in a rented truck with end tables, a Ping-Pong table, a set of twin beds with headboards for the women counselors' cabin, one walnut bookshelf and a credenza for the far end of the dining room near the stone fireplace.

The following week, Mrs. Beabots had donated the tables and chairs the children now ate at for every meal. Just thinking of the octogenarian's generosity brought an emotional lump to her throat.

"Nice rug, too," he said, tapping the red, gold and black wool rug.

"Thanks, I hooked it myself."

His eyes darted to her face. "You're kidding?"

She shrugged. "I hook rugs. Mea culpa. I do it in the winter when the days are lonely and bleak here at the camp. It keeps me busy at night."

His face went solemn. He blinked and shook his head slightly, as if he didn't believe her. Then he took out the recorder.

"So, for the record, how long have you had the camp?"

His voice took on an intimidating tone that matched the physical strength of the man. She was amazed at how quickly he could bounce from pleasantries to business. Then again, that could be a self-criticism since it was so easy for her brain to remain in idyllic fields and grasses of splendor. Anywhere to avoid the shards of reality, most of which had to do with her shrinking financial status.

"Three years and a few months," she answered. "But we've only been open two summers. I spent a great deal of time—not to mention my small inheritance and all my savings—on upgrading the camp. It's been a financial struggle, I'll tell you, but I've done it. I've put in the regulation wheelchair ramps, and we have very safe recreation equipment. I've upgraded all the electrical, bought new beds, linens, kitchen equipment. If you didn't know, the camp was built in the early 1950s. The bones of the place are solid as a rock. But the rest… Frankly, I have to admit that from a financial perspective I would have been better off bulldozing it down and starting over with new buildings. The bank would have been happier. But I loved this place too much to tear it down. Anyway, the bank did give me a loan for the new plumbing and electrical system."

"And that's all up to code?"

"Absolutely!" She ground her back teeth. Man, but she hated officiousness. "I have the inspections and permits if you need to see those."

"I'll take your word for it. But keep them handy if it comes up."

"Comes up?" She glared at him.

"I'm trying to help you, Bee… Beatrice. If there was an incident last night, my chief might ask for documentation of your inspections."

"Why?"

"If that fire had crossed the road then your camp would have ignited. All it would have taken was a strong wind for the sparks to carry. City regulations are there to protect you. In an emergency, do you have enough power to run electrical equipment? Enough water to feed fire hoses once the pumper is empty? I see you have a little lake. You could use the water from that lake, but you'd need a sump pump to extract it. And that sump pump would require an electrical feed."

"I understand."

"I'll have to make sure everything is in order."

"Mr. Nelson..." She took a deep breath, but it didn't calm her at all. In fact, she felt she was about to ignite with indignation, which happened nearly every time she defended her camp. "I bought this place because I loved it when I came as a kid. It was lovely here. I met real friends here. You see, I grew up in Chicago, in the city, actually, and life was all about concrete and traffic and buildings. I didn't have a yard. I had an elevator. I never had a dog or cat. When I came to camp, I felt I was me, for the first time."

"You never had a cat?"

"No."

"And you don't have one now?"

"I still want one. But we've had a few kids with allergies."

"Let me guess, cat dander. Dog hair."

She mimed shooting him with her pointed finger. "You got it."

He pursed his lips. "I have a cat." He paused. "And a dog."

"Don't tell me—it's a dalmation."

He lifted his shoulders.

"No way."

Then he laughed. "I'm kidding. Jack Russell terrier. He can't even jump up on my lap. He was the rescue dog of all time."

"You saved him from a fire?"

"No. I saw his owner dump him at the fire station. He was just a pup. I rushed to get him before the idiot drove over him with his car. He was high or drunk. I called 911 and gave them his license plate."

"Did they catch him?"

"Uh-huh." He grinned and for the first time she noticed a dimple in his left cheek. "But I kept the dog."

She couldn't help it. She should be wary of him, this official in his black jeans and shirt "uniform," but impossibly, he won her over. She needed to keep her mind on the issue at hand. "You're lucky. But I have to think of the kids, and funneling all the money I have into making this a great space for them, albeit a low-tech one. Kids here learn to swim, fish, row a boat, dive and give CPR. There's no video games or motorized vehicles. They've got Ping-Pong, board games, puzzles and group activities. Art classes, tennis, badminton, tetherball and no swimming pool. The shallow lake out back is for kayaks and rowboats—small, new and very watertight rowboats.

"My garage-sale finds, I save for me, Amanda, the cook, and the counselors. The kids get the best of everything."

"Albeit low-tech," he added, echoing her.

"Right."

"It does sound like a dream."

"Thanks." She gave him a slight smile.

"The kids. Tell me more about them. Like Eli, for example."

"Some of the kids have special needs, but Eli and Chris are foster kids. We get several of those a year. Most of the foster children's fees are paid by the state or the county, which you pointedly addressed earlier."

Rand cleared his throat.

Was that an apology for accusing the innocent before being proven guilty? Or did he just default to guilt? And why? she wondered.

"You were saying?" he urged.

Beatrice continued. "Zoey Phillips from DCS has recommended my camp to other Child Service Departments and thanks to her and others like her, we are booked weekly until school starts. We'll stay open on weekends only up 'til Thanksgiving, when the weather gets too cold."

"I never heard of a camp staying open so long."

"Frankly, I need the income. And this year, there's a demand. Look, Mr. Nelson—"

"Rand," he interrupted.

"Rand. The foster kids can't afford a cell phone or tablet. I believe all children need fresh air and sunshine, time to play and be kids. Those needs don't know a season. If I could afford the kind of heat it would take to stay open all winter, I'd do it. I'd have skating lessons on the little lake. Ice hockey, tobogganing, cross-country skiing. This is the land to do those things. The outdoors is the only place to live one's life fully."

He stared at her. "I agree."

"I want to show these kids how wonderful life can be in the out-of-doors." She knew her words came out in a passionate rush, but she didn't care how carried away she got. She believed in her purpose. She'd bet all her life savings on this kids' camp. She'd cleaned, scrubbed, painted, pounded nails, replaced pipe and hammered in roof shingles to save money to provide the best camp she could. And he wasn't going to take it away.

Just then, there was a firm rap at the door.

Beatrice looked up into the face of a middle-aged, medium-height man with thinning brown hair. He wore a short-sleeved summer shirt, tan trousers and sneakers. He carried a plastic kit that looked like a fishing tackle box.

"Rand, we're finished. I'll be sending my formal report to the chief."

Beatrice assumed this man was the head of the forensics team.

Rand bolted to his feet, his face stern, his eyes obsidian stones as he looked at the man.

Beatrice could see that Rand was braced for bad news. "Arson?"

"Afraid so," the man answered.

Rand turned to her. "Beatrice Wilcox, may I introduce Art Bishop, our forensic investigator. Art, this is Beatrice."

"Mr. Bishop." Beatrice nodded but bit off her words so sharply, she hoped both men would feel the sting. "No one would deliberately set that forest on fire," Beatrice countered.

"Sure they would. It could be you, Miss Wilcox. Maybe you wanted to burn this old camp down. Collect insurance money to pay off debts."

"I just spent the last few minutes trying to convince Mr. Nelson how preposterous that idea is!"

The man shrugged his shoulders. "We see it all the time. People who do that wind up in prison."

Beatrice looked into Rand's dark, unforgiving eyes and felt her heart turn cold.

CHAPTER SEVEN

RAND HAD SUSPECTED arson all along. It was the only probable explanation. His eyes darted to Beatrice. He was convinced now that she would never destroy her camp. She'd poured her heart out to him, relating her dreams with so much passion, he'd felt his own heart kick up a notch. But Art Bishop brought them both back down to earth.

"You are very mistaken." Beatrice refuted the forensic expert by slapping her desk with her palm.

Art stepped up to her desk. He handed her a business card. "My card. The fire chief can provide a more extensive report if you wish. After the report is filed, I can answer any questions you'd have." He looked at Rand. "Can I talk to you? Outside?"

"Sure." Rand followed Art down the hall and to the front drive.

"What did you find?"

"I went directly to the area where you said you found the woman and the younger boy.

My guess was that the little kid didn't stray that far from the fire's origin." He reached in his pocket and pulled out a plastic bag. "It's burned, but that's a Hershey bar wrapper. And this is a kid's metal toy car."

"Hot Wheels. I used to collect these."

"So did I," Art said. "I figure he dropped it or it fell out of his pocket when the fire started and he ran."

"My guess is it was accidental. The kids could be charged with reckless burning. Which would mean detention hearings, attorneys, dispositional hearings, review hearings. Time in detention halls. That's a lot of trauma for a kid."

"That's gonna be your call. I have to write it up as arson because it was man-made. You talk to them. Find out all you can."

"Still, there will be consequences," Rand said sternly.

"There's always consequences. The sooner these kids learn that, the better their lives."

Rand shoved his hands in his pockets and looked back at the dining-hall building.

"You got any idea who did this?" Art asked.

"I do."

Art gazed up to the crystal blue sky. He didn't lower his head as he spoke. "Kids. A crude fire in a small clearing but unfortunately not far enough away from all those dry pine nettles and grass."

"Probably didn't even take much wind to get it going, did it?"

"Nope. There was a lot of dry kindling around. Broken limbs. Twigs from storms. The usual." Art pointed down the gravel road. "I saw that you noted there is only one hydrant out here. Code is three."

"I noted that, yes," Rand replied in a low tone. "If it hadn't been for the change in weather, the wind dying and the rain, the fire would have been worse and taken us longer to extinguish. I've already surmised Miss Wilcox is running this place on a shoestring. And she may not have been aware of that code—it's only a year old."

"Following it is for these kids' safety."

"I know." He scratched the back of his neck roughly as if spiders were crawling down it. "I'm just doing my job, so why do I feel so guilty?"

"Can't say." Art glanced around at the camp. "I remember this place. I came here as a kid. I'm glad someone reopened it. She do all this?"

"Says she did."

"Amazing woman. It's a lot of work." He

clicked the side of his mouth, making a snapping sound. "She's pretty, too."

"I noticed."

"Did you?"

Rand cleared his throat. "Yeah. Last night when I saw her at the hospital."

"You? Went to see a victim?"

"She's strong. Tough. She'd do anything for these kids. Lay down her life. And so sweet—like a honeybee. I've never met anyone like her."

Art stared at Rand with rounded eyes. "I see that."

Rand stared off. "And I'm the one who keeps delivering bad news to her."

"Yeah. That'll make it hard to get on her good side."

"Impossible, you mean."

Art put the plastic bag back in his pocket and shuffled his forensic kit to his left hand so he could extend his other hand to Rand. "Thanks for reminding me I take care of the small stuff."

"Would you shut up?" Rand slapped him on the back. "You coming over for barbecue this Sunday? I'm doing ribs. My entire family will be there."

"Can't say. Did you call Alice? She keeps our social schedule."

"I did. She accepted."

"Great. I'll bring beer and my famous Boston baked beans. See you Sunday. About five?"

"You got it." Rand gave him a thumbs-up, then went back to Beatrice's office. He rubbed his nape again.

Rand had written over a hundred reports during his career. Handled all kinds of investigations. Real arson. Accidents. Chemical explosions. He'd never had a problem sorting out the truth and reporting it.

So why did this particular investigation pierce him like an arrow? It was his responsibility to make certain the kids were protected. That's what city and county codes were for.

It didn't take a wizard to see just how much Beatrice was struggling financially with this camp. It was his bet she didn't even charge enough for the kids' visits. Particularly foster kids like Eli and Chris. State funds were not exactly extravagant. He'd bet she'd let them stay for free if she could.

She had that kind of heart. Tender. Vulnerable. Giving. The kind of heart that could knock a man to his knees.

The problem with big-hearted people, though, was they expected others to bend rules for them. Make concessions because that's what they would do if the situation was reversed.

But ever since smoke-jump training in Idaho, he'd learned to play by the rule book. Because if he didn't, others would—and did—get hurt.

Get a grip, Rand. You're just doing your job.

She was on the telephone finishing a call as he came to stand in the doorway.

"I'd like to speak to Eli and Chris, if I may," he said once she hung up. "I have a few questions I'd like to ask."

"No."

"Excuse me?"

Her eyes darted to her landline receiver. "That was my attorney. He says I shouldn't consent to anything until I see the formal report from the fire chief."

Rand was surprised. He'd thought they'd started to bond. And perhaps they had, but that was before Art Bishop had entered with his findings. The landscape had changed then as quickly as a brush fire sweeping across a sun-scorched prairie.

"I'll get that report for you, but it's not complete until I conduct this interview."

She rose slowly from the desk and hobbled

around to the side. "You need to understand something, Mr. Nelson."

Uh-oh. We're back to formalities. "And that is?"

"These kids are not just campers coming to spend a week or weekend at Indian Lake Youth Camp. They are my responsibility. They look to me for guidance. I'm here to help them whether they have parents or not."

He stepped closer. "I don't mean any harm to you or these kids. But I have a job to do and I'm going to do it. I'll be back with the report. I'll expect to talk to Eli and Chris at that time."

She crossed her arms over her chest. "Fine."

He didn't quite understand why he couldn't take his eyes off her. *Step back, walk away.* But he couldn't. There was something about her that held him like steel to a magnet. He admired her strength and her passion for the kids. He enjoyed talking with her when her feathers were ruffled. But now she looked at him like he was the enemy. He wanted to remind her that he'd saved her life, and Eli's, only a matter of hours ago, but he doubted that would change anything.

Not now that the law had intervened.

As it always did, when wrongdoing was involved.

"Can I ask you something, Mr. Nelson? Professionally?"

"Sure." He braced himself.

"Do you think I'd burn my camp down?"

"No. I do not."

"Then you really want to blame the kids? I can't believe for a minute that Eli or Chris would deliberately set a fire."

"You might believe that, but I don't know them. I can't say what was going through their heads. But let's say I give them the benefit of the doubt and find there was no intent. They still might be guilty of reckless burning. And that's a punishable offense."

"But they're children!"

"Agreed. So their sentence would be lighter. My guess is that a detention judge would offer them informal diversion. It's a program that allows for community service as a sentence. If the kids comply, they won't go to court."

"And that's the best they can hope for?"

"Yes. Reckless burning is serious. As the Earth's climate changes and we see staggering increases in forest fires due to drought and alien pests that cause diseases in our trees, the forests have to be protected more than ever."

He had to give her points for the way she stood her ground. Her eyes didn't flicker when he'd hit her with the severity of the situation. Now was not the time to tell her that his report—and his alone—could make all the difference in Eli's and Chris's futures. If he went hard on them, they'd be in detention hall. And if he discovered a lack of remorse in the boys, Rand had no choice but to comply with the law.

He'd been honest when he told her he didn't know these kids.

But he also couldn't deny that this wasn't just a simple case for him. After all, he'd been the one to catch Chris when he fell from the tree. Something had happened to Rand at that moment.

"I'll be back," he said finally.

"Make sure you call me first. I'll have to schedule you in."

"I'll do that," he said, feeling the sharpness of his own words on his tongue.

He marched down the hall and shouldered open the screen door to the dining room as he walked into the blazing sun. He stuck his Ray-Bans on his face, walked to his truck and got in.

Rand wiped his palms on his jeans before turning the ignition.

He wasn't quite sure what there was about Beatrice Wilcox that tossed his emotions from fascination to irritation faster than a rogue wave, but he'd never been bounced around by a woman quite as much.

One thing was for certain—he sure set her teeth on edge. He supposed he couldn't blame her. She probably saw him now as an enemy. Once his investigation was over, he would be very happy indeed to put the Indian Lake Youth Camp and its owner on his list of accomplishments completed.

He rolled down the window, hung his arm over the edge and drove the truck carefully over the gravel so as not to disturb the white and gray stones.

SHOCK WAS NOT a new experience for Beatrice. She'd taken many blows in her life—from the day her father was shot and killed in the line of duty, to her mother's announcement that she was moving to Los Angeles to star in a daytime soap opera, to yesterday's fire, when Eli and Chris had gone missing in the inferno.

But this time it wasn't just her who would suffer.

Knowing young boys, and Chris's authority issues, she feared Rand would find that Chris and his brother did have something to do with why the fire had started.

And Beatrice didn't doubt Rand's inference that his testimony would weigh heavily with police and in a court of law. If it came to that.

She swept her palms over her face and realized she was perspiring. Her nerves affected her body in random ways. She could break out in a sweat on a subzero day. Start shivering in the middle of a heat wave. Her hands had a tendency to shake when she reconciled her checking account. A person prone to such tendencies probably wasn't the best role model for children.

The kids.

It was the children that forced Beatrice to get a grip. Their trusting expressions and heartfelt, unselfish hugs gave her life meaning.

Beatrice knew how it felt to be abandoned. To be alone. Without real family. Once she'd moved out of Chicago and come to Indian Lake, she'd found real friends. To her, Mrs. Beabots, Maddie Barzonni, Sarah Jensen Bosworth were family—the big, huge family she'd always dreamed of.

Eli and Chris had been cast into the world with the worst of parents. A drug dealer for a father and an addict for a mother. They'd been raising themselves for years. She understood what that was like. That's why she would do just about anything for them. Their lives had been far too difficult, and if they were accused of setting the fire, they'd be headed for a juvenile correctional facility. For a kid like Chris, who already had an "attitude" problem, he would emerge even more jaded, if not completely corrupted.

Beatrice had read too many testimonials from kids who'd been incarcerated and then released. The "scars of the bars" were burned on their souls. It took strength of character to overcome those years, and without some kind of parental love, somewhere in their past, they would never be rehabilitated.

Even if Chris purposefully set the fire, Beatrice couldn't sentence him to that fate. He didn't need the book thrown at him; he needed love.

But how to convince Mr. Rules-and-Regulations of that?

CHAPTER EIGHT

TRUE TO HIS WORD, Rand called Beatrice to arrange for an interview with Chris and Eli. They settled on later that day. He wasn't quite sure if Beatrice had stalled for time by demanding this formal request, or if she simply didn't trust him.

Probably both, he surmised as he pulled into the camp drive and turned off his truck. He glanced at his reflection in the rearview mirror and stared at the Ray-Bans he was wearing and his official ILFD short-sleeved black summer knit shirt with the banded collar. *Hmm. Beatrice was right.* He would look intimidating to a kid.

He whipped off the sunglasses and stowed them in the console compartment between the seats. He'd spent so much of his life being the official on the job—as a fire marshal, the captain of his smoke-jumper team, a smoke-jumper trainer—that talking to a group of frightened kids was intimidating to *him*. It was a fine line between making his point and scaring them enough that he didn't get through or they wouldn't let him in.

The devil of it was that he liked kids. Loved them, really. But when it came to safety rules, ones they should obey for their own good and welfare, he did get hard-nosed. He knew it.

But in the end, he couldn't help it.

If he was a bit hard on the kids, maybe they would remember him and they'd heed his sound advice and experience. After all, the terror of potentially losing Chris and Eli to the flames was fresh and raw. Even to Rand.

He grabbed his cell phone, then the stamped and recorded forensic report from the passenger seat and the report from his captain.

As he got out of the truck, he rolled his neck around his shoulders to try and relax. It did no good. His muscles were taut, prepared for battle.

He walked across the gravel drive to the door. He cleared his throat and prepared himself for the interview.

He placed his hand around the latch, but the door was opened from the other side.

"I saw you drive up," Beatrice said with a smile, but the tiny, tense lines between her eyebrows told him she was faking her kind greeting. She was nervous.

Did she suspect the kids of being guilty, too? Was she hiding pertinent information that by law she was required to divulge to him? Or was she going to hide behind her attorney again? And if she did, was that how their relationship was going to advance?

Relationship?

Where had that thought come from?

"Hi," he finally said. "Sorry to be a little late."

"Absolutely," she said. "Chris and Eli have been waiting in my office."

Swell. How long had they been waiting? Both boys must feel like they were already on the hot seat. Anticipation like that could make a kid go left on him. Lie. Snark his way around the truth. Quibble and generally evade every question Rand would pose. He wished she'd allowed him to interview the kids hours ago, when he was first here. They would have been unprepared for his questions. He might have had a chance to get through to them.

But Beatrice had only been following her attorney's advice and legal protocol. She'd impressed him again.

"Lead the way," he said.

"Can I get you anything?"

He wanted to ask if the front door was the quickest exit. "No, thanks. I'm good," he said quickly.

She hobbled on her crutches toward her office door and he couldn't help noticing the scent of flowers and summery spices she wore. Rosemary and eucalyptus. Jasmine and rose. Then he noticed her burned hair. Obviously, she put the kids first and thought of herself last.

He lifted his hand to touch the crimped ends of her hair, where the raging flames had nearly taken her life. She probably had no idea how close she'd come to death, but that was his job, his experience. He shivered, though there was no air-conditioning in the building. Au naturel, Beatrice had explained. The place had filtered fans to sift out harmful airborne allergens and pollens, but the air was untouched by ions and artificial Freon.

It was pure and free.

Like her.

"Mr. Nelson." She turned to him and caught him with his hand in the air.

"Um. Yes?"

She hopped away from the door, gesturing with her head for him to enter her office.

"Eli and Chris are waiting for you. Aren't you, boys?"

"Yes, ma'am," they chorused.

"You may sit at my desk, Mr. Nelson," she said.

"That's okay, I'll stand."

Beatrice moved behind the boys' chairs as Rand walked in front of them. He looked up at Beatrice, who frowned and shook her head. She pointed to the chair. "Truly, I don't mind if you sit," she said with the terse direction of a school principal.

Rand gave her a single nod and went around the desk. He sat down.

"Better?" she asked.

"Um, better." He squirmed under her glare. She was right. If he'd been one of these boys, he would have been scared out of his wits to look up at a guy who was all muscle and, in his work boots, nearly six feet five inches tall. *Good call*, he thought. Though he didn't particularly like the idea that Beatrice was calling the shots before his interview even got started.

His eyes latched on hers. "You don't need to stay, Miss Beatrice."

"Oh, but my attorney insists that I do."

Her attorney. Again. Sounded to him like they had been conversing a good deal. Rand knew now he had to get the truth out of these kids in the next few minutes.

"Chris, I'll start with you. Why don't you tell me exactly how you two came to be over there in the woods—"

Chris slammed his arms across his chest. "I'm not sayin' a word."

"Why not?"

"I want my own attorney."

Rand lowered his chin and rolled his eyes up at Chris. "This isn't a court of law, Chris. It's just an informal question-and-answer period. I'm just trying to find out what happened."

"No, you're not."

"Excuse me?" Rand barked.

Beatrice coughed.

Rand ignored her.

"Chris, just tell me what happened."

Chris cocked his head backward, toward Beatrice, but never took his steely eyes off Rand. "If she can have an attorney so can we. It's the right of the land. I know about these things. All you want to do is pin something on me and Eli so's you can send us off to some juvie hall or correction center. Then neither you or Miss Beatrice have to deal with us. Now or ever."

"That's not true!" Beatrice exploded with sorrow-filled emotion.

"Now, just a minute, Chris. It's nothing like that at all," Rand said. "I have a right to the truth, and so does Miss Beatrice. She's been very kind to you and your brother from everything that I can see. So tell me what happened!" He hit his fist on the desk.

Quickly, he slid his hand underneath the desk. He'd gotten carried away. Blast it! But then, he'd been in one too many situations when a junior fire jumper hadn't listened to him, had not obeyed the rules. Had taken risks—and lives had been lost.

Chris was only a kid, but if he'd started the fire, he was at fault.

While Rand stared at Chris, he'd forgotten that Eli was even in the room. The skinny kid had inched away from his brother to the far side of his chair. His hands were clasped in his lap and his head was lowered, his chin so far into his little chest, Rand was certain it had left an indelible dent.

Rand's eyes slid surreptitiously to Eli and then back to Chris, who was still glaring at him.

Beatrice put both hands on Chris's shoulders and massaged them gently. She whispered something into Chris's ear, then kissed the side of his cheek.

Rand saw Chris's eyes slowly close, as if he was taking in every single gesture of affection she gave him. The boy's cheeks flushed pink, though that faded fast, as if he wasn't used to endearments or caresses.

Rand felt his heart pinch. His own mother had done all those things to him so many times growing up. Heck, just last Sunday she'd given him a hug for grilling the family some bratwurst. She'd kissed his cheek when she left and there had been love in her eyes, and more, pride.

What had it been like for Chris and Eli to have never seen pride in their parents' eyes?

"We stole stuff," Eli mumbled.

Rand's head whirled to the younger boy. "What?"

Beatrice moved to Eli and leaned down to him. "What are you saying, sweetheart?"

Eli's voice warbled like a newborn baby robin. "We—we snuck out of our cabin."

"Eli, shut up!" Chris shouted.

Eli kept his head down and didn't look at his brother or the adults in the room. "No, I have to tell the truth, even if you hit me."

"I'm not going to hit you, Eli." Chris

reached for his brother's forearm. "But don't do this. They could send us to jail."

"I don't care. I don't want anything bad to happen to Miss Beatrice. Don't you see? She loves us." Eli raised eyes that were swimming with tears to his brother.

"Just what did you steal, Eli?" Rand asked with a voice he hadn't meant to be quite so gravelly and accusatory.

Beatrice shot him a quelling I'll-kill-you-later look. To the little boy, she said, "Eli, sweetheart. You know there is nothing here in the camp that isn't meant for you children to use. You know that, right?"

"I do," he sniffed.

"Then what did you steal?" she asked, whisking his tears from his cheeks.

"Me and Chris never had s'mores like you made for us. We couldn't believe it. Graham crackers and marshmallows and all that chocolate melted together! I told Chris I thought we were living in heaven. There were so many times when we had no food and Chris gave me his. So I wanted him to have another treat. I told him I would go to the pantry after lights out and get us the stuff to make more s'mores. Plenty of chocolate. It was his idea to go out into the woods across the street, where no one would see us. We'd make a little fire so we could melt the marshmallow and chocolate, just like you did, Miss Beatrice." He looked at Beatrice as a new round of tears filled his eyes, magnifying the size of his irises, a sea of blue in a forlorn face.

"Go on, honey. It's okay," she urged Eli, but it was Chris who continued.

Rand sat spellbound.

"It was a small fire," Chris said. "I only had a few sticks and some pine nettles."

"But the ground was strewn with dry pine nettles that quickly caught fire, too," Rand said.

"It was so dark." Chris lowered his voice as regret rattled through his voice. "I didn't see them. I didn't know…"

"It's my fault," Eli said. "I wanted Chris to have that s'more. He likes them." Eli gulped back another round of tears.

Beatrice hugged Eli to her chest and rubbed her hands on his thin back. "It's okay. It's okay."

Chris stiffened his neck and pinned Rand with his eyes. "So are you going to press charges against us?"

"Son, I'm only making out a report. That's not my call."

"But your report could send us to juvie hall," Chris said firmly.

Beatrice cut in. "Mr. Nelson has told me that you would have had to deliberately set the fire to be punished with time in a juvenile detention center. And this was an accident." She looked at Rand with pleading eyes.

Their story had softened Rand's heart to butter. He'd write the most favorable report for them he could, and if circumstances did put the boys in front of a judge for a hearing, he'd speak up for them and request community service. Their restitution would be minimal.

But at the moment, he still needed them to see him as an authority figure. Rand stood up. "Forest fires are increasing all over our country, guys. Civil authorities don't take these fires lightly anymore. Because more and more houses are being built close to forests, a fire can endanger homes and people. When a fire starts, it's like a living being who is very mad. It wants to wreak havoc. Firefighters risk their lives to contain these fires."

"Like you did for us," Chris said.

"I did."

Rand held Chris's eyes for a long moment and Rand finally glimpsed what he'd hoped to establish with Chris when he'd asked the boy to fall into his arms: trust.

As imperious as Rand must have seemed to Chris, the boy still had faith in him. Rand would cling to that.

"So you know, Chris, Eli—I'm following orders with this interview. I have to obey my superiors and they report to the county commissioners. But I will promise you this. Because I know you love each other, and you didn't mean any harm, I will do all I can to explain the circumstances to the city and the county. There may be restitution you will have to pay. Counseling or community service. But I'll plead your case. I'll do what I can. The rest is out of my hands."

Chris had held his breath until he finally said, "Fine. Can we go?"

Rand waited for a long moment, thinking he would get an apology or even a thank-you, but he didn't receive either. "I think that would be best," Rand agreed.

Chris swooped out of his chair, grabbed Eli's hand and urged him away from Beatrice. "C'mon. We'll miss badminton."

The boys left.

Beatrice watched them leave and then turned back toward Rand.

"You got what you came for."

"I did." He swallowed, wondering how she managed to do that—put Loctite under his boot soles so that he couldn't move.

"Thank you for going to bat for the boys." She paused. "What about me? What are the consequences of your report for me?"

He didn't mean to frighten her, but she should be aware. Based on his report, she could be found negligent. The county could cut her funding for the foster kids. And there was no predicting what the very overloaded child protective department would do.

He knew she was running on a thin financial cord. The loss of the foster kids could break it.

He wanted to quell her fears, but he knew it was impossible. He was the messenger pulling the alarm. It was his job.

"I can't say," he responded finally. "But the report will mostly focus on Chris and Eli. Those boys need guidance. They have to understand that there are consequences to all behaviors."

"They need love, Rand. Bushels and bushels of it. I don't know if anyone has a heart big enough to give the kind of love that would fill the empty space that Chris has."

"You do," he said aloud. And he meant it.

Her blue eyes misted, her face softened

and a radiance from some deep part of her soul shone through her face. Beatrice was all heart. Nothing but heart.

He'd never met anyone like her.

And something told him, he never would again.

CHAPTER NINE

"YOU WANT A cup of coffee?" Beatrice asked. She had to do something. Say something. Standing here with Rand's eyes locked on her face didn't make her nervous in the least. It was just the opposite. She felt comfortable and secure, and that was the most frightening feeling of all.

He was the guy who could close her camp down, send the boys to juvenile hall, cite her for negligence, cause her to lose everything. But there was something about Rand that encouraged her to trust him, and heaven help her, she wanted to know what it was.

She told herself that the fact that Rand was attractive had nothing to do with it.

She saw a dichotomy in him, and she wanted to discover who the real Rand was. The official who was just doing his job, or the near-fantasy hero who carried her through a flaming forest?

No. Rand was real. Heart-poundingly real.

"Yeah, sure," he said.

Using the crutches, she managed to hop to the kitchen. He followed. At this time in the afternoon, the place was empty.

"Wow. Great kitchen. And an old Wolfe gas stove. I could go crazy in this place," he said.

"You cook?"

"A hobby. Grill, roast, smoke and steam." He grinned. "But I'm pretty good at it, so my family and friends tell me."

"That's great."

She leaned the crutches on the counter and went to the pantry to withdraw coffee. "You want cream or sugar? Sweetener? Milk? I have everything."

"I'm easy. Just black."

As she put filtered water from a jug into a kettle to boil and pulled out a French press she said, "Do you really like it black or is that because you're always in a hurry?"

She glanced over her shoulder for his reply and was glad she did. He grinned at her and cocked his head.

"How did you know?"

"I'm betting you really like it with frothed milk, cream maybe, and...hmm. Raw sugar is my guess. The big-granule, brown kind."

"I do. What are you, psychic?"

"No. But since you like to cook, you couldn't

possibly be a splash-and-go kinda guy. You're different."

"I am? I mean, I am." He chuckled. He pointed to her ankle and the air boot. "Hey, I should be doing all this. You should rest."

"Don't be silly. I know where everything is and you don't."

"I could learn," he answered quickly.

Beatrice stopped midmotion. Did he mean that? Why would he want to learn about her kitchen?

He got up and went to the windowsill over the sink, where a long, narrow pharmacy box sat. "This for your burns?"

"Yes," she said, scooping espresso into the carafe. Then she took out organic milk from the refrigerator and placed it in front of him. He watched as she hobbled around the room using the island counter for support rather than the crutches.

"Have you treated your burns today?" he asked accusatorily.

"Not since dawn. I've been busy." She reached for a box of raw sugar.

"Here, then. Let me," he replied and walked over to her. He took out the tube and unscrewed the top. "Give me your arm."

"I'm making your coffee," she argued.

"Stop taking care of the world and let me

do this for you." He took the spoon from her fingers, and she felt that same warmth and comfort she'd felt before from him. He lingered over her fingers, as if inspecting them for more burns. Or was he still gathering information? Judging from the slight upward curve to his lips, he liked what he found.

"You admiring my hand?"

"You have a piano player's hands—long and tapered. And they're soft. I didn't expect that, since you're the camp's, well, handyman and all-around fixer of things." He chuckled.

"Well, you're right about that. I'm the only one to do simple repairs, and there's always something."

He held her forearm in his large hand. "Do you scar easily?" he asked as he smeared the ointment on her arm, taking his time.

"Do you think the burns will scar?" She looked at her arm. It was peppered with blisters. The blond hairs on her arm were singed and some appeared to have melted away. She wondered if they would grow back. Maybe not. Another reminder of the change in her world since the fire.

"Hard to say. What about those on the back of your neck?"

"I couldn't get to them."

"Turn around," he ordered.

Rather than argue, she turned and lifted the stray tendrils that had fallen out of her ponytail band. She'd worn cheap gold hoops in her ears. Her only concession to fashion during camp days.

His fingers were large, but when he touched her, the pressure was no more than a feather against her skin. She shivered.

"You okay?"

Not really. No. "Yeah."

"Not used to being touched, are you?"

"Not since I was a kid, really."

"Why's that?"

"My dad was the one in my family who was big on physical affection."

"Lucky you. My dad was rigid. The opposite of my mom. But I loved him."

"Yeah. I loved my Dad, too. When I was very little on cold winter nights we'd sit by the fireplace and he'd brush my hair dry after my bath."

"Your mom didn't do that?"

"No. She was too busy brushing her own hair. Or trying on clothes or practicing lines for another audition."

"She's an actress?"

"Yes. Fortunately, right now, she's employed. She's in LA. She's got a soap."

"That's good, right?"

"Very good. She's occupied. Not broke or calling me for a loan."

"Hmm. I can see that would be difficult."

He smoothed more ointment on yet another burn. This time, it smarted. "Ow!"

"I'm so sorry!" he said.

"It's okay."

She pressed her fingers near the edge of the burn and laughed. "I always tell the kids that a kiss makes things better. Maybe not in this case."

"I can give it a try…"

The next thing she knew, his lips, which were full, soft and warm, were pressed against the back of her neck. It was a purposeful and reverent kiss. Her body relaxed, her boot slipped ever so slightly and she leaned against his rock-hard chest. His right arm slipped down to her waist to steady her, but it didn't leave. His fingers gripped her as if holding her to the spot, keeping her close to him.

Through her back, she could feel his heart thrumming, then pounding as if he'd started to run, but he was as bolted to the floor as she was. She wouldn't move if her life depended on it.

Beatrice didn't dare question what was happening to her because she wanted it to happen. Not being attracted to Rand was almost out of the question. She didn't know him, but through some sacred passage in her heart, she believed she knew just what kind of man he was.

He was a protector, a hero.

The same qualities that had gotten her father killed.

She started to pull away.

"Did that help? Is it better?"

"The doctor said this ointment would do the trick," she answered, turning slowly around.

He didn't move his hand from her waist. And when she gazed up into his brown eyes, she could see that he was shaken.

She'd expected lightheartedness. Flirting, maybe. But not this emotional questioning she saw in his eyes. He was looking at her as if she'd changed somehow.

"My mother said love heals all wounds."

She sighed. "I wish that it did."

He looked as if she'd slapped him. Maybe that had been her point.

"Well, you said you loved your father."

"I did. But he was an adventurous man. He took a lot of risks in his career as a Chicago police detective. And that's why he was shot and killed in the line of duty."

"I see."

Coffee aroma filled the kitchen. "Coffee's done," she said. She poured them each a huge mug of coffee and plenty of milk and foam.

"Let's sit here," Rand said, pointing to two garage-sale, mismatched stools at the counter. "Tell me more about him, won't you?"

"Is this part of investigating me?"

"Yes, actually. The more I know, the better I can make my assessments."

"I understand. I think."

She sipped the strong coffee slowly, wondering if it was wise to tell him anything more about her background. Sure, her friends in Indian Lake knew it. Mrs. Beabots certainly knew about her father's tragic death and why she bought the old camp. If Rand wanted to find out her life history, it wouldn't take long. Why not tell him now? Besides, she was enjoying talking to him.

"I wasn't always sentimental. After my father died, everything in my life changed. I thought we'd been such a close family, but then when he was gone, I realized it was a fantasy. My father and I had had each other. But my mother was, and is, very self-centered. I'm not sure she ever really loved my father. I think he knew it, too. That's why I became so important to him. But—" she looked down into her coffee "—even that wasn't real. I wasn't as important as his police work. He chose that life-and-death life over his family—"

"That's not fair," Rand interrupted.

"Sure it is. When you're a kid abandoned by your parents, it's utterly fair," she said caustically. "Jenny—that's my mother—had to struggle to support us. She blamed my dad's dangerous job for all our bad times and her bad breaks. I just blamed him for leaving me with someone who didn't want to be a single parent. Or a parent at all."

"Even when I was little, my mother often said she was afraid every time my father went to work. She was terrified he'd be killed. She obsessed about it. She warned me that loving a man who chooses danger over his family is a torturous way to live."

Rand gripped his mug and drank. He peered at her over the rim. Watching. Assessing.

She knew he'd already drawn the conclusion, but she pressed on. She needed to make her point. "That's why I vowed never to get involved with a man who worked in a dangerous job."

"Like cops…and firemen?"

"Exactly like cops and firemen." His handsome face was heartbreakingly compassionate at that moment, but she'd struck him down again.

"Listen, Beatrice. I'm a highly trained and skilled firefighter and smoke jumper. I'm certainly more careful going into a fire than you were. I know what I'm doing. Seriously."

"It's still dangerous. You're not an accountant who sits in an office behind a computer all day. You risk your life for others!"

"I certainly do," he replied proudly.

This had to stop. With each moment she spent with Rand, their attraction grew. No. It was more than that. Her heart was opening to him, and she couldn't let that continue.

She had to make certain he got the message loud and clear.

"There's one other part of my past you should know."

"Do I want to know it?"

She lifted her chin, struggling to find strength. "I was engaged several years ago. He was a nice guy. Then he suddenly decided to switch from forensic work to become a police detective."

"Just like good old dad."

"Just like. Yeah."

"And you broke off the engagement?"

"I did."

Rand didn't respond. His face was granite. She couldn't tell what he was thinking; he must have learned long ago how to mask his emotions when necessary. But then, he was conducting an official interview.

That's what he'd said. But that kiss hadn't been part of his on-the-job duties. How much of this had been for the investigation? And how much was just for Rand?

Slowly, he put down his mug. His smile was faint and polite. "That was very good coffee," he said politely. "Thank you. I should be going now."

A part of Beatrice wanted him to know more of her past. To be convinced that as the daughter of a cop, she would never do anything illegal or jeopardize her camp or the kids in it. And she would also never consider a relationship with a man who'd chosen a dangerous career.

But another part of her grew queasy with uncertainty, as if warning her that she'd made the wrong decision.

He turned and walked out of the kitchen.

Beatrice didn't say goodbye.

He closed the door quietly, leaving the room filled with silence.

CHAPTER TEN

BEATRICE SLID HER palm down her flushed cheek and circled her fingers around to the place on her neck where Rand had pressed his lips. The moment had frozen into a memory she suspected she would revisit often.

She found herself spinning on a carousel of attraction and mistrust. Hesitation and excitement. Sure, she was injured and was dependent on others for help. But that would end. She would heal.

But the real jolt to her life had come from Rand. He was a conundrum to her. He dropped his gruff and bureaucratic attitude when he was with her.

At first she'd assumed he might not have been comfortable with kids. But when Eli broke down and told the truth, Rand's face had softened. His dark eyes had shimmered as if Eli had uncovered something emotional in Rand's past that connected him to little Eli.

Then again, it might have been her imagination.

What she was not imagining was the danger in his career. He'd certainly put his life on the line for her, Eli and Chris.

What was there about danger that drew men like Rand? Like her father? Was it an adrenaline high, similar to the kick an addict gets from his drugs? Was it a need to prove themselves mightier than the fire? Or the bullet?

Or did it come from their drive to protect? Rand was strong in body and will. He would persevere through just about any peril to fulfill his responsibilities. Perceived or real.

No, men like Rand were as lethal to her as poison. She'd done the right thing to step back. Way. Way. Back.

She hobbled to the window and looked out at the scorched forest and the skeletons of pine that had been full, lush and green only two days ago. Life was like that. One minute everything in one's world was verdant and thriving. People were employed and children were cared for. Then, in the flash of a lightning strike, a twist of fate—she looked down at the boot on her foot—altered everything. Sometimes irrevocably changed someone's life, like when her father had been shot and killed.

The one truism she'd known in her life

was that her father had danced with danger and he'd left her.

She and romance were sparring partners at best. For some reason, fate kept bringing the wrong guy to her.

First there was Heath. They'd actually gotten to the diamond-ring phase before he did a one-eighty on her and their relationship went up in flames.

Upon reflection, Beatrice had to admit that she should have known Heath wasn't happy in his career. Her dreams, even then, had been about children and making a real family. She'd hoped that the void of her past could be filled with a real home. He'd been more focused on his career.

Now she was older and, she hoped, wiser. Though the camp wasn't what most people would think of as a family, it was hers. She'd built it as an oasis for forgotten kids like she had been, who needed love. They came here broken, sorrowful, angry, arrogant or just plain lonely. She hugged them all and loved them all.

She'd accomplished a great deal with the camp, and though it still had a long way to go, she would get there. It might take her twenty years, but she had a lifetime to devote to these children. She didn't care how many hours she worked, or how many obstacles fate rutted her road with—she would persevere.

"Rand Nelson's investigations or no. I won't stop."

"What did you say?" Amanda asked from the kitchen doorway, causing Beatrice to jump.

"Oh, you surprised me."

"Just got here. So, what were you saying? Are you worried about what Mr. Nelson will put in his report?"

"Frankly, yes. I have no idea how we will be affected."

"Don't borrow trouble, I always say," Amanda replied with a half smile. "Don't look at me like I'm nuts."

"Nuts? No, you're not nuts. A Pollyanna, though, yes."

Amanda shook her head. "Not true. I'm old and I'm wise." She shook her finger at Beatrice. "The rule of the universe is that if you put negative thoughts out there, that's what's going to come back to you. Think happy things instead. I always do. And look at the kids. They're happy to be here. This camp was their wish all winter. They depend on you to shore them up like you always do."

Beatrice hopped over to Amanda and

hugged her. "You're so right. I have let my-self wallow a bit, haven't I?"

"Wait 'til the verdict comes in. Whichever way it goes, we'll deal with it then. In the meantime, I made my cherry lemonade."

"Cherry, huh?"

"Yep. I just got a peck of sweet cherries from my friend up the road in Michigan. Her trees weren't hurt by the late-spring frost."

"However did she manage to escape that?"

"She has a positive attitude." Amanda began to turn, then lowered her voice. "And fire barrels to heat the trees in the orchard during a frost."

Rand wore his full gear of Nomex suit, pig-skin gloves, thermoplastic helmet and heavy boots as he held up the fire hose that was pumping one hundred and fifty gallons of water a minute at the flames.

The warehouse fire had gained strength and power before the alarm had even been triggered. The building had been built in the late 1880s. The wiring had been updated, and a sprinkler system installed fifteen years ago, but the place had not had a tenant for over a decade, the chief had informed him. The place was the definition of a tinderbox.

In larger cities, these old buildings were

demolished and replaced by high-rise condos or parking garages. But not in Indian Lake, where town residents preferred to refurbish their historic stores and houses.

Luckily, there was no one inside this warehouse. Rand and the crew were battling the flames, but the fire would no doubt eat the remaining walls. The roof had caved an hour ago. The contents were a goner. Their goal now was to make certain the fire went out and stayed out.

His biceps flexed as the water rushed through the hose. Had it only been a couple of days ago that he'd held this same hose after rescuing Beatrice and the boys? A few days ago that he'd sat in the camp's kitchen and been more moved than he'd ever been in his life?

He'd kissed her neck. He hadn't meant to linger over her skin. Hadn't meant to close his eyes and inhale the floral-and-spice scent she'd worn. It had been all he could do to take his hands from her waist. He'd liked helping her keep her balance.

Though he'd wished she'd reached out for him as well, because he felt as if the floor had melted under his feet. He'd kissed plenty of women in his life—and technically, he hadn't yet kissed Beatrice. He'd only touched his lips to her burned, very tender neck. But he'd felt her pulse stop and then race under his lips. She'd warmed to him, whether she knew it or not. More than her response was his reaction of wanting to know everything about her. She strummed a deep chord of harmony in him he'd never felt. As if everything in his world had been made instantly right and complete.

It had been days ago and he was still reverberating.

How was that possible?

It wasn't. Pure and simple. It had to be some kind of delayed reaction to the adrenaline he'd experienced saving her from the fire. That had to be it.

Once, he'd found an elderly man overcome with asphyxiation near Bear Lake in California. The guy had been fishing, then started a campfire and had passed out. When the wind picked up stray sparks from the campfire, an inferno had resulted. Blessedly, the fire had been near the lake and hadn't gone far, but the man had awakened and been dazed. Rand found him wandering, disoriented and terrified. But Rand had gotten him out and the fire had been contained quickly. Three days after saving the man, Rand still had tingles of triumph running through his body. He'd done his job and he'd done it well.

Back then, Rand had been young and naive. The adrenaline rush that accompanied firefighting falsely led him to believe he was invincible. He'd thought he could save the world. Years later, after the incident at jumper school, Rand had realized how wrong he was. The strict rules and guidelines of firefighting and the laws accompanying his work were based on experience and a long history of lives lost. Fire codes and regulations were established to save lives.

Rand abided by them now as if they were his bible.

But kissing Beatrice and being with her was not the same victorious energy he'd experienced when he'd saved her life. It had been something different. But equally thrilling.

He'd never met anyone like her. Most people put a guard on their heart. Certainly he did. That was a space meant only for special people. His mother. Brothers and sister. Close friends like Luke Bosworth. Nate, Rafe, Mica and Gabe Barzonni. Austin McCreary. He trusted all those guys. He'd known them his whole life. They were good people.

Beatrice had no guard on her heart when

it came to her kids—but when it came to men, she had electrified guard gates around her, complete with very large No Trespassing signs. Particularly if a man held a dangerous job.

He'd gotten the message loud and clear.

Well, if that was what the lady wanted, then so be it.

But was that what she wanted? He couldn't help remembering her strong and distinctive pulse that had jumped when he'd touched his lips to her neck.

And why in the blazes had he done that? Sure, it was an impulse. *Sure. Sure. Kid yourself, Rand.*

He'd been wanting to taste her from the moment he'd seen her in the hospital. He still wanted to kiss her. Really kiss her, like he'd bet she'd never been kissed before.

"Hey, Nelson." Captain Bolton jogged up to Rand.

Refocusing on the job at hand, he turned off the hose. He realized the fire was mostly out.

"We're done here. Pack it up. I'll see you in the truck."

The other two guys on the team, Curt Sauers and Jim Peyton, were already gathering the last of their equipment.

"You gonna drive?" Curt asked Rand as he pulled the hose to the truck to rack it.

"Sure." He might as well. Maybe the drive back to the fire station would help get his mind off Beatrice.

Captain Bolton called to him from the passenger seat, "Nelson!"

Rand held the engine door open as he doffed his helmet. "Captain?"

"I want that report about the youth-camp fire on my desk by the end of the day."

"Sir. Yes, sir."

Rand climbed in the driver's seat and waited for Curt and Jim to settle in.

He started the engine.

The report. So much for getting his mind off Beatrice.

RAND STARED AT the document template on his laptop. He'd filled out plenty of these reports, so there was no reason this one should be any different. But it was.

He glanced at the report Art had submitted. He went over his own notes.

They'd both noticed the youth camp only had one fire hydrant. He read the regulatory document from the City of Indian Lake Utilities. Three hydrants were required by law for the size of her property. If Beatrice didn't install two more hydrants, the city had every right to shut her down until the water lines and the hydrants were operational.

That could end the camp for good.

But an even greater issue was how he handled the issue of Chris and Eli.

The boys' futures were in his hands. The laws had been tightened in recent years, and the new severity of the charges could change the course of Chris's and Eli's lives.

Rand had never been in such a quandary. He believed both boys were good kids despite the deplorable childhood they'd endured. They were strong and independent. He liked them. Incredibly, he wanted to get to know them better, and he wanted the best for them.

If he did not come to their rescue, Beatrice would never forgive him.

He'd never forgive himself.

At the same time, he had to think of the other kids at the camp. Beatrice was responsible for their safety, and due to his involvement now with this report, he was responsible as well. He was bound by duty and the law to do the right thing.

"The right thing."

He swept his palm across his forehead, smoothing away a thick lock of hair and a good bit of nervous perspiration. He didn't like being the bad guy. Nobody did. But darn it, she should have known about these regulations, despite the fact that they were recently enacted.

"She should have…" He rested his forehead on his palm and exhaled deeply.

None of this was going to go well. She would blame him if her camp closed. And if there had ever been the slightest chance they could explore what was between them, this report would kill it.

Rand looked at the report form. He filled in the blank that required the cause of the fire. He wrote "Accidental."

He went on to describe the incident of the s'mores and the boys' innocent and naive participation in the cause of the fire. He purposefully requested leniency for the boys. If there was to be any sentence at all, he suggested community service, and that he be assigned to oversee the boys' sentence.

As for the necessity of the hydrants, Rand filled in "Failure to comply to code."

Captain Bolton rapped on the open door to Rand's office. "Can I get that report?"

Rand hit Send. "It's on its way to your inbox."

"Thanks."

Rand watched his superior's back disappear into his office down the hall.

Rand turned off the laptop and left the office.

CHAPTER ELEVEN

BEATRICE WORKED WITH Maisie on yet another Excel spreadsheet listing their growing expenses.

"You can't take on any more foster kids this summer," Maisie said.

"Why not?"

Maisie jabbed her finger at the list of numbers that swam in front of Beatrice's eyes. These days those numbers had a life of their own. They taunted her, teased her and threatened her. Beatrice inhaled and took the printout. "Don't answer that. I know why. The state doesn't cover their expenses."

"It doesn't. Each week we're fifty to seventy dollars short. Over a month's time that's two hundred to two hundred-eighty dollars in the red. Per foster kid."

Beatrice dropped the sheet. "Those foster kids need me, er, the camp. I can't let them down."

"You mean kids like Eli and Chris? The

ones who've caused the most harm since we opened this season?"

"Yes! Just like them," Beatrice ground out. "The neediest ones are the reason to keep the camp going. We're changing lives here, Maisie."

Maisie placed her palm on Beatrice's hand. "Your heart may be made of gold, but we can't cash it at the bank."

Beatrice peered at her associate. As young as she was, Maisie was as business-savvy as they came. Maisie had yet to pass her CPA boards, but when she did, the young woman could have a job in any accounting firm in Chicago. Beatrice wondered if Maisie would choose to work here at the camp at a much lower wage. Despite her hard talk, Maisie didn't fool Beatrice. She loved the kids and sympathized with their plight as much as Beatrice did.

"I'll talk to Zoey Phillips and see if she can get us more money from the state."

Maisie rolled her eyes. "The state? Which is already overburdened with the skyrocketing number of foster kids thrown into the system on a daily basis? That's not going to happen and you know it."

"What's the solution?"

"We could cut some of these expenses.

Regular milk instead of organic. Tap water rather than bottled water. We'd save over a hundred a month right there."

"All right. And we can substitute canned or frozen veggies for fresh."

Maisie took out Amanda's shopping list. "I say we buy our flour, sugar, syrup and some of these canned goods in even larger bulk. I talked to a wholesaler in Indian Lake yesterday—"

Beatrice cut her off. "A wholesaler? Who? How?"

"I was at the tractor supply looking at bulk packs of granola bars. Actually…" Maisie started to blush. "He wasn't the wholesaler. He was making a delivery. We met in the parking lot."

Beatrice smiled knowingly and propped her chin on her palm. "And his name was…"

"Clay. It's his uncle's fish-and-produce wholesale company. The place has been in business for over a hundred years. Don't you think that's amazing?"

"Uh-huh."

Maisie's blush had grown to a crimson stain that now ran down to her throat. "He's a native of Indian Lake."

"Right. And when are you going to see him again?"

"At the fair." Maisie stopped abruptly. "How did you know he asked me out?"

Beatrice sat back in her chair, picked up the Excel sheet again and said, "Oh, just a wild guess." She gazed down at the paper. "I think you're right. There are places to be more cost-efficient. Buy cheaper laundry supplies instead of the expensive green powders we use. Then I want to talk to our insurance company and see if I can lower our monthly premiums in any way."

"That's a good idea."

"Look, Maisie, I have no intention of cutting the staff or of lowering salaries. I don't want you to worry."

"Oh, I wasn't worried."

"Liar." Beatrice smiled and Maisie breathed a sigh of relief.

"We all love it here, Beatrice. We love you. Working with these kids is more than a dream. It's satisfying in a way I can't explain. You're so right. These kids need us. Even the ones with loving homes blossom in ways that show their real potential to learn and grow. Each week when they leave, I see the changes. They're happier. They've learned new skills We've given them responsibilities and they love it."

"I know. That's because we don't coddle

them. We have expectations and they want to meet our vision of them." Beatrice rose from the desk and went to a bulletin board where she'd pinned photos of two years of camp kids. "But the foster kids mature the most in the little time they're here. I like to think the guidance they get from us will last a lifetime. Even if I never see them again, I know we made a mark on them. A good one."

"We do, Beatrice."

Caught in the moment of fond and fulfilling reflections, Beatrice almost didn't hear the first knock on her door.

The second knock was nearly a pounding. "Sorry to disturb. Are you Beatrice Wilcox?" The man in the doorway was middle-aged and rail-thin, and wore his starched cotton shirt and starched knife-creased khakis as if he was a wooden board draped with fabric. His skin was pale to the point of being a bloodless gray and his wire-rimmed glasses slid to the middle of his long, hooked nose.

"I am."

"Percy Smith. Inspector for the City of Indian Lake."

Beatrice hadn't met this inspector before. He must have been newly hired.

His voice was clipped, emotionless and thin. He didn't offer his hand. Instead he opened a plain manila folder and withdrew a stapled group of papers. He shoved the papers toward her, narrowly missing Maisie's face. "I'm here to inspect your water hydrants. Or lack thereof."

Beatrice looked at the official stamp at the bottom of the document. "We have one hydrant."

"Says that here." He pointed at the paper. "City code is that for an establishment of this size you need three."

"Three?" Beatrice's voice squeaked with shock. She cleared the rattle from her throat. "I don't understand. I was given a list of all city requirements when I began renovations nearly three years ago."

"It's an update."

"Update?" Beatrice and Maisie chorused.

"New code. You received a notice about it."

"No, I did not."

"I'll check that. Perhaps an oversight. Which is possible. This, er, discrepancy might have gone overlooked for quite some time if it hadn't been for this recent fire." With his head he gestured to the documents on the desk. "We learned about it from the fire chief's report and the court ruling. It's all there."

Beatrice felt her legs wobble. Quickly, she sat back down in her chair before she fainted. She held on to the chair arms. "Fire chief. And the forensic team. Yes. They were all here."

"Apparently," Percy said.

All the upgrades she'd installed and the enormous cost flew across her mind like a swarm of banshees. She'd spent all her inheritance. She'd gone through her savings. She'd bet everything she had on this camp. She'd been so certain she'd covered all the bases. But this was a new development. One she couldn't afford to cover.

She picked up the papers. She flipped to the second page, which was the official report on the fire. Anxiously, her eyes skimmed the text and the lengthy explanation about Chris and Eli's participation in the cause of the fire. Her heart hammered in her chest, fearing the worst.

Then she read the final line:

Accidental. No intent. No damage to private property. No injury or death to human or animal.
Court of Indian Lake: Christopher Dunning found not guilty of reckless burning.

It was deemed an accident.

She breathed a sigh of relief—Rand had been lenient with the boys, as he'd promised.

But halfway through the report was the order from the fire chief for two more hydrants to comply with the city and county code #4530898.

Her hands shook as she put down the papers.

Yes, she had to figure out how she'd find the money for the new hydrants, but Chris and Eli were saved from legal trauma. She could deal with everything else.

Somehow.

At the bottom of the report were two signatures. Those of Fire Chief Bolton and Rand Nelson.

Beatrice felt a stab in her belly.

On the one hand, Rand had come to the boys' rescue. On the other, he'd delivered her camp a crushing blow.

She'd told him she'd struggled to get the camp up and running. Maybe he didn't understand how difficult it was to take a ramshackle place like the camp and refurbish it.

Rand.

Beatrice had never been one to cast blame on others for her situations or crises. She put her hands around obstacles and tackled them. Alone.

But in this case? Beatrice felt her anger boil. Rage. Seethe.

The inspector cleared his throat. "You have two weeks to present the City Water Commission with two construction bids for the hydrants and thirty days to begin the construction or the city will install them for you."

"And the cost?"

"It's there in the paperwork. Four thousand."

Beatrice swallowed hard. Anger, hurt and fear cut off her airflow.

"Thank you, Mr. Smith. You may proceed with your inspection."

"I need to take some photos, is all. I won't be long."

He left without a single pleasantry. Beatrice didn't blame him. It had to be tough being the messenger of ill fate.

Maisie's eyes misted over with tears. An unusual response from her analytically minded counselor. "Oh, Beatrice, what are we going to do?"

"Do?"

She rose from the chair and grabbed her crutches, which were perched against the wall by the window. Then she took her keys from the desktop. "I won't be long."

"Where are you going? And should you be driving?"

"To town. And physically? Yes. I can drive and should drive. Though I might have to restrain myself from plowing my SUV into a particular fire station."

A TOOL BELT around his waist, Rand stepped back to watch the fire engine's hydraulic platform rise into the air. "That's it, Curt. I think I fixed it."

"Yeah, much smoother," Curt shouted from the aerial apparatus basket. "But let's check if we can crank it up farther."

The tower-ladder fire engine was parked outside the fire station on the concrete drive. The hot summer sun had baked the ground and the driveway since dawn. Rand ran the sleeve of his black T-shirt along his sweating forehead. "Will do."

He was just about to go to work when a familiar SUV sped around the corner, nearly on rails, and shot up the drive and jerked to a stop.

Beatrice got out of the SUV, hauling the crutches out behind her. Awkwardly, she slammed their rubber poles against the concrete and stomped, with somewhat of a wobble, toward him. Anger spewed out of her mouth before she said a word.

"Rand Nelson!"

Oh, boy, he didn't like this Beatrice—at all. "Bee. Beatrice." He walked up to her. "What can I do for you?"

"I think, sir, you have done enough."

She'd seen the report. *That was fast.* He figured city offices and bureaucracy being slow, he should have had a week or more to think of how to break the news to her. Gently.

Better toss that game plan.

"Come again?" Stalling was the new game plan, apparently.

She balled her fists at her sides, as an element of composure crossed her face. "First, I suppose I should— I mean, I want to thank you for what you did for Chris and Eli. That…well, it was decent of you. Though I still don't think children should be formally accused of accidents…"

He held up his hand. "Don't go there. It's moot. It's the law. I'm not the lawmaker."

"Right. And so, yes. Thank you."

"But…?"

"You know precisely what I'm talking about. Seems my camp is not up to some new city water code I didn't have a clue about. I have a citation sitting on my desk that if I don't have two bids from construction companies in two weeks, and begin the installation of not one, but two—" she shoved two fingers in his face "—water lines and two hydrants, the city will do it for me."

"That's the law, yes."

She clamped her mouth shut.

He jumped in. "Look, Beatrice. This is all for the safety of the children, the counselors. You. We got lucky with this last fire. If there was another one, we might not be so fortunate. What if I hadn't saved you? Or the kids? Did you think of that?"

He'd seen anger before, but not directed so piercingly at him. His guilt over his part in her crisis rained down on him like rocks from the skies.

But why did he feel guilty? He was right. Positively right.

"Yes, Mr. Official. I thought of that. But you know that I don't have the financial resources to do all this right now. At the end of the summer—"

"Might be too late. If we don't get some substantial rains—and soon—to wet down that forest, another blaze could spark. One lightning strike—"

"Stop." She cranked up a palm. "I don't

want your lecture. I get it, okay? I paid attention when you talked to my kids."

Sarcasm wasn't her thing, he thought. He liked her better when she was hugging children. Or letting him put his hand on her waist. This defiant, angry and hurt Beatrice cut him to the bone. He guessed his pain was nothing to compare with hers, however.

She turned awkwardly on her boot, adjusting the crutches, and marched toward her SUV.

"Beatrice, wait," he said and strode after her.

"Hey! Rand!" Curt called from his platform in the air. "I'm up here, remember?"

"Be there in a sec."

Curt laughed. "I think you're done."

Rand's eyes flew to Curt, who blew him a kiss. Rand turned his gaze to Beatrice. Her anger had come down to a simmer. A breeze lifted her blond hair off her shoulders. She'd finally gotten it cut. Her blue eyes shone in the sunlight. Other than some lip gloss, she didn't have a stitch of makeup on her tan face. If she wasn't so mad at him, he would have tried to hug her. Console her about the monster who had done this to her.

But I'm the monster.

"What?" she asked.

"I just want to say that I'm sorry. But I was doing my job."

"Your job?" She pursed her lips and looked at the concrete, then back at him. She moved a step closer, leaning on the crutches. She lowered her voice so that Curt couldn't hear her. "Fine. You do your job, Mr. Nelson. I'll do mine. I'll find a way to make this right. Comply with regulations and give my kids the summer dream of their lives. I'm not going to let you stop me."

"I'm not trying to stop you, Beatrice. I'm trying to help."

"Could've fooled me."

He stared at her as she turned and opened the SUV door. He grabbed the door handle and put one hand on her shoulder. "I have a friend at the bank…"

"Don't bother. I'm at my credit limit." She put the crutches in the SUV. "Without more revenue, they won't loan a dime to me until I pay off my existing loans. Yes. That's loans, plural. You have no idea…" Her voice caught. Tears filled her eyes. "Oh, forget it," she spat and climbed into the vehicle. He closed the door for her. Gently. Safely.

"I can't forget it, Beatrice."

"Try," she said and started the engine, backed out of the drive and sped away.

He stood at the end of the drive and watched as she drove around the corner and disappeared.

"Hey, Rand!" Curt shouted and hung over the metal white bar of the platform. "I gotta tell you, man, your technique sucks. Unless you were trying to get rid of her. In that case, you were aces, man."

"Yeah. No question. She's written me off—for good."

Curt gave Rand a thumbs-up.

CHAPTER TWELVE

IT WASN'T GUILT that shoved Rand into his truck and steered him toward the Indian Lake Youth Camp later that day, or at least that's what he told himself as he watched the setting sun blister the clear blue sky with fingers of flaming red, orange, lavender and gold.

He'd left three voice mails for Beatrice and she hadn't answered. He wasn't about to let the sun go down on this day without talking to her.

The camp's gravel drive crunched under his tires as he entered. Before he got out of the truck, he heard the clanking and clanging of pots and pans being washed and put away. The dining hall was empty of kids. He saw the cabins' interior lights coming on as the sun sank in the horizon and the sky turned dark, studded with twinkling stars.

He heard muffled sounds of giggling kids through the screen doors of the cabins. Kids getting ready for bed, talking to their camp mates about the fun they'd had that day.

As he got out of the truck, he spied several duffel bags outside the cabin doors. Some kids would be leaving in the morning. New kids would be coming in.

New little spirits for Beatrice to influence. Guide.

"Love," he said aloud as he took in the scene around him.

Night swooped in on dark wings, and the yellow bug lights outside the cabins automatically turned on. Combined with the lights from inside, it created a nostalgic look that Rand could have taken from his own childhood, when he'd camped with his father and brothers up in Michigan.

Tree frogs chirped in the forest and crickets joined in their song. Lightning bugs flitted from the cabins across the gravel road to the burned forest. As the last vestiges of twilight gleamed, he saw neat rows of pine saplings had been planted across the street. Debris had been raked and cleared. Three old metal watering cans were perched near a large rock.

Beatrice must have organized a reforesting project. Without rain, the saplings wouldn't make it, but if she and the kids watered the trees, they might live. He knew she wouldn't abandon those infant trees any more than she would walk away from her camp.

Codes or no codes.

At the end of the row of cabins, set back closer to the woods, he saw a larger cabin, its lights blazing.

Beatrice stood on the porch, her hands gripping the rail as she stared at him. Even at this distance he could feel the Arctic blast from her.

He walked up the inclined path to the bottom of her porch steps.

"I'm surprised to see you. Why are you here?" she asked, crossing her arms over her chest.

"I wanted to talk to you about the citation."

"There's nothing to say. It's done. Now, please leave." She pointed to his truck.

Despite her blatant disgust with him, he was fascinated by her passion and commitment. She was a fighter. And that intrigued him.

He took another step forward, though gingerly. "I just want to apologize. I didn't mean to hurt you. Or the kids."

"Well, you did."

He wondered if she'd ever warm up to him again.

He walked up the first step and paused, trying not to intimidate her. "I think what you're doing here for these kids is great. Needed. Fantastic."

"Thanks." She jutted out her chin. "But your apology doesn't help me or them. I don't have the money for those water lines or hydrants or the next code I haven't complied with. Which I'm sure you'll find somewhere in that long list of regulations that mean so much to you."

"Look, Bee…" He took another step but stopped when she shook her head.

"Don't do that."

"What?"

She clenched her jaw and looked off to the forest. She sniffed.

Was she fighting tears?

"My father used to call me that."

"And I'm dishonoring him by using that name, too? Bee fits you."

Her shoulders hitched as she pursed her lips. "He used to say I was as sweet as a honeybee."

Right now, Rand could only think of the stinger she'd attacked him with at the station. "I can see that."

"Really?" She heaved a sigh but continued staring at the forest.

He followed her gaze. "Did you do that? Plant those saplings, I mean."

"Uh-huh. Well, the kids and I did. Bruce dug the holes and we planted them. Amanda and I water them every morning and evening."

"They'll be strong trees with all that attention."

She looked at him with a smile so faint he wasn't sure if shadows were playing tricks on him. "I love trees. They're my friends. When I was a kid and came here to the camp, I used to walk in the woods and talk to the trees. I even hugged them. Stupid, isn't it?"

"No. It's real. I'm the same way. That's why I risk my life for them. I've always thought that because trees live such long lives, they could tell such great stories. I hate it when I see a tree being cut down, even by us firefighters when we know it's the only way to stop the fire from spreading."

He'd come here to apologize, but he liked that they were getting back to the warmth of the conversation they'd had in her kitchen.

And then what, Rand? You don't "do" relationships and she clearly told you she'd never consider one with someone like you.

But if there was chemistry between them, shouldn't they explore it?

Rand walked over to one of the two rockers on the porch and sat. He patted the arm of the rocker next to him. "What did you tell the trees when you talked to them? How much fun you had at camp?"

"My sorrows, mostly. I was missing my dad so much back then. He was my world and my mother was so into herself. I felt…"

"Abandoned."

"Exactly," she said softly.

"It's not easy to admit to being alone." He looked down. "Or lonely."

"You can't feel that way, though. You said you had a large family."

"I do." The sides of his mouth went up involuntarily. He always smiled when he thought about his mother and siblings. "My brothers are my best friends. We kid around, probably too much for my mom, who's really cool about our taunts to each other. And my sister, Cassie, she's the gutsy one. Owns her own business."

"Really?"

"I admire her for that. Did it all on her own." He peered deeply at her. "Like you."

"Oh."

Was she blushing? He wasn't sure. Beatrice always seemed to glow when he was around her.

"And your dad?"

"He died when I was young. Similar to your experience." He looked down at his hands, realizing he was uncomfortable talking about Richard Nelson.

His father, though, had been a hard man. There were times when Rand believed the man had ordered his children into existence with his commander's voice, rather than them being birthed naturally.

A navy admiral, Richard had run every part of his life as if he was the leader of a warship. But he'd been honest, responsible and protective of those less fortunate until he'd passed away when Rand was fourteen. Rand held his father in the utmost esteem for that, and strove to emulate Richard.

Of the four Nelson brothers, Rand looked the most like his father. His mother called him handsome, but Rand didn't see it, what with his broken nose and one awkwardly placed dimple. Didn't handsome guys have a dimple in their chins? But he was strong like his father; it was his powerful body that saved lives.

For that he was abundantly grateful. And he didn't take his physical gifts for granted. He did not misuse his body, take drugs, drink or smoke. He was the vigilant type. Always ready to respond to a crisis.

Still, it was his mother's nurturing and loving care that had molded him and all his siblings into the responsible and respectable adults they became.

His mother's softness and gentle spirit had bent his rigid father to her will time and again. It had always amazed Rand that his father's blasts and orders to him and his brothers and sister to do their chores, clean the garage, do their homework, were silenced by the crook of his mother's finger or the caress of her hand against his arm.

Richard would get a silly look on his face that Rand hadn't understood until he was in high school and had a crush for a full semester on Mary Kate Harrold.

He lifted his eyes to Beatrice. Already she was having that kind of effect on him. Astonishingly, he liked it.

"My siblings and I have been known to be a rowdy bunch. A bit intimidating to outsiders."

"Why? Do they all look like you?"

"Not my sister. She's slim and blonde."

"Really? I wouldn't have guessed that— you being so tall, dark and— I mean, you're, uh, the opposite."

Rand laughed, watching her stumble over her words. He hadn't meant to make her uncomfortable. But he did want to win her trust. And a whole lot more.

For Rand, there was no doubt in his mind—he'd never met a woman like Beatrice. Maybe that's why he hadn't ever had a serious relationship. He'd told himself it was because of his career. He was always on the move. But perhaps that wasn't it at all. Perhaps he was just particular.

He wasn't commitment-phobic. No. He wanted a wife and family one day. Funny how that "one day" had moved into his present.

But he'd only just met Beatrice. He strove to keep the conversation light for now, until he could get out what he'd come to say.

"Cassie looks like my mom. She gets her green eyes and hair from her. She's got a soft heart like my mom, too." *And like you.*

"Oh."

Beatrice worried her bottom lip and looked away from him. She hugged herself with her arms tightly.

He rose but remained a distance from her. "Look, Beatrice, you've got to be overwhelmed by everything that has happened to you. The fire, nearly getting killed, the risk the kids took out there in the forest. The legal threat to them. Your burns." He pointed to her foot. "Not to mention your foot."

"Don't forget my burned hair." Her laugh was forced.

She was on the edge of losing it.

"I came out here tonight, Beatrice, because I want to help you."

She snorted. "You? Want to help me? After that citation?"

"I had to do it, Bee. It was my job. My duty."

She dropped her arms. "I know. And truthfully, I get it. But the fact is, I'm broke, Rand. I can't afford these repairs. I can barely keep these kids fed." She pointed to the cabins. "They deserve the best from me. And I failed."

"No." He moved closer. "You didn't fail. Not in the least. This is just a hiccup."

"Yeah. A nearly four-thousand-dollar hiccup that will choke the life out of my camp."

"Hear me out. I have a friend, Luke Bosworth, who has a construction company here in town. He's a gifted carpenter, but he takes on all kinds of jobs. I'll talk to him tomorrow and get him to give you a bid. He can get this set up for you, maybe for less than the city quoted you." He took another step toward her and put his hand on her elbow. "Please, Bee, let me do this for you."

"Beatrice," she insisted.

"Bee fits you better," he replied. He looked down into her blue eyes as the moon's silver beams danced across her face, making her look ethereal. Angelic.

She took his breath away. He had to get a grip. This wasn't the time to allow romantic fantasies to cloud his mind. She might be softening to him, but in the end, he was still the bad guy to her.

"What do you say, Beatrice?"

Her eyes scanned his face as if she was looking for a flicker of a deceit. Some offense to charge him with.

"You really do want to help me."

"Yes."

"Why?"

"Because I like you. Okay?" He dropped his hand from her elbow and shoved both hands in his jeans pockets. "And right now you've got me pegged as an evildoer, right up there with Darth Vader and Bernie Madoff. I don't want to be the bad guy."

"Always the hero?"

"Why not?"

She heaved a sigh. "I don't know that I need a hero right now. I need a miracle."

"You could play the lottery."

"Now you're making fun."

"I was. I apologize. This is serious and I'm all in." He leaned his face toward her until their noses almost touched. "Say yes."

She pursed her lips to hold in a chuckle. "Okay. I accept."

He straightened. "Good. I'll call Luke and see if he can help. Can I call you tomorrow?"

"Sure."

"Good," he replied and started down the porch steps.

"I'll walk you to your truck," she said and turned to grab her crutches from the porch railing.

"No need. I can see the way."

"Good night vision, too, huh?"

He decided he didn't want their time together to end, so he stood at the bottom step as she followed him down. "You're getting pretty good with those things."

"I'm trying," she said and walked alongside him to his truck.

He stopped, turned and moved so close to her he could smell her floral scent. And was that peanut butter on her breath?

"What I meant to say, Rand," she breathed, her eyes falling to the ground, "was thank you for saving my life. Eli's life… Chris's…"

Before she said another word, his lips touched hers in an excruciatingly soft kiss that sent Rand's mind tumbling as if he'd been pitched over a cliff. He was falling and he didn't want to ever hit bottom.

He deepened the kiss and felt a jolt of excitement and warmth straight through to his heart. She kissed him back with an eagerness he'd never experienced.

She broke the kiss, but kept her lips next to his so that he felt every movement of her breath against his lips.

He kissed her again with the full comprehension that this could be the most irreparable decision of his life.

It was Beatrice who tore herself away once again. She put her hands on his chest and pushed him back. Not so far that he felt shunned, but far enough that he knew she wanted distance.

"I'm sorry," he said.

"For…offering to help, or for the kiss?"

"The kiss. I don't know what came over me." He rushed on. "I'm going to blame it on the moonlight."

She shook her head. "Too much of a cliché." Her face was mirthless.

Had he gone too far? After all, they didn't know each other all that well, though now he sure as heck wanted to change that. No, she'd enjoyed that kiss as much as him.

"What is it, Bee?"

"Maybe," she began, "you only kissed me because you feel sorry for me. My finances... My foot and being dependent on these stupid crutches." She looked down. "Which are lying on the ground now." She kicked one of the crutches. "Useless as they are."

"Nah." He pulled her close and kissed her one last time to get him through the long night. "That's definitely not why I kissed you."

He turned and opened the truck door. He had to escape, and fast, before he was completely overwhelmed by her.

He climbed in, shut the door and rolled down the window. He couldn't take his eyes off her. Silver strands of moonlight wove through her golden hair and her eyes sparkled as if reflecting starlight. He knew she hadn't the slightest idea how magical she looked.

"Just remember I'm here for you, Bee."

He started the engine.

She leaned toward the window. "You saved my life, Rand. But helping me? I think that's over your pay grade. Good night." She spun away, picked up her crutches and hobbled toward her cabin.

He watched her in the rearview mirror. She didn't believe him. She didn't believe in him. And that bothered him. A lot.

CHAPTER THIRTEEN

"I DON'T WANT to leave you, Miss Beatrice," Susan Kettering said, sniffing back a sob as she clung to Beatrice's neck. "I'm having too much fun."

"Me, too." Jessica was next to bury her face in Beatrice's neck, her cheeks wet with tears. "We were going to stay the whole summer, but when we finally told Mom about the fire yesterday, she wanted us to come home."

Both girls were set to leave camp that morning.

"You have to talk to her, Miss Beatrice. You just have to," Susan pleaded. "Miss Maisie was starting knitting lessons and I really like it."

"And I painted a rock hippopotamus like Mr. Bruce taught us."

"I know." Beatrice hugged them tighter.

The Kettering girls weren't the first kids whose parents had wanted them to return home after learning about the fire. Little

Ricky's parents had left with him less than an hour ago.

Luckily, none of the parents so far had asked for their money back, but Beatrice's real fear was that they wouldn't send their kids to the camp again next summer. And if they spread the word to other parents that the camp was unsafe, more cancellations could follow.

Beatrice had spoken to Ricky's mother, but she hadn't managed to convince her that Ricky was in no danger. She had to do better with Mrs. Kettering.

The Mercedes sedan pulled to a stop in front of the dining hall. The driver's door opened and Rhonda Kettering—tall, model-slim and dressed in white slacks, a silk aqua-colored blouse and yellow espadrilles—whipped off her designer sunglasses as she spied Beatrice and her daughters.

Rhonda waved. "Jessica! Susan!" She rushed forward without closing the car door, clearly concerned about her children. A summer breeze blew Rhonda's shoulder-length curls around her face.

"Mom!" Jessica waved back but held on to Beatrice's hand.

Susan just stared at her mother and stepped back a pace.

The kids were holding their ground. Beatrice hadn't expected support troops, but she had them.

Out of the corner of her eye, Beatrice saw Maisie and Cindy come to the kitchen screen door to watch from the sidelines. Amanda was bolder. She pushed past them, stepped outside onto the steps and pretended to dry her hands on a kitchen towel. Bruce appeared from inside the boys' cabin.

Beatrice realized her staff knew the significance of the Ketterings' leaving early. They were depending on Beatrice to win this confrontation.

Beatrice held her breath, trying to think of the most persuasive argument, but nerves jangled up and down her spine. This was worse than racing into a burning inferno. She'd relied on guts then. This was a matter of confidence, and right now, Beatrice had none.

"Mrs. Kettering. Rhonda. How was the drive?"

"Not bad. Though all those semitrucks make me nervous." She looked down at the girls. "Don't I get a hug?"

Jessica tightened her grip on Beatrice's hand. "We want to stay, Mom. We have the rest of the summer. We're learning so much and having a good time."

Well, Beatrice thought. Maybe she didn't have her arguments planned out, but Jessica did. The kid should go to law school.

"Yeah, Mom. We're just fine." Susan looked up at Beatrice with admiration in her un-patched eye. "And I really like the kids here."

Rhonda had opened her mouth to speak but closed it. "You do?"

"Yeah," Jessica insisted. "And they like us. You know how hard it's been for us to make friends."

"Yes, but..." Rhonda examined Beatrice. She took in the fact that both her daughters were practically clinging to Beatrice. Rhonda strode closer. "Is this true? They've been making friends?"

Beatrice smiled down at each child. "Of course. The other kids love them. What's not to love? You have the sweetest, most endear-ing kids I've had the pleasure to know. The counselors and Amanda, our cook, we all love them."

"And they obviously return the sentiment." Rhonda paused.

"Mrs. Kettering, the fire was an unfortu-nate incident, but we are taking enormous safety precautions to make certain all the children are protected."

"But Ricky's mother said two of the other children started the fire. What safety precautions are you taking against these troublemakers?"

"The boys started the fire by accident. They wanted to make s'mores. They'd never had a s'more in their lives and were fascinated and delighted when I served the treat to the children at our weekly campfire. They tried to make it for themselves and inadvertently sparked the fire."

"They'd never had a... Why, it's nearly hard to believe."

"The boys have had to survive without a lot of things. They don't have a loving mother like you, Rhonda, who would drop everything and drive all the way here at a moment's notice to see to the welfare of her children. They've been abandoned. Forgotten. I want to show them that someone cares. I care."

Beatrice's passion had run away with her mouth again, and that familiar clump of tears in her throat returned, choking off her words. She took a deep breath.

"Now you make me feel heartless, Beatrice."

"I didn't mean to."

"I know you didn't." Rhonda went over to Jessica and pulled her into her arms. "I love you very much, Jessica." She held out her left arm for Susan to join in her hug. Susan went to her mother and flung her arms around Rhonda's neck.

"I love you, Mommy," Susan said. "You are the best mommy. Just like Miss Beatrice said."

Rhonda looked up at Beatrice. "They do love it here, Beatrice. When they came home last summer they started counting the days until they could come back."

Now there were tears in Rhonda's eyes as she rose and put her hand on Beatrice's arm. "You believe these boys are not a menace?"

"I believe they're good kids," Beatrice said confidently.

"Then I'll take you at your word." She gave the girls another hug. "You and Susan can remain until the end of the summer."

"Oh, Mommy!" Susan squeezed her mother's waist. Jessica did, too.

"Thank you, Mrs. Kettering. Your faith in me and this camp means a great deal."

Beatrice tapped Jessica's shoulder. "You girls take your duffels back into the cabin.

If I'm not mistaken, Miss Amanda is going to teach you girls how to make pie crust."

"Yay!" the little girls chorused and after kissing their mother, they raced off to their cabin to drag their bags inside.

Rhonda glanced at Beatrice. "Pie crust? From scratch?"

"It's to die for. Flaky and delicious. She uses lard." Beatrice winked at Rhonda.

"Really?" Rhonda's eyes widened. "Maybe I should stick around."

RAND CLATTERED THROUGH a group of tools in his garage searching for his pickax, a sledge-hammer and the new sharp spade he'd bought last month. Finding the tools, he put them in the back of his truck alongside the wood stakes he'd bought at the lumberyard. He also had four balls of twine, blue chalk markers, sheers and four gallon jugs of water.

The sun winked across the eastern horizon, but Rand spotted clouds in the distance.

"A good rain would make my job easier," he said to himself as he climbed in his truck, started the engine and drove out of his driveway.

Last night he'd confirmed with Luke Bosworth that his friend had made it out to the camp and had come up with a competitive bid. Unfortunately, Luke had told Rand that the city's estimate was fairly accurate. But Luke would do what he could to reduce the bill if he could keep costs down.

That was when Rand had come up with his plan.

He wanted to help Beatrice. Yes, even impress her. Apparently, carrying her out of a fire wasn't enough. Nope. There was no hero worship in her eyes when she looked at him now. He saw distrust. Guarded fear.

He had to prove to her that she could count on him. But he had to do it without compromising her pride.

She was the kind who didn't ask for help, otherwise she would have done just that a thousand times already. She'd been on her own for so long, rebuilding that wreck of a camp when no one in their right mind would take on such a task. But she'd done it. Admirably. There was personal victory in such an accomplishment.

Rand figured the best way was just to show up and start putting his plan into action. Better to ask for forgiveness…

Rand pulled his truck to the side of the road in front of the camp and turned off the engine. He took out the city engineer's survey drawing of where the water lines should be placed. As dawn crept over the land, he saw the tiny blue flags the city surveyor had placed for the proposed hydrants. Orange spray paint ran in two lines from the blue flags to a larger yellow flag, purportedly the water main.

Rand took out a hammer, the twine and the stakes. The ditch for the water lines needed to be eighteen inches wide and two feet deep. He measured the distances and placed stakes at three-foot intervals and then curled the twine around the stakes to make certain his trench was straight.

He took his tools out of his truck and placed them on the ground next to the staked-out water lines he would dig.

Slinging the pickax over his head, he chopped the first hunk of dirt. The first six inches was like hacking through rock, but below that, the soil softened.

After forty-five minutes of cutting through the earth, Rand's T-shirt was soaked with sweat, the sun blazed in the east and the clouds he'd seen earlier had disappeared.

"Dang! Just my luck." He swiped a palm over his forehead to wipe off the sweat. He slid his hand down the side of his shorts.

Behind a row of elderberry bushes to the left of him, he saw movement and an unmistakable red shirt and blue camp shorts. A dark-headed boy peeked through the berry bush.

"Eli?"

The boy went rigid.

"Is that you?"

Rand wiped the stinging, salty sweat that had rolled into his eyes and peered at Eli. As his focus sharpened, he saw Chris standing several paces behind Eli.

"Chris?"

"Hello, Mr. Nelson," Eli said, straightening from his crouch position. He stepped away from the elderberry bush.

"How long have you been there?"

"Not long. The counselors watch us like hawks. After the fire…" Eli said.

"I'm sure Miss Beatrice will worry if she doesn't know you're out here."

Chris walked up to stand by Eli. He put his hand on Eli's shoulder. "We didn't do anything wrong. Besides. It's not breakfast time yet."

"I see," Rand said, watching Chris's protective instincts surface once again.

"What are you doing?" Eli asked a bit excitedly.

"What does it look like? Digging."

Chris snorted. "We got that."

"I'm helping Miss Beatrice. She needs two new fire hydrants…in case of another fire."

"That was our fault," Chris said.

"Yes. It was your fault, Chris." Rand put his hand on his hip. "What are you going to do to make it up to her?"

Chris stared at Rand.

Eli's eyes tracked from his brother to Rand and back. "I could help you."

"Yes, you could. In fact, you both should. That's a good way to make restitution for what you did," he said, staring directly at Chris.

"No way," Chris said. "We'd only get in trouble for using dangerous tools. They'd find something to pin on us. Come on, Eli."

Chris pushed his brother's shoulder but Eli deflected the gesture and spun away from Chris. "You go," Eli said, sliding his eyes toward Rand.

Rand stood still and firm, keeping his expression purposefully neutral, though his eyes remained on Eli, hoping the younger boy would not cave.

Chris pointed at Rand. "You think he's some kind of action hero? Well, he's not. He's like all of them." Chris spat on the ground and hurled a spite-filled glare at Rand. "Just like…" He swatted the air with his palm. "Aw, what's the use."

Chris stalked off toward the dining hall.

Eli watched his brother for a moment and then turned back to Rand and gave him a wary look. "Is he right?"

"About what?" Rand felt his breath hitch in his lungs. What was he doing? Would he disappoint this kid? And even if he did, what was it to him?

It struck Rand at that moment that this boy, whose life he'd saved, the one who'd spoken the truth about the origin of the fire and confessed to stealing the marshmallows and chocolate, the one who loved his brother with an open heart, deserved something better than what life had served him up already.

Rand felt a surge of compassion.

Eli took a cautious step forward. "That you're not a hero. I think you are. You are for me and Miss Beatrice. If it weren't for you, I'd be toast. Or crumbs." Eli snickered at his little joke, macabre as it was.

"I was just doing my job," Rand retorted. "Any other firefighter would have done the same. I just happened to be there at that time. It was no big deal."

"It was to me. And Miss Beatrice told us that everything happens for a reason."

"She did, did she?"

"Uh-huh." Eli kept walking toward a large shovel. He leaned down and picked it up.

Rand thought Eli looked like a Lilliputian with the shovel. There was no way the kid could lift it filled with dirt. But he had to give him credit for trying. That was determination. Guts. Maybe the kid did have what it took to help.

Eli smiled tentatively. "I bet Miss Beatrice told you about us, huh?"

"Some."

"Like that my dad's in prison? My mom took off. She left me and Chris alone in our apartment. I like Zoey Phillips—she runs the foster kids' place where the cops took us. She said she's trying to find a home for Chris and me, but it won't happen."

"Why not?"

"We're too old. And there's two of us. I couldn't leave Chris. It makes me sad to even think about being busted up."

"He takes care of you?"

"Yeah. He used to do a lot of things for me. But now, sometimes I wonder…"

"What?" Rand slung at the ground again, sweat pouring from his head. He turned his ball cap around so that the bill would shield his neck from the sun once it started rising in the sky. He wiped his forehead with his bare arm.

"If I'm smarter than him. But that doesn't make sense cuz I'm younger."

"I dunno. Smarts don't necessarily come with age." Rand pointed to the left. "Now, you stand out of the way while I sling this pickax. I don't need to race you off to the ER because you got too close. And this hard dirt can go flying everywhere."

"So, you're going to let me help?"

Rand kept his head down as his arms vibrated with the force of the ax striking through the hard dirt. "I am."

"That's good."

"Yeah? Why's that?" Rand asked, slinging the ax again.

"I've never been picked for a team before. Not even here at camp. Everybody thinks I'm too skinny and frail. I get on teams by default."

Rand held the pickax in midair and looked at the kid. "Default?"

All his life, Rand had been the strong one. He'd been gifted with his father's brawn and muscle. None of his brothers, though they were fit, were as naturally ripped as he was. In school, he'd been the captain of every team he played on—football, basketball, wrestling and track. He didn't know what it was like to be puny, unloved. To live the misfit role, as Eli had.

"Well, you're no default player to me, Eli."

He put down the pickax and strode over to his truck, where he had a sharp small spade. As he turned around, he spied movement in the bushes to the far left. At first he thought it was a stray dog, as it stayed close to the ground. Then he realized it was a child.

Chris.

He hadn't left.

The boy was curious about what Rand and Eli were doing.

That was a good sign.

He'd been right to suspect this other side to Chris. If Rand continued to come to the camp, perhaps he could foster the trust he'd seen in Chris when he'd jumped into his arms.

Pretending not to notice Chris, Rand handed the spade to Eli.

"This is more your size. Start there at the end where I broke up the ground. Shovel those pieces into a pile alongside the trench we'll dig together. Then after the pipe is laid, we'll easily fill in the trench. You think you can do that?"

Eli's pale face lit up as if someone had

flipped a switch. "Oh, yes, sir!" He saluted Rand. "I can do that." He took the spade with both hands as if weighing it. His smile was as wide as his cheeks. "I like this tool. It's just my size!"

Rand paused. "That's right. As if it was made for you." Rand eyed the bushes. Chris was listening intently.

"Yes," Eli replied, staring at the spade as if it was made of gold.

Rand realized this might have been the first time in the kid's life he'd ever been given a real job. One with responsibility. It wasn't just a spade Eli was holding. It was a chance to prove himself worthy.

And what about Chris? Was he enjoying that chip on his shoulder, or was he feeling left out? Both boys needed guidance, he was sure about that. They needed the love and affection that Beatrice gave them. But they needed more. Rand hoped that Zoey Phillips could find them a real home and not bust them up.

Knowing what little he did about the foster system, he suspected the prospects were dim.

Rand felt his throat tighten with emotion. "Yeah, well… Time to work." He went over and put his ball cap on Eli's head.

"What's this for?"

"I don't want your pale skin to get sun-burned. Miss Beatrice would be very angry with me about that."

"Yeah. You're right. She's protective."

Rand chuckled. "A real helicopter mom, huh?"

Eli shook his head. "What's that?"

"Uh, like my mother. Always worrying about her kids."

"Oh. That's what mothers do?"

Rand's eyebrows hitched. "Some mothers."

Rand picked up his ax and flung it into the hard ground. The dry earth cracked under the onslaught of the long javelin-shaped tooth of the ax. The runners of the fissures scattered under his feet.

The kid made Rand feel responsible for him in a way he hadn't felt in years. Not since Idaho. His eyes slid over to the bushes as he watched Chris run back toward the cabins, where the counselors were starting to rouse.

Rand shoved away the thoughts of that other time—that failure—when his life had turned upside down and he'd been anything but a hero.

CHAPTER FOURTEEN

THE BRIGHT FINGERS of dawn pried Beatrice's eyes open. She smoothed her hair from her face and sat on the edge of her bed, wiggling her toes against the rag rug. She tried to write some of the letters of the alphabet with her toes, but zings of pain shot up her leg. She suffered through the letters until she hit *z*.

She stood, stretched and went to the window. The kids were still in their beds, and the camp was quiet—except for an odd pounding noise she didn't recognize.

Following the sound, her eyes widened when she saw a familiar black truck. "Rand."

Swinging an enormous pickax over his head, he assaulted the ground with a force she thought surely was mighty enough to cause a rumble across the land and straight up to her cabin. His sweat-soaked T-shirt was plastered to his chest and arms, outlining the massive cut of his muscles. She drew in a breath.

It was a sight to behold.

She had to find out what he was doing. She awkwardly hurried to the bathroom, washed her face, shoved her hair into a band, brushed her teeth and then put on a clean camp shirt, shorts, one sock and her sneaker. On the other foot, she correctly secured the air boot. She'd learned to properly balance on the boot, so she left the crutches behind.

Beatrice had only gone a short distance away from her cabin when she spotted Eli shoveling dirt with a small garden spade. He wore an ILFD ball cap, several sizes too large on his head. To the left, she saw Chris scooting away from the scene.

What's going on?

"Chris?" she called, but he ignored her and kept moving toward the dining hall.

But Bruce had also noticed Chris and motioned for the boy to come to him.

"I've got this," Bruce called to Beatrice.

She gave him a thumbs-up and marched over to Rand.

"What do you think you're doing to my property without *my* permission?" Beatrice demanded as Rand yanked the pickax out of the dirt.

Rand beamed at her with a smile so charming that she nearly lost her train of thought. Nearly.

"He's making improvements," Eli answered proudly. "And I'm his number one helper."

"You shouldn't be here, Eli. You could get hurt."

"It's all right," Rand assured her in a deep, authoritative voice, one that clearly stated that it would be all right. No one would get hurt. Not with Rand around.

Rand's eyes were focused on her, and the warmth in his gaze reminded her of their kiss. She remembered achingly well the way his fingers had tightened around her waist...

All things she had no business remembering.

"Eli, Amanda has your breakfast ready." She stared at Rand, her hands on her hips.

"But I don't want to go. I'm doing a good job, aren't I, Mr. Nelson?"

"Yes, you are, Eli. I couldn't ask for a better apprentice." He gifted Eli with one of his smiles.

Beatrice was shocked that she almost felt jealous. "I agree with Mr. Nelson. But you need your nourishment. Doesn't he, Mr. Nelson?"

"Yes, Eli," Rand agreed. "You get your breakfast. I have to talk to Miss Beatrice."

Eli carefully laid down the spade. "I'll be back."

"No, you have kayak lessons today and a water-safety class," Beatrice replied pointedly.

"Oka-a-ay." Eli trudged off with slouched shoulders, dragging his feet across the dry dirt and dead grass.

Beatrice watched him leave. She turned back to Rand, who hadn't moved his eyes from her—which she liked, but shouldn't. "You didn't answer my question."

He lifted his chin, and he looked even more handsome as the sunlight played off his chiseled jaw.

She admonished herself for noticing.

"I talked to Luke last night," Rand responded. "He said that the biggest cost was the labor to dig the trenches. I figured if I got the trenches ready for the pipes, it would save you some money."

She shook her head. "I don't understand."

He looked down at the two-foot-deep trench he'd built. "It's gotta be this deep for the pipes. It's a good thing we don't have to remove any tree trunks. That always takes a lot of time."

"No. I mean why are you doing this?"

He dropped his smile, his eyes penitent in his face. "Because I'm sorry, Bee."

She almost felt guilty for making *him* feel guilty.

"I've been thinking about this," she said. "It's not your fault. Eventually, the city would have cited me. I would have had to put the lines in sooner or later. This isn't necessary."

"Oh, but it is. And I'm not doing it just for you. I'm doing it for the kids, too."

"Really?" She folded her arms over her chest. "The kids? Like Eli? Even Chris?"

"Yeah. Like them."

What could she say to that? She had to admit that the boys would benefit from a male influence. Besides, she did need those trenches dug, and it would save her a lot of money.

"All right. But I'll be watching you."

"I hope so."

With a flush, Beatrice hobbled away.

As Rand worked on the trenches over the next several days, Beatrice found it difficult to keep her mind on work and the kids. Okay. *Absolutely impossible.* The man was amazing. In four days, he'd slammed through the hard topsoil and finished one complete trench and in a day or so, he'd complete the second.

Cindy had clicked plenty of photos on her phone to record the progress. Beatrice also noticed the shots were not only of the trenches, but also of Rand's biceps in action. Beatrice could barely lift the heavy pickax he used, much less sling the thing up and down for hours on end as he had.

But it wasn't Rand's physique that kept capturing her thoughts. What kind of guy would spend his free hours working like a prisoner on a chain gang solely to help her? What kind of guy took it upon himself to encourage two somewhat wayward boys into joining him in the work?

The first day Rand had won over Eli. By the third day, Chris had tired of lurking in the bushes and had started bringing water out to Rand and Eli.

By the end of that day, Chris had taken over Eli's shoveling and instructed Eli to rest under the forsythia bushes. Chris was still closemouthed about his participation, but Beatrice had caught the two brothers walking back to the dining hall after Rand had left, joking around about who would get to wear Rand's ILFD ball cap after dinner that night.

Beatrice had always suspected that Chris

wasn't quite the hardened delinquent he portrayed himself to be. With each day with Rand, Chris's arrogance melted.

Just last evening, she'd walked in on an activities' group and Chris was showing Jessica how to weave blue yarn around popsicle sticks to make stars that the kids would string across the dining hall for Jubilee Night, the last night in camp for most of the kids.

As glad as she was to see the change, it also made her anxious. Rand was only working at the camp for a few days, and he had a very demanding—and dangerous—job. She didn't want the kids to get too attached. It had to stop.

She found him knee-deep in dirt.

"Mr. Nelson?"

"Rand," he said, not stopping.

"Rand. Can I talk to you?"

He rested the pickax on the ground and gazed up at her. "Sure. Of course."

"It's about Chris and Eli. I don't think they should help you anymore."

"Why? It's good for them, Chris especially."

"Maybe in the short term. But I have to consider their long-term welfare. What happens after you finish these trenches?"

"There's other work to do."

"Okay, but after that? You have a job you have to go back to. A life. One that doesn't include two little boys."

"I still don't see how that's a problem. I'm enjoying being around them."

"Hmm. That surprises me."

"Why?"

"Well, if you enjoyed being around kids so much, how come you don't have any of your own?"

She realized the question was too personal, but he answered.

He leaned on the handle of the pickax. "My job as a firefighter and smoke jumper doesn't allow me time for relationships."

"Oh?"

"Yeah, just last autumn I was gone for over three months fighting fires in California. Before that I was up in the Upper Peninsula of Michigan."

"Yes, I see how that would be a problem. I guess if you wanted to settle down, you could just stop smoke jumping, right?" She'd meant it as more of a rhetorical question, but a dark shadow crossed his face at her words.

"Stop? No, I can't stop."

"So no matter who you leave behind, you'll just run into the next fire, the next dangerous assignment?"

"That's my life, Bee."

"I see," she repeated lamely. "Well, if you're so committed to that life, maybe reconsider leading these boys on. I gotta go help Amanda with breakfast." She turned and hobbled away as fast as she could.

RAND WATCHED HER leave then went back to work.

Well, he thought, she'd wasted no time unearthing his Achilles' heel.

Idaho.

The past was a territory Rand didn't step into without massive protection. Not even his family knew all the details.

Rand had thought too much of himself back when he'd been a smoke-jumper trainer in Boise, Idaho. He'd been too lenient with a cocky recruit. He hadn't followed the rules, but someone else had paid with their life.

So now he took his responsibilities seriously, both as part of the ILFD and as a jumper. Mistakes were unacceptable.

His job was everything to him, and that left little room for relationships. "Flexible" was the definition of a smoke jumper's life. Forest-fire season started in May and could continue even into December in some places in California. Technically, Rand was "on call" for fires in all the national forests around Michigan, Ohio, Wisconsin and Minnesota. But if any of the nine smoke-jumper crews in America gave him a call, he'd gladly volunteer. Last summer he'd gone to Alaska for three months.

His job had forced him to lead a somewhat nomadic life. He wasn't husband material, and he certainly wasn't the right kind of guy to be a dad.

Beatrice, on the other hand, was all about permanence and planting roots, like she had with those saplings. He'd thought at first it might be possible to explore their chemistry, but she was not the kind of "summer love" girl he could leave behind. She was different, and that bothered him because he'd never been attracted to a woman like Beatrice.

Her expectations would be high and he would err, as he had in the past. If he opened his heart to her, he would end up hurting her. And that failure would cause a new anchor of pain and guilt that would drown him.

Rand was not willing to feel that kind of pain.

He was right to keep his heart closed off.

Besides, what woman would want to be with a guy who was risking his life for two-thirds of the year? Certainly not Beatrice, who'd already lost a loved one to a dangerous career.

He didn't want to hurt her. Or the boys.

Perhaps she was right; it was best to keep his distance. He'd dig these trenches for her, but tell the kids they had to stay with the counselors. Then he'd walk away from the camp, and from Beatrice.

He checked his phone for the time. Crap, he'd have to get a move on to make his shift at the station.

THE STATION HOUSE was a hive of excitement and activity when Rand walked in for his shift. He went up to Chief Bolton. "What's going on?"

"We got a call for volunteers to go fight a blaze in Copper Country State Forest."

"Where's that?"

"It's in the far western part of the Upper Peninsula in Michigan. It's a big fire, and being that Michigan has the largest forest system in the nation, we can't let it rage."

"I'm there, Chief."

"Good man. Nearly every smoke jumper in our region has volunteered."

"When do we take off?"

"Three hours." Chief Bolton slapped Rand's shoulder. "Thanks."

"Anytime."

Rand went to his locker, but instead of focusing on what he'd need for the mission, his mind was on Beatrice.

Would she care if he left? Would she send him off with a wave and not another thought?

She'd said he would jump at the next dangerous challenge. For him, it was his job. His mission. He had to go.

But how did he explain that to Beatrice? Or to the boys?

Sadly, he knew they would never understand.

CHAPTER FIFTEEN

BEATRICE WAS ON her way out of her office when the camp landline rang.

"Indian Lake Youth Camp. Beatrice Wilcox speaking."

"Bee. Beatrice. It's Rand...Nelson."

She couldn't help smiling and leaning back in her chair when she heard his deep voice. "Hi."

"I tried your cell phone but you didn't pick up."

"Sorry. I was working in my office. Obviously—"

"I figured," he interrupted. "I'm calling because I'm going out of town and I won't be out tomorrow to finish that last trench."

Out of town? Why? Where? She didn't want to be intrusive. What he did with his life was not her business. "I can't thank you enough. And thank you again, Rand. It was a lot of work."

"You're welcome. I was hoping to smooth

them out a bit more. Every little bit helps you with the cost."

"I know. I appreciate it."

"I was happy to do it. So, listen. Luke Bosworth said he finished up the bid for you and he's going to be out there later today or tomorrow morning. He'll take over from here."

"Take over?" Her hand grasped the receiver tightly. She had to ask. "So, you're leaving for a while?"

"Bee, it's a smoke-jumping job. I'm there for as long as I have to be."

"I know…"

Was she disappointed that he wouldn't be around? Or was it something else?

"Where—where are you going?"

"Copper Country State Forest in the Michigan Upper Peninsula. They needed volunteers."

He volunteered? "So, it isn't required that you go?"

"No. It never is."

Never. She choked back what felt like a sob in her throat. It burned all the way to her belly.

She'd been afraid of this. Had tried to protect herself and the boys. But it still hurt.

She reminded herself he was skilled and exceedingly well trained. He trained other jumpers, for goodness sake. The Forest Service was lucky to have someone like him. But she couldn't help remembering Rand carrying her and Eli out of a raging fire. "You be careful."

"Always," he said lowly. "Listen, Beatrice. I promised Eli and Chris I'd show them some of my videos of smoke jumpers when I came out there tomorrow. If I send you an email with the videos, would you see that they get it?"

"Sure, I will. But I think you should speak to them yourself."

"I'd like to. I want to explain about the job."

"They should be coming up to the dining hall in about twenty minutes. I'll have them call you."

"Super. My personal cell is 555-805-9999. You, uh, could make a note of that number as well."

"I will."

"Good. You know, I think Chris is genuinely interested in firefighting. Eli is young and probably just enamored of my ball cap and the fire trucks. But once we started working together, Chris asked some intelligent questions."

"Like what?"

"Oh, like the kind of training I had to complete. I told him the first-aid classes you gave at the camp were the first order in becoming a fireman or a first responder. He was fascinated."

Beatrice twirled her finger through the coiled phone cord, as her thoughts jumped from warning herself to keep Rand at arm's length to wishing he was in the same room with her. She sat up straight. Where had that idea come from? She was best off keeping a distance between them. He was a smoke jumper, through and through. He had his own life. She had hers.

"I'll tell them where you're going."

"Maybe you could point it out on the map for them."

"I will."

"Thanks. It's funny, you know? Other than my family, I've never had anyone tracking my progress when I go out on assignment."

"Really?"

"Oh, that reminds me. If I'm gone more than a week, call my mom. Her number is 555-393-0001. I told her about Chris and Eli. She actually wanted to come to the camp and meet them. Er, they will be at the camp, won't they? Did you secure more money from Zoey Phillips for them?"

"A little. It wasn't exactly enough. Zoey pitched in."

He paused. "Then I'll pay the rest."

"What? You can't do that."

"Why not? Is it against the law?" He laughed.

"No. It's just— Well, that's very generous of you. And the boys will benefit from your kindness so much."

"No, Bee. It's your affection they need. I want them to have that."

Beatrice didn't like the wrenching emotional sound in his voice as if this was a last request. In case he didn't come back. Was that what he was thinking? If so, she'd been right to cut off any connection she or the boys had established with him.

So why was she so worried for him? "Rand, would you do me a favor and let me know how you are? Where you are?"

He was silent.

She continued. "I want to make sure that you're all right."

"Why, Bee. I didn't expect that from you. You surprised me. I like it."

"Well, I didn't expect it, either," she replied, realizing she was smiling. How could she smile when he was going off into harm's way and she had no idea if he would return?

Not that she had any claim to him. It wasn't as if they were longtime friends or anything more than that. But there had been those kisses...

"I'll try to call. I have to go, Beatrice. Tell the boys, okay? And don't forget, Luke will take over. It's going to be all right. Everything will be all right."

His words should have been reassuring but they caused her to bolt out of her chair. "How can you be so sure? You're going into the face of who knows how much danger. You might not even come back. You could die out there and I'll never..."

"Never what, Bee?"

"See you again." That errant sob returned, lodging in her throat. "Oh, sorry. I didn't mean to say that."

"Bee, we both know I'm not the guy for you. That guy is a stable, come-home-every-night kind of man who works a nine-to-five job and has his head and heart safely tucked next to yours. No worries. No fears. Me? I can't get close enough to the flames. I don't even see the danger anymore. So you shouldn't give me another thought."

"I'm not the woman for you."

"No, you're...not."

The taste in her mouth was like battery

acid. And why was that? He was only stating the obvious, what she herself had said. "Then I guess we're A-OK."

"We are."

"I'll see you...sometime."

"Sure," he replied and hung up.

Beatrice stared at the black receiver as she placed it in the cradle.

CHAPTER SIXTEEN

SIX DAYS AFTER Rand's phone call, Beatrice sat in the doctor's office. The doctor assured her she was healing perfectly. Because she'd already tossed the crutches, she was fitted with a more flexible walking air boot. After walking around the office, she found the new boot greatly improved her mobility.

"Either I'm getting used to having a medical device on my leg, or my sense of balance is going to be permanently disabled after this is all over."

"You're doing great, Beatrice," the nurse said as she checked out Beatrice and gave her an appointment card for the next checkup in three weeks.

Rather than head straight back to camp, Beatrice stopped by Maddie Barzonni's Cupcakes and Cappuccino Café to pick up the order of cupcakes she'd placed online. Maddie was behind the counter working on a tray of cupcakes with Chloe Knowland, who had been working at the café for years and was now in acting school part-time in Chicago.

"Maddie, hi!" Beatrice said cheerily.

Maddie wiped her hands on her pink-and-white-striped apron. "Beatrice! How super to see you. I thought you'd be buried out there with the kids all summer." She looked down at Beatrice's foot. "How's the foot?"

"Great. Healing perfectly."

Chloe barely glanced up as she finished placing the cupcakes on the tray. "Hey, Beatrice. I heard about the fire out there at the camp. Is everyone okay?"

"Oh, yes. Absolutely," Beatrice assured them, but changed the subject immediately. She didn't like probing questions about how the fire had started or the fact that there even *had been* a fire. Particularly not in front of a café full of patrons. "So, Chloe, I heard you were trying out for a part at the Merle Reskin Theatre in Chicago. Is that right?"

Chloe beamed. "I am! And I'm so nervous."

Maddie hugged Chloe. "She's always nervous for these auditions." Maddie waved Chloe on to deliver the cupcakes.

"Heaven help us once she actually gets a part," Maddie said. "But I'm driving her in to the city tomorrow while I check on my newest café opening. She'll be pacing until the director calls her name."

Beatrice stifled a chuckle as Chloe came back. She narrowed her eyes and said to Beatrice, "Truthfully, Maddie was just as nervous when she was trying to get her franchise off the ground. I remember those days."

"Be quiet," Maddie scolded. "Don't you have something to do?"

"No. You've got this place so organized, I could take a break." Chloe winked at Beatrice.

The bell over the door chimed as Sarah Jensen Bosworth and her three children crowded through the door. Annie Bosworth, now twelve years old, rushed up to Chloe.

"When was the audition? Did you get it?" Annie asked excitedly.

"Audition's not 'til tomorrow."

Annie's eyes rounded. "Tomorrow?" She spun around to her mother, who was holding eighteen-month-old Charlotte. "Mom, can I go with Chloe to Chicago?"

"Annie!" Sarah gasped. "You haven't been asked. That's not polite to invite yourself."

Annie dropped her chin. "Sorry."

Maddie put her hands on Annie's shoulders. "I'm driving Chloe into the city. If you'd like to come, Annie, and if it's okay with your mom, I'd love to have the company."

"Hey!" Timmy chimed in. "What about me? I'm going to be an actor, too."

"You are not," Annie countered. "Last week you said you wanted to be a firefighter."

"That's because I talked to Mr. Nelson at Lou's diner with Dad. He told me all about it."

Beatrice tried not to flinch. She'd wanted the conversation as far from the subject of fires and firemen as possible, but that clearly wasn't happening.

Timmy continued. "He's really brave." He looked up at Maddie. "I'd still like to go to Chicago with you. Maybe this will solve the conundrum about my future career." He blinked and grinned.

Sarah's eyes fell on her son. "Since when do you know a word like *conundrum*?"

"Dad told it to me. He said that I'm in a muddle of confusion about what I want to do with my life. A man has to think of these things if he's going to provide for his family."

Beatrice had to bite her tongue not to laugh. Timmy was far more adult than most of her campers. But he'd had to grow up fast after his mother died six years ago. Luckily he'd been blessed with Sarah as his step-mother, who loved him like her own.

Beatrice felt the sting of regret. How would her life have been different if she'd had a loving mother like Sarah?

"Timmy," Sarah said. "You have a long time until you have to worry about providing for your family."

"Sarah, I'd love to take both the kids with me to Chicago. We'll watch Chloe's audition, then have some lunch afterward and come home together." Maddie turned to Chloe. "They won't mess you up, will they?"

"No way. It would be great to know I have a cheering section. They won't tell me for days if I got the part."

"Oh, cool," Annie and Timmy chimed.

Sarah sighed. "I'm afraid they're getting bored with summer. I have an overload of designs to do at the drafting table and Charlotte is so demanding of my attention that Annie and Timmy get lost. No wonder they're champing at the bit."

Beatrice looked at Annie and Timmy as they sidled away from Sarah and began inspecting the cupcakes in the display case.

"They're bored?"

Sarah nodded. "Bible camp ended last week. And their piano teacher is on a two-week vacation out of town. Timmy says he's read over fifty books on his summer reading list, even though his goal is one hundred by September first. I'm running out of ideas."

"The kids at my camp are in the middle of first-aid classes. Kayaking races are this afternoon and when the new kids come in next week, we'll be teaching them about our pioneer garden."

"Pioneer garden? What's that?" Annie asked, diverted from the cupcakes for the moment.

"We have a large vegetable garden near the apple and pear orchard that we started in the spring. We rigged up wooden stakes that look like tepees for the beans to grow up into the air. We did the same with pie pumpkins so that the pumpkins don't rot on the ground. We have tomatoes, corn, zucchini, cucumbers, yellow squash, onions, green peppers, jalapeño peppers and just about every herb you can think of. The kids learn to till the earth, fertilize it and tend the plants. Then Amanda, our cook, conducts cooking classes every other day. There's always something to do at camp."

"Sounds cool," Timmy said. "I'd like to go to your camp."

Sarah shook her head. "Beatrice's camp

is for kids who come to stay for a week or more. Isn't that right?"

"Yes. They're usually from out of town."

"Bummer." Timmy went back to the cupcake case.

"Sarah," Beatrice said. "I know your kids would love a day camp, but I'm focusing on kids who aren't as fortunate as Annie and Timmy. They need the camp so badly..."

Sarah touched her arm. "I know. But, Beatrice, maybe it's time for you to think about it. It's another revenue stream you haven't considered."

"Maybe I will. Thanks, Sarah. I'd better get my order and drive back."

"I have it right here," Chloe said, picking up a brown-and-white-striped box with yellow ribbon. "Thanks for your business."

"Hey, your cupcakes are the best," Beatrice said. "And I don't have to drive all the way to Chicago to get one." She hugged Sarah with her free arm. "You take care. See you again soon, I hope."

"Absolutely. Oh!" Sarah held up her forefinger. "I nearly forgot. Isn't Luke working up a bid for you?"

"Yes. He is." Beatrice forced a smile. She didn't want anyone to know she was worried about her finances. Or a certain someone.

"He was supposed to get that to you last week, I think he said. I'm so sorry. It's been really busy this summer for him. He got behind on a commercial job and he's just now getting caught up. I'll remind him."

"I would really appreciate it, Sarah. I've got a time restriction on this construction. I need to get moving soon." She hadn't followed up with Luke because she'd been trying to figure out how to come up with the money to pay him. But the fact was that the clock was ticking. "I look forward to hearing from him."

Beatrice finished her goodbyes and went to her SUV.

She drove across town to the fire station. Around the redbrick building were planters of red geraniums, blue salvia and white daisies. The grass had been newly cut and edged, and due to its dark green color, she could tell it was generously watered. On both corners of the building were American flags waving in the breeze, and across the front door was a red-and-white-striped swag with a blue jabot with white stars in the center. Though it was past the Fourth of July, the place was an icon for small-town Americana at its patriotic best.

"As it should be," she said to herself as she

took the box of cupcakes from the passenger seat. Closing the door, she was approached by a very young-looking man dressed in regulation ILFD black T-shirt and black slacks.

"Hello. May I help you?" he asked politely.

"Actually, um, yes. I'm a…friend of Rand Nelson's. I was wondering, er, hoping to find out if any of you had any word on the jumpers up at Copper Country State Forest."

"I'm not allowed to share department business. Perhaps you should ask his family."

Beatrice's hand flew to her mouth as she gasped. "I promised Rand I'd call his mother, and I did, but there was no answer." She stared at him.

His expression was implacable.

"What is it? Has there been an accident? Is he hurt?"

"I can't divulge…"

Beatrice was desperate. She had to know why this man was withholding information. They did that when someone was hurt or killed, didn't they? They had to notify all the living relatives first. Then they got around to friends. Maybe. "Please." Her hand shot to his bare forearm. She wanted to hold on to him in case her knees gave way.

"Hey," he said, "Miss…"

"Wilcox. Beatrice Wilcox."

His eyebrow hitched up. "You're her?"

"What?"

"The one who drove in here and reamed him out." His eyes took in her air boot and his face broke into a grin. "I'm new here, but that story was one of the first I heard." He kept grinning as if he knew something about her she didn't.

Embarrassment colored her cheeks. "I had a bad day, all right? Now tell me what's going on with Rand."

He shrugged his shoulders. "He and a few others from the station are still in Michigan. It's a monster of a fire. I wish I was there," he said wistfully as if risking his life was his dream come true.

Maybe it was, she thought. "How long do these things take?"

"Weeks. Months sometimes. Rand will come back after his shift. In a week or so. But he'll only be home a few days before returning to the fire. They'll keep rotating in and out until the fire's contained."

"I see."

"You can follow their progress, you know."

"How?"

"The reports are on a satellite station." He patted his pockets and withdrew a pen and a small writing pad. He held up the pen. "I'm a rookie, so I'm always taking notes. This comes in very handy."

"I'll bet it does."

"These are the call letters of the satellite feed." He wrote them down and tore off the sheet of paper. "This way, you'll get the information you want and I'm not breaking regulations." He grinned again.

She held out her hand. "Thank you very much, Mr. ....?"

"Mason Conners. You have a good day, Beatrice Wilcox."

The satellite-feed call letters swirled on the paper as she looked at them. She'd wanted to know how Rand was doing. She'd wanted information, but this way, would she hear a blow-by-blow description? Would she hear the particulars of the fire, the dangers, a list of injuries? Lives lost?

They were wrong for each other, and he'd clearly made a personal decision that he had no room for her in his life. The fact that she couldn't get him out of her mind and that she'd begun to care for him was her dilemma.

She started to go and stopped. "Oh, I almost forgot. These cupcakes are made by a friend of mine. Maddie Barzonni. She owns the Cupcakes and Cappuccino Café in town. You should try it sometime."

"Thanks. The guys will love these. That's very kind of you."

"Well, I felt I should do something to apologize to everyone for making a scene a few weeks ago."

"Aw. It's okay. Like I said, you're practically famous around here. A real legend." He gave her a thumbs-up.

Beatrice got into her SUV and carefully backed out of the drive. "A legend." *Terrific.* She could just imagine what the firemen thought of her. First Rand saves her life and to thank him, she bawled him out…in front of another firefighter. "Some legend I am."

When she got back to camp, she folded the paper and put it away. She decided she'd wait for Rand to call. He'd said he'd try to give her an update at some point. Of course, then he'd also made it clear that he wasn't right for her, and she wasn't right for him. But that didn't mean he wouldn't call, right?

But as the days passed with no word from Rand, her anxiety intensified. Logically, she knew he was in the midst of a battle, just as if he'd gone off to war. He couldn't communicate with her. No cell coverage. He probably had little time to sleep.

But the hours had slowed to a standstill for

her like never before. She was heartsick that something had happened to him.

She hadn't planned on this overwhelming emotional reaction to the void his leaving had created. It was a void filled with fear and terror like she hadn't felt since her father was alive.

And whenever she scolded herself for thinking about him and promised herself that she was better off without him, the more she needed to hear from him.

She'd called his mother, as he'd asked, but her call had gone to voice mail. She'd explained she was a friend of Rand's.

But even as she'd said the word, she knew she wasn't a friend in that way his other friends were. She was the woman he'd been investigating. The person who blamed him for putting her camp in jeopardy. The woman he'd left behind without a second thought.

She shoved her fingers frustratingly into her hair and slipped a lock behind her ear. Rand.

Finally she decided she had to stop arguing with herself and tune in, as soon as she was alone in her office. She had to know if Rand was safe. She took the paper and placed it in her pocket.

Beatrice left her cabin and found Joshua's

parents had arrived to drive him home. Changeovers were at noon and the new arrivals were due in between three and four o'clock on Fridays. Joshua held Beatrice's hand as he explained all the fun things he'd learned at camp.

"Next year I want to come back for a whole month!"

Joshua's father smiled indulgently. "That's a long time to be away from home. I'd miss you."

"I'd miss you, too, Daddy, but I'm growing up now and you have to get used to letting me go."

"Whoa. Where did that come from?"

Beatrice shrugged her shoulders. "Joshua is a bit more forthright than other kids his age. But we would love to have you for a month next summer, Joshua. And don't forget, you can come back for a weekend in the fall, perhaps. We have botany field trips through the forest and down to Indian Lake. You think about that."

"Okay," Joshua said and put his arms around her waist. "I'll miss you, Miss Beatrice."

"I'll miss you, too, Joshua. More than you know."

He turned to his father. "Okay, Dad. We better go before Miss Beatrice starts to cry."

"Goodbye."

Beatrice wasn't sure how Joshua knew she cried when the kids left. These kids left indelible marks on her heart. She waved at Joshua, who sat in the back seat, waving to her.

Cindy walked up with her ever-present clipboard of departures and arrivals. "You have one hour until the first of the newcomers arrive. Maisie needs you in your office."

"Is there a problem?"

"Just some budgetary items."

"She probably wants more board games. And baseball gloves. Thanks," she said and headed for her office.

Budgetary items. While it was true the kids deserved all kinds of new games, brain teasers and bats, balls and baseball gloves that fit properly, she doubted that was really what Maisie wanted to discuss.

She'd been careful not to dwell on her financial issues in front of the staff. She wanted them all to focus on the kids and making their camp experience fun, educational and memorable. If all the kids could be like Joshua or the Kettering sisters, she'd never have to advertise again. Kids would book the entire summer.

If only…

She walked into her office but Maisie was nowhere in sight. She reached in her jeans pocket and withdrew the piece of paper Mason Conners had given her. One of the few indulgences she'd allowed herself when she first rebuilt the camp was satellite radio and a satellite dish. This far out of town, however, there was poor to nonexistent television coverage.

She tuned the office radio to the call letters Mason had given her.

The feed was a computerized weather and atmospheric service alert system for the Lake Michigan area, covering all the surrounding states. It gave data on the tides, nautical winds and air temperatures. When the report started for Copper Country State Forest, Beatrice sat straight up in her chair and leaned forward, not wanting to miss a word.

"Winds southwest at twenty-three knots. Waves, one to three feet. Small craft advisory. Copper Country National Forest fire is reported to cover one hundred fifty acres. One hundred acres burn. Fire contained north sector. Firefighters on scene."

Then the report moved on to give temperatures for the Upper Peninsula, daybreak and sunset times.

"That's it?" She switched off the radio.

Maisie stood in the doorway. "What's 'it'?"

Beatrice lifted her eyes. "Nothing."

Maisie walked in. "Sure, 'nothing.' You were hoping to hear about Rand."

"How do you know that?"

Maisie plunked down in the wooden chair. "Because you told Amanda he was going away to fight some forest fire. The UP, I think. Amanda told Cindy. Cindy told me. I told Bruce."

"Is no secret safe around here?"

Maisie touched the tips of her fingers to both hands and steepled them. "Oh? Rand is a secret now?"

"Would you stop?" Beatrice purposefully glared at her. "And did you want to see me about something?"

"Amanda says we need more maple syrup. But the pure stuff just went up another twenty bucks. I could cut costs way back if we get those huge jugs from the wholesaler. Clay says—"

Beatrice cut her off. "No high-fructose sugars and it's fine with me." Beatrice pulled her cell phone from her back jeans pocket. Still no text from Rand.

She frowned.

Maisie leaned forward. "Beatrice. Are you all right?"

"Huh? Oh, yeah. Of course!" She beamed a fake smile.

"Liar. But have it your way." She rose. "I'll take care of the syrup and the other cooking supplies."

Beatrice looked at her cell again. No voice mails, either. Rand was battling a raging fire. He had to be exhausted and surely cell coverage up there was nonexistent. Being honest with herself, she was hoping he thought about her. Deep down, she had to admit that she wanted to mean something to him. And right now, she felt rejected. And lonely. Despite her argument that he was totally wrong for her, she couldn't stop her growing affection.

"Beatrice?"

"Huh?"

Maisie cocked an eyebrow and pointed out the window. "The kids? You're greeting the parents. Hyping the camp. Doing promo."

"Got it. Yes." Beatrice shoved the phone in her back pocket as she rose from the chair. "I'm on it."

"Way to go, boss." Maisie rolled her eyes.

"What?"

"It's just that since Rand Nelson went away, you've been watching your phone like a hawk. You never did that before. Now you're listening to the satellite radio? Since when?"

"Your point is?" Beatrice knew she sounded defensive.

"My point is that it's obvious to me that you're more than interested in him. I'd say you're invested."

Beatrice dropped the pretense. "I don't know if he's injured. Alive. Dead." She had to hold her hands to keep them from trembling. She blinked back tears as she looked at Maisie. "I'd be acting just the same if it was any of you going into danger like that. I care about you."

"I know that. I do. You've got the biggest heart of anyone I've ever met." Her eyes tracked over to the radio. "But I think your heart has drawn Rand in as well."

Maisie waved and left.

Maisie had a point, but the cruel truth was that these days of worrying about him and his safety had shown her that she did care about him. Probably more than she could ever admit to herself.

He was everything she'd look for in a man—kind, generous, thoughtful, and he was a lifesaving hero as well. But he craved danger. He needed to walk that tightrope between life and death. They weren't even in a relationship and she was crazy with worry already. A life of this would be her undoing.

And, eventually, fate would grab him, and Beatrice would be left alone and brokenhearted.

There was no place for their relationship to go.

It was best they remain apart.

CHAPTER SEVENTEEN

BEATRICE MET LUKE BOSWORTH outside the dining hall when he arrived at the camp early the next morning. He was tall and dressed in jeans and a banded-collar white shirt with his construction company logo over the pocket. Offhandedly, Beatrice wondered if all Rand's friends were as good-looking as he.

"Hi." Luke smiled and held out his hand. "We haven't formally been introduced, but you've met my wife and kids." He stood back and studied the camp. "Sarah and my kids can't stop talking about what you're doing here. I didn't grow up in Indian Lake like Sarah did, so I don't know how it was back then, but you've done a wonderful job." He gestured to the burned forest. "That's a shame, huh? Rand told me about it."

Beatrice shielded her eyes from the sun with her palm. "Yes. It was. But it will grow back. The kids and I planted new saplings. And of course, the forest is full of pines that resprout themselves from the cones that spew seeds during a fire."

"Right. Good lumber, that pine," Luke said.

"You have my bid for me?"

"Oh!" He smiled and jabbed his thumb over his shoulder. "In the truck. I'll get it." He withdrew a set of papers from the dashboard. "I took the surveyor's report that Rand gave me." He handed the papers to her. "And I've come up with a fair bid."

Beatrice looked at the final figure. "Uh. Um. Is this right?"

He glanced down at the line where she was pointing. "Yes, ma'am."

"This is more than I'd planned. The city doesn't charge this much."

"The city doesn't include several of the labor costs that I did. That's another reason I don't like working with them. I know for a fact that the utilities commissioner has a brother-in-law who has a construction company, and that commissioner is notorious for sliding building contracts to said relative. Then when the construction is going full tilt, the client is hit with increased costs."

Beatrice dropped her jaw. "That's illegal. Or should be."

Luke shrugged his shoulders. "It's been

going on for years. You'd think that guy would be voted out of office." He smiled confidently. "That's why Rand wanted me to handle your job."

"I see. Well…" She heaved a sigh. "If you'll follow me, I'll show you where the new water lines and hydrants are to go."

They walked around the line of apple trees and forsythia bushes and came up to the trenches Rand had dug.

Luke whistled. "What's all this?"

"Rand dug them."

"By himself?"

"Uh-huh." She didn't dare tell him that two young campers had lifted a spade or two to help. "He's the kindest man."

"I'll say. That's a lot of work." Luke scratched the back of his neck. "Of course, for Rand Nelson, it probably wasn't so much. In the winters, I go to the gym with him and Trent Davis. He's a police detective. Rand can outlift both Trent and I together."

"I believe that."

"I was in the navy and Trent was a Green Beret. So the three of us understand each other."

Sarah's husband had been a military man? A man who risked his life for others? Sarah seemed the essence of peace and calm to

Beatrice. How had she managed to come to grips with his need for danger?

Of course, Luke was in construction now. He wasn't out there fighting flames like Rand was at this very minute.

"Did you hear me?" Luke asked.

"Sorry." She shook her head. Too many thoughts of Rand weaving gossamer webs in her mind. "What did you say?"

"He saved you a great deal of money."

"He did?"

"Yeah. Fifteen hundred dollars, I'd say. Maybe more."

Beatrice exhaled deeply. "That's good."

"Sure is. That should help the bottom line."

"Oh, it does. Though not completely. And all this is coming at a bad time. But I have to have this work done. And soon. How do you prefer to be paid?"

"We ask you to put a third down on signing the contract. Another third when we're halfway finished and the balance on completion."

"I see. And how long will it take to get it done?"

"Less than a week."

"A week." She felt her eyebrows zing to her hairline. She'd have to have all the money in a week's time. It had been a few months since she went to the bank and asked for a loan, but she was going to have to do it now. She would never hire someone to do work unless she had the funds to pay.

"Is that a problem?" Luke asked.

"I have some financial transfers I need to make, is all," she hemmed. "Can I call you tomorrow? I don't want to sign the contract until I know for certain that I have everything in order."

"Sure, that's fine," Luke replied. He pulled out his aviator sunglasses and put them on. He started walking back toward his truck. He pointed to the dining hall. "Is that where the kids eat?"

"Yes. Three meals a day, plus snacks, fruit and milk for them around three in the afternoon. One night a week we have story hour around a campfire and Amanda, our cook, and the counselors make s'mores for the kids. It's really fun. Sometimes Bruce will play his guitar and we sing songs."

"Wow." He stopped in his tracks. "My kids would love that. Have you ever thought of having kids from town as day campers?"

"Actually, I did, but I wanted to focus on kids with special needs. I felt they would benefit the most from my camp. Though I have a few vacant spots right now…" With her need for income increasing by the minute, maybe it was time to make some changes. "Are you interested? For Timmy and Annie?"

"We sure are."

"Let's give it a try," she suggested.

"Great. Sarah can drop the kids off before she goes to work, or I could bring them out. And then pick them up before supper."

"I appreciate your help, Luke," she said knowing that tuition for two children was a dribble in the bucket. But she'd take it. "We have plenty of activities for the kids. When would you like to bring Annie and Timmy out here?"

"Let me talk to Sarah. How about Saturday?"

She held out her hand. "Mr. Bosworth, you have a deal. Saturday morning at eight o'clock we start nautical flag lessons. Bruce is starting classes on sailing. All we have is a small sailboat but he will teach the older kids the basics."

"Wonderful. Aw, Beatrice, you're a lifesaver!"

"Hardly that." She thought of Rand's work on the trenches. He was the real hero.

BEATRICE TIED ELI'S sneaker as the boy shoved a too-large piece of waffle into his mouth.

Syrup dribbled down his chin. Chris instantly picked up a paper napkin and wiped his brother's chin.

"You're such a slob," Chris said.

Beatrice put Eli's foot down. "That was a thoughtful thing you just did, Chris, wiping Eli's chin for him. But why did you say what you said?"

Chris stared at her like she was nuts. "He is a slob."

Eli shook his head until his thick hair fell down over his forehead. "Nah-uh. I'm not. I'm hungry."

Beatrice walked behind Chris, put her hands on his shoulders and leaned down to whisper in his ear. "That was a loving thing you did for him, but your words hid your true feelings. I'm guessing that's how your parents treated you. Is that right?"

Chris was silent. His right forefinger traced the tines of his unused fork. "Maybe."

"Your actions always show me that you care about Eli a great deal. But the words out of your mouth can be hurtful."

Chris tilted his face toward her and whispered, "I don't want to hurt him. I want to help him grow up."

"I want that, too." She smiled. "Very much." She kissed his temple.

"What did you do that for?" Chris asked.

"Because I care about you, too."

"Beatrice. There you are." Maisie's voice carried across the dining hall as she raced in the front door.

Beatrice looked up. "What is it?"

"The day campers are here." Maisie glanced over her shoulder.

"Finish your breakfast, Eli. Bruce is starting those nautical flag lessons today."

Eli grinned. "Yes!"

Beatrice crossed the room as quickly as her boot would allow and followed Maisie.

Coming up the road and onto the gravel drive was Sarah's red SUV.

Luke and Sarah got out of their red Envoy. "The kids are excited about your camp," Luke said.

"I want to thank you and Sarah," Beatrice said, watching as the back door opened and Mrs. Beabots got out.

"Mrs. Beabots!" Beatrice exclaimed and hugged her. "I'm so happy to see you."

"I couldn't wait to visit, Beatrice. You know, I used to come here all the time, back in the day." She gazed over at the dining hall. "I'm thrilled you didn't tear anything down."

"No, I refurbished it all. I'm still at it," she said glumly.

"That's what Luke tells me. He and a few others. Hmm. Well, I wanted to help, so I made a half-dozen pies for the children for their snack time."

"Thank you, Mrs. Beabots. Why don't we go up to my office to finish the paperwork. Maisie will take the kids." The kids ran off with Maisie, and Beatrice turned to Sarah and Luke. "Thanks for bringing Annie and Timmy. I need all the help I can get."

"That's what Rand told us," Luke said, picking up Charlotte.

"He did?" she squeaked. Beatrice clamped her lips shut, realizing she'd sounded offended.

"Please don't be angry." Mrs. Beabots put her hand on Beatrice's arm. "We want to help you preserve the camp. The thing is, we just didn't know you needed us. And, sweetie, friends like to know they're needed."

"You're too kind." Her eyes misted as Mrs. Beabots put her arms around Beatrice and hugged her.

"Beatrice. We're here for you. You've done so much for these children. Now—" Mrs. Beabots took her hand "—help me with these pies."

Luke lifted the hatch. There were two rows of double-crusted pies dusted with sugar.

"There's blueberry, apple, blackberry and peach. I wasn't sure what the children would prefer, so I made all four," Mrs. Beabots said.

"Yeah," Sarah chuckled. "She went crazy."

Beatrice led the way to the kitchen, where they deposited the pies and she introduced Amanda to everyone.

Leaving Mrs. Beabots with chatty Amanda, she took Sarah and Luke to her office, where she'd laid out the paperwork.

"It's pretty standard. Mostly contact information so that we can get in touch with you." She always shied away from mentioning "emergencies." After the fire, she didn't want to bring a single negative vision to anyone's head, including her own.

Once the paperwork was finished, Beatrice thanked them and walked Luke and Sarah and Mrs. Beabots back to their vehicle.

Mrs. Beabots hugged Beatrice and said, "You know, when I used to come out here, they had roses all around the dining hall."

"I saw photographs of how it used to be. The roses were lovely, but I haven't had the, er, uh— What I mean is that landscaping hasn't been in my budget."

"Well, I think I can take care of that for you. I'll have Lester MacDougal clear out some of my roses from my gardens and bring some plants out here for you. He's got the greenest thumb."

"Not as green as yours," Sarah said.

"True. But I've taught him nearly everything he knows. Except, of course, for the things your mother, God rest her soul, taught him when he first walked into town."

"Thank you so much, Mrs. Beabots. Roses would be wonderful. I wonder if Lester would consider giving the children a lesson on horticulture."

"Why don't you ask him, dear? I think he'd be delighted," Mrs. Beabots said as Luke held the door for her.

As they drove away, Beatrice's mood sank.

She was grateful for her friends' help. But it didn't cut it.

She was out of money. She'd cut back on food, laundry supplies and new games and equipment. The budget had been whittled to the bone, but she still didn't have enough money to cover Luke's contract.

After all this work, would she still lose everything?

CHAPTER EIGHTEEN

THE DAY AFTER Rand returned, he headed to the camp. Chris and Eli spotted his truck and ran to see him.

He handed ILFD ball caps to Chris and Eli, and both boys eagerly fit the hats on their heads.

"There," Rand said. "Those are perfect. My old one was too big for either of you."

"And smelly." Eli wrinkled his nose as he beamed up at Rand.

"That, too."

Chris smashed the bill down on his forehead. "That's from working hard." Though he didn't smile, Rand saw something in Chris's eyes he hadn't seen before. It nearly bordered on respect. He felt his heart trip.

He'd talked with the boys once from Michigan, and assured them he'd see them soon. He'd kept Beatrice's warnings about not letting the boys get too attached in his mind, but he hadn't wanted to let them down, either.

"You guys helped me a lot."

"So, we made restitution?" Chris asked timidly.

"Yes, Chris, you did."

"And me, too," Eli added.

Rand smiled. "You sure did." Rand carried his pickax and shovel to the end of the long trench.

"What are you doing now? I thought you were finished," Chris asked.

"I talked to Mr. Bosworth this morning and he told me that I'm about two feet short on this end. It's not much, but I don't want anyone to accuse me of imperfect work."

"So, can we help you again?"

Rand pulled a pair of work gloves out of his back jeans pocket. "Since I only brought one shovel, you'll have to take turns." He gave the gloves to Chris. "Use these. I know they're too big, but they might help."

Chris put them on, but they were much too large. He handed them back to Rand. "You need them more than I do, anyway." He took the shovel, his eyes still cast downward. "But thanks for...offering."

"Of course."

Rand noticed that Chris watched him with a different kind of intensity than he'd experienced from the boy on previous visits. "Something's on your mind. I can tell."

"I was wondering. Eli and I were wondering…"

Eli sprang across the area and stood close to Rand. "We want to see your station. Would you take us sometime?"

"To the fire station?"

"Yeah," Eli said. "I want to get inside the truck. Maybe turn on the siren."

"No sirens," Rand replied. "Those are for official use only."

"That's okay," Chris began. "We won't touch anything. But I, uh, um, we both want to see what it's like."

"Yeah. Do you have a pole and everything?"

"Yes." Rand put his hand on Eli's head. "We have a pole that we slide down. It's faster than stairs."

"Oh, cool." Eli grinned.

Rand's eyes tracked to the more serious Chris. "I suppose you want to slide down the pole?"

"No. I want to learn how to do what you do."

Rand cocked his head. "And what is that? Exactly?"

"Protect people."

Rand felt his heart stop. Like an ax sliding through a burned-out tree, Rand fell for the kid.

Initially he'd misjudged the boy. Those first days, Rand would have bet that Chris's ability to polish his arrogance to a cynical gleam would never be tarnished. But somehow, Rand had gotten through to the kid. Or the fact that he'd nearly caused his own brother's death had straightened him out? Whether it was circumstances or Rand's skills or a bit of both, he might never know. But Chris was reaching out to him now.

Rand reached back, shoving aside the voice—that sounded suspiciously like Beatrice's—that he was getting too close to the boys. Maybe he could even invite them to the family barbecue on Sunday.

"Yeah, let me set that up for you both. I'll talk to the captain."

"You'd do that for us?" Eli asked.

"Sure, I would."

Chris pursed his lips together. To keep them from trembling? Rand wondered. Chris glanced to his brother. "Thanks."

"You're welcome."

Rand noticed that Eli didn't take his eyes off Chris. The younger boy moved a step closer to his brother and simply stood next to him as if buffering him from the world or showing that he would be Chris's pillar if he broke down.

"Well, we'd better get to these trenches."

Rand measured out the distance and marked it with a line he drew into the earth with the end of the pickax. He pointed to Eli. "You stand aside and out of the way of flying debris. I don't want you to get a rock or dirt in your eyes."

"I'll be careful," Eli assured him with a bright smile.

"And, Chris, you wait 'til I have this trench area dug deep enough before you try to shovel. Once I start working, my mind stays pretty focused on the labor and not much else."

At least it always had before. But as he began digging, Rand was keenly aware of his surroundings.

He'd had a hard time focusing on the work up in Michigan, too. Visions of Beatrice surrounded by fire haunted him like a never-ending nightmare. And the more he tried to wipe her from his brain, the more he thought about her.

Swirling around his visions of her were his thoughts about the boys.

He hoped they'd understood why he couldn't call again, and believed him when he said he'd be back soon. He'd wanted to call, but it had been impossible. The smoke-jumper team had been deep in the forest, and their only connection to the outside world had been the radio to base camp and their radio to the pilots dropping water.

The last thing he wanted was further disruption in Chris's or Eli's life. Instead, he wanted somehow to give them a sense of security in their shattered lives.

Rand remembered how small and alone he'd felt when his father died. Though Rand had been just in his early teens, the impact of losing his father had been devastating.

Rand couldn't imagine how lost Eli and Chris felt. They had no one.

He wanted to help them, despite Beatrice's warnings.

Beatrice.

He'd thought surely the raging fire in Michigan would burn away whatever connection had been building between them.

But once they got within a hundred miles of Indian Lake on the way back from the Upper Peninsula, Rand began to watch the mileage signs on the side of the interstate like a kid anxious to arrive at a theme park. The soles of his feet itched to get home. All so that he could find some excuse to come out here to the camp and see her.

But then what?

He'd practically shoved her out of his life, and yet, here he was throwing down a pickax on her property—without her permission.

He didn't care if she blew her stack with him. He'd think of something to make it right with her.

But what was it that he wanted? Could they be friends? He hoped so.

"When did *you* get back?" Beatrice asked with a harsh tone as she approached the trench.

He looked up and squinted. She was wearing a summer dress of some kind of gauzy green material. He'd never seen her in a dress, but he liked it. Her tan, taut arms were folded across her chest. There was a gold necklace around her neck and she had white pearl studs in her ears. Her blond hair was clipped at the back of her head, though tendrils fell down the right side of her face. He realized she was dressed up for something. It was Thursday so she wasn't off to church.

"Uh, yesterday." He lowered the pickax and noticed the lime-green straw sandal she wore. It had long ties that wrapped around her tan ankle. The air boot was wrapped around the other ankle. She was a vision. "You're all dressed up."

"I went to town."

"Oh." He smoothed his sweat-soaked hair away from his forehead. He wiped his palm on his thigh. The sweat wasn't from the weather or labor. His discomfort was from the censure he saw in her eyes. "Well, wherever you went, you look…nice. Pretty."

"Thanks. I was at the bank."

"Miss Beatrice," Eli said brightly. "Mr. Nelson gave Chris and me new hats. See?" He took off his cap and rushed to show her.

She touched the hat and dropped her hand. Her eyes flew to Rand's face. "You bought them presents? Why?"

He didn't like her caustic tone. As if he'd slipped the kids something illegal. "They helped me out here." He gestured toward the trenches. "I wanted them to know I appreciated their efforts. They went above and beyond. They should be rewarded." He paused and shot her a quelling look. "Don't you agree?"

"I do. Thank you," she said grudgingly.

He didn't know what was going on, but he intended to find out. "So, the bank. How'd that go?"

"Fine."

"I'm not buying it."

She looked at Chris. "Boys, it's nearly time for snacks. Why don't you go up to the dining room and see if Amanda needs some help, hmm?"

Chris glanced down at his shovel. "But I haven't done much here and I..."

Rand watched her jaw clench. He put his hand on Chris's shoulder affectionately. "You better go on up, Chris. There's lots of ways to help. Thanks, though."

"You're welcome," Chris said and gave the shovel to Rand.

Rand waited until the boys were out of earshot before he asked, "Did I do something wrong?"

"Frankly, yes. A lot of somethings wrong."

"Okay. I'm sorry for just showing up today. I should have called first."

"I'm not talking about that."

"You're not?" He started to smile and dropped it when he took in the hard expression on her face. "Then what is it?"

"I already warned you not to get too familiar with Chris and Eli. They're fragile and impressionable. I don't want them thinking you're some kind of action hero, and with these grand gestures..."

"Grand? A couple ball caps and an invitation to tour my station house?"

"What invitation?"

He rushed past that question. "I like those kids, Beatrice. I'm beginning to understand what you saw in them weeks ago."

"What's that?"

"Potential. What if someone did adopt them? What if—"

"What if what? Are you going to adopt them?"

"Me?"

"See what I mean? You could easily give them all kinds of false hopes without meaning to." She looked away.

Was that what he'd done to her? Given her hope? He had said he'd call her if he could, but that hadn't been possible. He'd used his one chance to fulfill his promise to the boys.

Still, he could tell he'd hurt her, and that had been the last thing he'd wanted.

"Yes, I see your point. Beatrice, I don't want to disappoint anyone. My intentions are honorable. I only wanted to help. You do believe me, don't you?"

She looked back at him and her blue eyes held his for a long moment. For a split second he thought he'd convinced her.

Then her eyes clouded and grew stormy.

"Leaving aside the boys, I was only able to get two thousand from the bank."

"But you got something, right?" he said, trying to be cheery.

"I was hoping for twice that amount. Luke's bid was more than I'd anticipated. He said it had something to do with the quality of the PVC pipe he used versus that of the inferior grade the city uses. Granted, I want these water lines to last 'til the day I die, but I just didn't think it would cost so much more."

"Luke told you that the city's bids aren't necessarily accurate, right?"

"He did."

"And he mentioned he signed his kids up for day camp."

She chewed her bottom lip and dropped her eyes. "Yes, but two kids won't make much of a difference."

"So maybe you can get more day campers?"

"I mentioned that to the banker. He thought it was a good idea. Otherwise he wouldn't have given me the two thousand."

"And I've saved you a bit of expense by preparing the trenches."

She looked at the trenches. "Yes. Fifteen hundred dollars. Which was very generous of you, but there's still a large amount to cover…"

Daringly, he took a step toward her. A mistake. This close, he could smell her sweet perfume. "But that's not really why you're angry with me, is it?"

"Fine." She thrust her hands on her hips. "You were gone over two weeks and I didn't hear a word from you. I didn't know if you were hurt, or dead, or alive, or what."

"Would it matter to you?"

"Would it matter…?" She inhaled and held her breath. Her fists were balled so tight her knuckles were white.

"You're really angry with me."

"I am. With good reason."

"You should be. I said I'd try and call, but I didn't warn you that that might not be possible." He smiled. He couldn't help it. Even when she was angry with him, she filled him with happiness.

"I am." Her voice softened.

Rand felt his chest pinch. He was out of his mind. Toast. Lost it. He'd left town telling this woman he wanted nothing to do with her. He'd purposefully pushed her away. And yet, she'd been worried about him. He'd thought of nothing but her and the boys for days on end. His nights had been ragged and filled with taunting dreams about her.

Had he been wrong to push her away? Maybe they *could* be friends at least.

Standing this close to her, the summer breeze fluttering the skirt of her dress around her shapely legs, he thought he'd lose what minuscule remains of his brain existed. He wanted to reach out to her, hold her. But he didn't dare.

She looked like she wanted to slug him.

"Bee…"

"How many times do I have to tell you not to call me that?"

"Sorry." He glanced up toward the dining hall. "I was hoping to invite Chris and Eli to my Sunday barbecue."

"I just got through telling you the boys are vulnerable. I don't want them to have illusions about you."

"It's just ribs and hot dogs, Beatrice. My family will be there. I don't see what it could hurt. You were the one who said they needed more than direction and guidance."

"The boys have been entrusted to me. They are my responsibility and I'm their protector. I should be with them."

"Fine. You'll bring them?"

She folded her arms over her chest. "I will. What time?"

"One o'clock," he replied, seeing the hard glint of mistrust in her eyes.

"We'll be there."

CHAPTER NINETEEN

ON SUNDAY, BEATRICE was nervous. She didn't want the boys to idolize Rand. He was already a hero figure to them, but would more familiarization cause them to have unrealistic hopes?

Only a few days ago, she'd spoken with Zoey Phillips and had garnered another two weeks tuition for Chris and Eli. Beatrice had submitted a lengthy report on the boys' improvements in social skills. Zoey told Beatrice that because Chris and Eli had turned around so drastically, she was recommending Indian Lake Youth Camp as an ongoing program for more foster children. Zoey was sending three more foster kids to her camp for the last two weeks in August. Zoey felt that by working together, Beatrice and Zoey could submit a formal requisition to the state for next summer.

Beatrice wanted the best for the boys. She struggled daily to maintain a professional distance with them, both for her own protection and theirs. It would be wrong for the boys to think of her as a mother figure when she might not be part of their future. As wrenching as a placement out of town would be for them, she already knew it would rip her heart.

Rand's involvement in their lives could complicate things even more. If the boys' attachment to Rand grew too deep and Rand pushed them away, like he'd done to her, they could be forever damaged.

Still, she couldn't deny the boys the opportunity to have a good male role model, or to experience a loving family. But she'd been right to insist that she accompany them to the barbecue.

With Chris and Eli in the back seat, Beatrice pulled up to Rand's ranch-style house, which was located a couple blocks from Indian Lake. She had to park in the street since his driveway looked like a car dealer's parking lot. In addition to Rand's monster black Toyota Tacoma truck, an open-roof cherry-red Jeep Wrangler, a rusted white Ford 4x4 truck, a twenty-year-old black Ford Bronco caked in mud, and a spit-shined blue Electra Glide Harley-Davidson motorcycle filled every inch of concrete drive.

"Would you look at all that?" Chris said, slipping his seat belt out of the clasp.

"My belt's stuck," Eli said.

"Chris, help your brother," Beatrice said as she turned off the engine then gathered her purse and plate of fudge she'd made. "You boys stick close to me."

They climbed out of the SUV. Eli held Beatrice's hand as she walked up the driveway.

"Wow!" Chris said. "I never saw anything so awesome as this bike."

"It's an Electra Glide," Beatrice explained. "My father started out as a motorcycle cop. He was always reading a 'bike' magazine."

"Righteous," Chris exclaimed. "Do you think it belongs to Mr. Nelson?"

"I don't know. It's vintage. Maybe it was his father's. He was an admiral in the navy," Beatrice said as they moved away.

Rand hadn't told her much about his family. Only that his father had been rigid. Was Rand mirroring his father with his disciplinary rules and regulations? Or was the softer side of Rand his true nature?

Beatrice scanned the mud-caked Bronco and then her gaze fell to the gleaming Harley. Obviously, the family consisted of some opposing personalities. But he'd said they all loved his smoked baby back ribs.

As they went up to the front door, she noticed the precisely trimmed boxwoods and blooming red and white impatiens in the front beds. There were two white Adirondack-style rockers on the front porch with red-and-white-striped pillows that looked quite inviting. Huge Boston ferns hung in white wicker baskets from the porch roof and an American flag waved in the breeze.

She wondered what it would have been like to have Sunday barbecues for a large family and a mother who cared.

Her upbringing had not been one any kid would choose. Her parents had argued. Her mother was self-absorbed, and her father had had his own priorities. Her mother's fear that he would die while on duty grew to an obsession that slowly extinguished her love for Beatrice. For self-protection, Jenny's world eventually became only about Jenny. And what if Beatrice had felt cherished as a child, would she have developed such a deep passion for her camp? Would she need her camp kids as much?

She looked down at Eli's trusting blue eyes as he smiled up at her.

Yes. She would love her kids even if she'd had the best family life. She squeezed his hand. "Ready to meet Mr. Nelson's family?"

"Oh, yes!" the boys said in happy unison.

Beatrice rang the bell and waited. She smoothed the front of her navy capri pants. She'd worn a navy-and-white-striped short-sleeved T-shirt and clipped her hair up so she wouldn't be hot in the ninety-degree temperature.

She rang the bell again, but still no one came to the door.

"Nobody's home?" Chris asked.

Eli sniffed the air. "I smell food. Someone must be here."

Just then, she heard a deep boisterous laugh. It was the first time she'd ever heard Rand's laugh so fully and raucously. She'd witnessed him chuckle once or twice, but she'd never made him laugh.

"I bet everybody's in the backyard," she said.

"Let's go see!" Eli said, dropping her hand and running down the porch steps.

"Eli!" she shouted.

"C'mon, Miss Beatrice," Chris said as he followed his younger brother.

Beatrice couldn't help but smile. They were more than excited about their first barbecue. She was happy for them but her nervousness remained.

She took in the detached garage and a

six-foot-high white resin picket fence as she walked to the gate.

Voices, both male and female, filled the air—talking, teasing and laughing. Eli was too short to reach the gate latch.

"Here, let me," she said to him and opened the gate. "Hello?" She ventured into the backyard.

Just then a dog barked and a Jack Russell terrier came rushing up to them.

"Hey, there," she said and petted the dog's head as he swished around her air boot.

"A dog!" Chris said excitedly and reached to pet him.

Eli hugged the dog immediately. "I didn't know Mr. Nelson had a pet. Aren't you glad we got asked to come, Chris?"

Chris stroked the dog's head. "I am."

Then the dog rushed off.

Beatrice tracked the terrier's progress to a large flagstone patio filled with people. Happy people. Three good-looking men dressed in jeans, shorts and T-shirts. No question they were all related. The men were drinking beer, laughing at a joke.

Rand was at the double, long, stainless-steel grill. Next to it was a black cast-iron smoker. He wore a tight navy blue T-shirt and khaki shorts. Around his narrow waist was a food-stained white apron. On his feet were leather sandals. The aroma of smoking meat wafted to Beatrice's nostrils and made her salivate.

"It smells so good," Chris said.

Eli shuffled closer to her legs and looked up at her warily. "It's a lot of people."

She touched his hair and smoothed it down. "You'll be fine," she assured him. His smile was faint yet trusting.

There was also a young woman with a drape of shining blond hair nearly to her waist. She was dressed in skinny jeans, black motor-cycle boots with stainless-steel chains around the ankles and a black tank top. As they approached, the woman held a margarita glass to her lips and laughed at Rand. She punched his shoulder and he leaned over and kissed her temple. Beatrice guessed she was his sister and the Harley belonged to her.

A short, round-faced older woman with huge green eyes and streaked, cropped hair turned to Beatrice as they approached the patio. The older woman gifted her with a blazing smile that was so similar to Rand's that Beatrice knew in an instant this was his mother.

"Rand?" she called. "Your guests are here."

He spun around, holding up a long pair of tongs, and said, "Hi! You found us!"

"We did. I rang the bell, but clearly…"

"Sorry. I should have told you to come to the back. We never stay inside." He put down the tongs and walked past his brothers, who parted for him. They each lowered their beers and stared at her. Then at the boys.

Then they stared at Rand. Gaping.

Rand walked up to the boys and held out his hand to Chris. "I'm glad to see you, Chris. And, Eli, how're you doin'?"

"I'm good," Eli replied, still clinging to Beatrice's side, his eyes sweeping across the group of people.

Beatrice captured Rand's attention. "He's a bit shy today. What with so many unfamiliar faces." She nodded toward Rand's family, all of whom were staring at them.

"I'll introduce you guys. My family is anxious to meet you."

"Why?" Chris's shoulders instantly braced.

Rand leaned down. "Because I told them what a great help you were to me."

"Oh," Chris said.

To break the tension, Beatrice offered the plate of fudge to Rand. "I made this for you."

"That was very nice," he said, his gaze

latching on to hers as he took the plate. He blinked. "You look really pretty." He smiled.

"Thank you. I like your apron."

"Huh? Oh, yeah. It was my dad's."

"So he smoked his meat as well?"

"Yes. But he wasn't as good at it as I am." He looked at the boys. "Come meet my mom." He turned. "Mom!"

The older woman walked over. "I'm Laura. Mother to this brood of rascals."

"Beatrice." She held out her hand.

Laura shook her head. "In this family we hug."

Before Beatrice knew what was happening, Laura embraced her. Then to the kids she said, "This must be Chris and Eli. Give me a hug, boys."

Chris remained stiff as the older woman wrapped her arms around him, but Eli fell into the hug easily.

His siblings approached next.

Rand slapped one of his brothers on his wide shoulder. "This is my brother Ed. He's one year younger than me."

"Thirteen months," Ed corrected.

"Nice to meet you, Ed," Beatrice responded.

"Oh, very nice to meet you, Beatrice. You must be pretty special to get my brother to pay attention to anything other than the next forest fire or his barbecue."

"So are the boys," Rand said.

"We've heard a lot about you kids," Ed said. He gave them each a quick wave.

A sandy-haired man held out his hand. "I'm David. This is Jonas. Pleased to meet you."

She shook hands with David and Jonas.

Finally, Rand's sister elbowed her way past her brawny brothers. "They always leave me to last since I'm the youngest."

"The runt of the litter," Ed joked.

"Cassie Nelson." She hit Ed on the bicep, and though he flinched, Beatrice believed it would take more than a fist to cause that man any real pain.

"I'm glad to know you, Beatrice," Cassie said. "All these guys can get on a girl's nerves after a while. Just blow them off for a few hours. They come whimpering back."

"Is that a fact?" Rand scoffed.

"True words," Laura said and leaned over to Beatrice. "All my boys have soft hearts."

Not all of them. Beatrice kept her smile in place. "How can I help?" She glanced over at a table where food preparations were taking place.

"Oh," Laura said. "Cassie and I were

working on the salad. You can cut up the cucumber."

"But they're homegrown so you have to take the seeds out," Rand said, putting a hand on each of the boys' shoulders. "Come with me and I'll show you everything I've learned about smoking the world's best ribs."

Beatrice couldn't help but laugh. "That's modest. Eli, stay back from that heat."

"Yes, ma'am."

Rand opened the grill hood and turned ears of corn on the cob. "I hope everyone likes the corn. I've got a new recipe."

"What was wrong with the way Dad used to do it?" Jonas said. "Grilled in the husk for twenty-eight minutes, turned one quarter every seven minutes."

Laura nodded. "That's exactly right."

"Well," Rand said with a proud lift of his chin, "this way we can infuse the corn with flavor as its cooking. If it's bad, we trash it and go back to the old way."

"Goodness, what kind of recipe is this?" Beatrice asked, moving to stand next to Rand as he smeared a gooey mess on the cobs.

"Mayonnaise, salt, pepper, basil."

"Ugghhh," Eli groaned.

Chris looked at Beatrice pleadingly. "Do we have to eat it?"

"You should try it, but if you really don't like it, you can eat something else," she said.

"I like hot dogs," Eli said.

"Taste the ribs first. I bet they're gonna be good," Beatrice said, picking up a field cucumber and cutting it.

Rand proudly said, "I tested them already. Incredible. Don't worry, Chris. Everything is good."

"I love it all!" Chris grinned.

As Beatrice went back to preparing the cucumber, Laura explained that Rand grew heirloom tomatoes, field cucumbers, zucchini, green beans and herbs in his yard. She pointed to a small storage shed in the back.

"Behind the shed is his garden. It's not big and if he has to leave town, I come over and harvest the vegetables."

"Really? I had no idea he had a green thumb. I have a pioneer garden for the kids at the camp."

"Rand told us all about your camp," Cassie said. "I never went to a place like that."

"That's right," Laura said. "You were too busy helping us wash and fix the cars. As I remember it, you didn't want to do anything that didn't involve an engine."

"I'm still that way," Cassie said.

Beatrice finished peeling and slicing the cucumber. "What do you do?"

"I own the Harley-Davidson store here in Indian Lake."

Beatrice put down the paring knife. "You own it?"

"Oh, yes," Laura said. "She's quite successful. A born saleswoman."

"At least I'm not a lineman like David or a tree climber like Jonas."

"I heard that," Jonas said, as he walked over with a tray of icy glasses. "Tree surgeon," he said. "I don't do the climbing. Ed is the climber. He can shimmy up a tree faster than anyone I've ever seen." Jonas handed Beatrice and each of the boys a glass. "Lemonade."

Chris took a big slug. "This is really good!"

"I like it, too." Eli smiled between sips.

"Thanks," Laura said. "I make it from fresh lemons the way my mother did. Real sugar, too. No aspartame."

"What's that?" Eli asked.

"Something you'll never find at our camp."

"Yeah," Chris said. "It's supposed to be bad for you."

"How?" Eli asked. "Is it addictive?"

Rand stopped midmotion as he turned an ear of corn.

Before Beatrice could say a word, Rand jumped in. "They say it can cause cancer. Dangerous stuff."

"Hmm. But not as dangerous as being a firefighter..." Chris mused.

Beatrice caught Rand's sideways glance. "You know, Chris, I'm not the daredevil in the family. Ed is."

Ed guffawed. "Not likely. You and the other jumpers worked nonstop for over thirty-two hours when you first got to Copper Country. I don't know how you can stay awake that long much less have the physical endurance it took to fight the fires."

"Yeah," Jonas added. "Mom said she was crazy worried."

Rand turned the corn. "I told her I was fine."

Beatrice noticed that his eyes slid to her and then back to the corn. Even though he hadn't told her he was fine, at least he was thoughtful enough to alleviate his mother's fears.

Cassie licked salad dressing off her fingertip. "It was really lucky that tree missed you when it fell. And you were the only one who saw it coming when it rolled down the hill toward you and the other jumpers. Your warning shouts saved them. Boy, Rand, if it hadn't been for your eagle eye and that sixth sense of yours, one of the other guys might have really been injured."

Beatrice held her breath as if she was living the scenario in the forest all over again. She noticed that Chris's and Eli's eyes filled their faces as their attention went from Rand to Ed, then back to Cassie.

David joined in. "The delay in getting the tanker planes filled with water wasn't good, either. Have you ever had to wait over twelve hours for them before?"

"Uh, no." Rand checked the ribs and flipped them.

Ed and David continued talking about more of Rand's exploits, both daring and dangerous, when he'd been in the Upper Peninsula.

Chris and Eli were spellbound. Beatrice didn't know if they were reliving their own night of terror, or if their hero worship was being polished. Neither was advantageous for the boys. "Rand…" she said with more warning in her voice than she'd planned.

Rand slammed the grill hood, obviously taking her cue. "Okay, guys! Grub is ready. Get your plates and I'll fill them."

The conversation shifted to the food.

"About time," David said as he grabbed his plate and went straight for the ribs.

"Hey!" Rand said. "The kids are first." He handed them each a plate. "What would you like?"

"A hot dog," Eli said.

Rand placed a grilled hot dog in a bun and put it on Eli's plate. "What about you, Chris?"

"Can I have one of everything?"

Beatrice looked at Rand. Their eyes locked and they both broke out laughing.

"Of course you can, Chris," she said. "Here, let me help you."

"You guys sit over there at the table," Rand said. "Mom will get you chips, baked beans. The works."

Chris stared at his plate being piled with food. "Do you think I could learn to grill stuff like this?"

"Sure. Why not?"

"I never saw it done before," Chris replied sadly. Then he raised his face to Beatrice. "This is almost as good as watching you make s'mores for us."

"You know, Chris, you could become a chef someday. You just have to put your mind to it," she said.

"I want to do all kinds of things. Just like Mr. Nelson."

Beatrice glanced at Rand. She supposed to a young boy with few role models in his life, Rand seemed almost godlike.

And that was dangerous for both the boy and the hero should the god prove human.

As Beatrice helped the boys to the table she watched Rand joke with his brothers and sister; all of them acting as if he hadn't nearly lost his life in the Copper Country fire. As she smeared mustard on Eli's hot dog, her hand shook. Fear did that to her. Always had.

Rand hadn't given her any details of the fire. She hadn't been privy to special reports or the stories he'd shared with his family. Before he left, he'd deliberately pushed her away. He'd invited the boys to his barbecue, but she'd pushed her own way in. She'd forced him to include her. Had he suspected his family would talk about the fire and he didn't want her to hear the truth?

But in the end, it wasn't her pain that mattered. All she could see was heartbreak ahead for Eli and Chris.

She wasn't about to let that happen.

"Wow," Rand said as he came into the kitchen, where Beatrice was drying a stainless-steel pan. It was the first moment they'd had to themselves since she'd arrived at the barbecue. "You were a big hit with my family. They really like you."

"I liked them all, too." She put down the pan. "A lot. And so did the boys. You wanted Chris and Eli to experience how a loving family treats each other. Am I right?"

"Uh-huh. Is that bad?"

"No…"

"Look, Beatrice. If the boys are lucky enough to get adopted or at least be placed with a nice foster family, I thought they should see what family could be. Not that my family is perfect. The guys horse around a lot. And Cassie. Well, she's just Cassie. You gotta love her. I do."

"That's the thing, Rand. The love you have for each other just flows out of you all with no hesitation. Except…"

"Except for me?"

She lowered her head and put the towel over the pot. "Yes. As a matter of fact. Sometimes you can be so rigid. You wall yourself off. Why is that?"

He paused for a long moment as if considering a multitude of thoughts. When he faced her, she thought she'd never seen so much grief in a person's eyes.

"Rand?"

"His name was Perry Shoal. And, Beatrice, his death was my fault. I was lax. I was less than the trainer I should have been. I saw it coming and I ignored my instincts. I can never forgive myself."

"He's the reason you insist on following the rules?"

"Yeah. He was a hothead. Arrogant. Self-centered and manipulative. During his first weeks in training, I thought it was a personality clash between us. I just couldn't get through to him the importance of following regs. I pushed him. Tutored him. Gave him extra exercises. When he still flouted the rules, I wanted to assign him to a different trainer, but he begged me not to. He promised to improve and he did. He became an exemplary trainee. Or I thought he had.

"So when a fire broke out in the Idaho forest and the call came in for jumpers, Perry talked me into letting him go."

Rand stopped and swallowed hard before continuing. "It was a demon of a fire. The winds shifted, locking us in. Regs say in that situation you stick together, but Perry panicked. He took off into the fire thinking he could escape. I was the one who found him."

She grasped Rand's hand and held it with both of hers. "Rand. It wasn't your fault."

His head jerked up. His eyes were hard. "Of course it was."

"No. It wasn't. He manipulated you into letting him go by pretending to respect the rules. You couldn't have known that. He was probably the best option you had in that moment. You can't go on blaming yourself for his death."

"Sure I can." Her eyes delved into his.

"That's not what this is about at all, though, is it? You're using his death to keep you from a life of your own. So long as you guard your emotions, lock them up and over-commit yourself to your job, you don't have to feel anything." She paused. "That's why you pushed me away, and why someday soon you'll do the same to Eli and Chris."

"Stop. Okay?" He pulled his hands from her. "You're a fine one to talk. Did you ever stop to think that you do the same thing? You've used your mother's worries about dangerous careers and your father's death to keep you from making choices, too."

Her breath hitched. "I should get the kids and go," she said, moving over to the counter where she'd laid her purse and keys.

He was accusing her of avoiding dreams?

She'd been doing everything in her power to create a haven for kids…and herself—that was her dream.

But as her ire dialed down a degree, she saw the kernel of truth in what he said. Her issues with her parents had stuck her like porcupine quills and she used them to keep love away. Protection had been her modus operandi.

She lifted her purse strap to her shoulder. "Yeah. I guess I'm guilty as charged. You were right. We're as wrong for each other as they come."

"Yeah."

His voice was low and she detected sadness in his tone, as if he didn't like being right.

"Well, thanks for dinner. You're a good cook."

"Thanks."

"I have to get the boys." She turned away and waved over her shoulder so that he wouldn't see the tears in her eyes. "Goodbye, Rand."

CHAPTER TWENTY

RAND STARED AT the full moon once his family left, remembering Beatrice's words. Her "goodbye" had had a finality that he didn't like.

For the first time he felt a stinging void and he didn't quite understand where it came from.

Maybe he *had* been using Perry's death as an excuse to avoid making real choices about his life. Had he been guilty of slamming the wrong doors?

And in the process, he hadn't moved a single foot toward his own future, either. He was stuck, and though he'd convinced himself that where he was in his life was as good as it got, lately, since Beatrice, things were different for him.

He knew his career was a deal-breaker for her and she'd never consider being with a firefighter, but each time he was with her, he got the impression that she was fighting her feelings for him. But he was fighting his feelings, too. And restraining himself around her was worse than battling a fire. He wanted to hold her. But that was out of the question.

And the kids had affected him, too. Seeing them today had lifted his spirits more than he'd expected.

Yep. They'd burrowed their way under his skin. He wasn't sure how he was going to handle it when they were finally placed in foster care.

The thought of the camp without Chris and Eli chilled him. To Rand, those two boys were as much a part of the youth camp as Beatrice. The camp was her soul. Rand saw that.

But something had happened to him when he'd been in Copper Country. He'd realized that joy could be found in a child's smile. Joy was what Rand was missing in his life.

He swiped his face with his palm as his cat jumped into his lap. "Backdraft, where have you been?" He picked up the cat and leaned back in the Adirondack chair. "Prowling the neighborhood? Anyone catch your fancy?" He snuggled the ragdoll cat and massaged him behind his ears. "Boy, a couple of losers we are, huh?"

The cat meowed as if to answer him.

Just then, the terrier came through the doggy door.

"And Flint. I should have known you wouldn't let Backdraft get all the attention."

The dog barked and wagged his tail until Rand picked him up for a group cuddle. "Yeah. You guys like group hugs, huh?"

But as much as he loved his pets, the house seemed empty.

Rand heard rustling in his boxwood hedges. Then he heard another cat making sounds. "What's this?"

Holding Backdraft under his right arm and Flint under his left, he went to the edge of the porch and peered into the dark flower bed. The cloud that had briefly covered the full moon drifted away. In the silver light, Rand spotted a slim calico cat staring up at him. Or rather, at Backdraft.

Backdraft squirmed and Rand put him down on the steps. The two cats scurried away to the far side of the house.

"I guess I'm not the only one feeling a bit lonely."

Rand scratched Flint under the chin and then looked at his watch. It was only nine thirty. The building-and-plumbing supply store was open for another half hour. "I just might make it."

He took Flint into the kitchen and put him on his doggy bed. "Be back after a while, buddy."

Maybe he wasn't Beatrice's "forever guy," but he could help her find a bit more stability. And for her, that started with easing some of her financial problems. Sure, he'd helped her a little, but had he gone the full nine yards?

No.

He could do more.

BEATRICE HAD CHECKED on all the kids to make sure the lights were out, and that no one was chewing gum or eating snacks after their teeth had been brushed. She stopped to say good-night to Cindy and Maisie. Bruce's light had been out for half an hour. The dining hall and kitchen doors were locked tight. Windows were shut. All the motion-detector lights outside worked perfectly.

She hugged her arms around her as she climbed the steps to her cabin.

Once inside, she sat in the old upholstered chair she'd bought at a garage sale and stared at the empty fireplace. Five months from now, she'd need to fill the wooden crate with firewood to keep her warm through the winter. The counselors would be gone. Amanda would work for Olivia Barzonni and her mother's catering company, keeping Amanda busy through the holidays. But the camp would be empty with no one around but Beatrice.

The fireplace cavity yawned lonely and bleak.

It was difficult to plan for holidays without a family. Undoubtedly, Rand didn't have such thoughts going through his head. His boisterous and loving family would have all kinds of plans that would include him.

Come to think of it, most of her friends in Indian Lake had a family or someone like family.

What was it that Mrs. Beabots had said? *Friends like to know they're needed.*

Beatrice brightened a bit. Mrs. Beabots was right. Beatrice would call on her friends. Maybe she would have a gathering at the camp for all of them. Nothing fancy or extravagant, but she could certainly put together some punch, cake and homemade cookies for everyone.

She would make her holidays delightful not just for herself but for her friends as well.

She made up a guest list and wrote out a possible menu. Then she looked up a few recipes in a cookbook. Yawning, she got up, stretched and looked at the old clock on the fireplace mantel. It was after midnight.

"No wonder I'm tired," she said and went to the casement window to open it and let in the cooler night air.

As she did, she heard a strange thudding sound.

"What in the...?"

She went to the cabin door.

Then she saw a flicker of lights through the apple trees and forsythia bushes.

She grabbed a flashlight and carefully closed and locked her cabin door behind her. She put the keys in her pocket.

The lights were from the headlights of a familiar black truck.

Rand was smoothing dirt over one of the trenches when she came around the trees and bushes. She shined her light in his face.

He put his dirty hand up to his eyes. "Turn that off."

"It's after midnight. What are you doing out here?" she demanded, dropping her arm but not turning off the flashlight.

"Installing pipe."

She walked over to the edge of the open trench. Her flashlight glanced off the white PVC pipe in the ground. She gasped. "What is that?"

"High-grade PVC." He kept shoveling.

"Rand." She stared into the trench that was now outfitted with perfectly primed and glued long pieces of PVC pipe. "Where did it come from?"

"Indian Lake Building and Plumbing Supply."

"I don't understand. How did it get in my trenches?"

"I bought it. Glued it. Laid it."

He didn't look at her and kept shoveling, filling in the hole. The dirt skittered off the pipe and rolled in and around it. "I figured out some things, thanks to you."

"Such as?"

"First, I can't let anything happen to you or these kids just because of a few bucks. That money you got from the banker, you use that to buy organic food for them and first-aid supplies and maybe some new games or a chess set. You don't need to spend it on these water lines."

"Rand. I can't let you do this."

"It's done already. Okay?" He looked up at her with dark eyes, his face bordering on anger.

"But…why? We agreed—"

"That we're totally wrong for each other. And my job is dangerous. I got that loud and clear." He shoveled more dirt and tossed it with a vengeance into the trench. He stopped and rammed the shovel into the ground so it stuck. He stomped across the dirt pile, then he stopped. "I still want to be your...friend."

"So this is the let's-be-friends speech?"

"No." He grabbed her shoulders. "Look, I've never met anyone as openhearted as you. Not even my mother. I want to be more like you. You've been an inspiration to me. What I admire most about you is that you never boast about what you've done. No exploits or heroics. You just love—"

Beatrice stopped him by grabbing him and kissing him. His arms went around her and he pulled her close to his hard chest. She felt her mind go blank and all she could do was feel with her heart. Of all the men in the world, he was the one she could never let herself love.

But that was the thing.

She did love him.

In that moment with his lips against hers, she knew it. She was in love with him.

And she could never let him see it.

Beatrice moved her hands to his chest, feeling his thrumming heartbeat under her palms.

Everything about them was a mistake.

How many times had they said that to each other now?

But Rand was a stubborn, principled and generous man. If she didn't stop him, the next thing she knew he'd want to put new gutters on the dining hall or build another cabin.

She pulled away, already sad that his lips were not on hers. "You can't do this, Rand. I mean…I'll find the rest of the money on my own. I want you to leave."

"I *will* do this, Bee." He ground the words out as if they were gravel.

"No. I don't want to see you—" she swallowed hard "—anymore." She lowered her head. How was it those words stung like acid?

He stared down at her, standing firm and strong, and yet she could see pain in his eyes as the truck headlights illuminated his face.

She felt her resolve ebbing. If she gave in, he'd come to her. Then there'd be another fire, or maybe it'd be the one after that, but something would happen. He would die. And she would lose all over again.

He pointed to her cabin. "I'll leave when I'm finished. Go away, Beatrice."

She was riveted to the spot, feeling his bitter words wash over her.

"I mean it, Bee. Go!"

Beatrice spun around and fled, using the flashlight to guide her back to her cabin.

CHAPTER TWENTY-ONE

BEATRICE SPENT THE night smacking her pillow and pacing her cabin. She couldn't get Rand out of her mind.

By dawn she'd convinced herself that she'd never hear from him again.

Then, just before breakfast, she read his name on her caller ID.

"Hi." She felt her voice tremble. She had no right to hope he'd call, but she had.

"Beatrice. I'm glad I caught you."

"Yeah, I was just heading for breakfast."

"I know you're probably in a rush, but I wanted to talk to you about a field trip for the kids."

"What field trip?"

"To come to my fire station. I promised Chris—"

"That's not a good idea."

She heard his intake of breath followed by a long pause.

She continued. "Rand. I've told you how I feel about you encouraging the boys. They already idolize you. Bringing them to the fire station would only create false impressions of you and your men."

"You're wrong, Beatrice. If anything, a trip here might show them how mundane most of our job is. The endless hours of waiting for a call. I'd actually like to show them that I learned to be a good cook in fire stations."

"Cook?"

"Chris expressed an interest in cooking at the barbecue, and I figured I might foster that idea. A person doesn't have to be a firefighter to become a chef."

"No, they don't," she replied. Maybe Rand wasn't hoping to polish his own stars. Maybe he truly did have the boys' best interests in mind. Was she being too tough on Rand? Too distrustful?

And if she was, she'd be shutting off the boys from a learning experience.

"Seriously, Bee— Beatrice. I did promise the kids, and that means something to them. Don't let them down."

"Now I'm the bad guy?"

"Not you. Never. I'm sorry. I sprang this on you. Please, Beatrice."

"Okay. Fine. I'll announce it to the kids. When?"

"How about tomorrow? Ten in the morning."

"Fine. But, Rand, I still have misgivings about this."

"Duly noted," he said and hung up.

She put away her phone. "I'm going to regret this."

"THIS IS THE most important, bestest day of my life," Eli said as he climbed into the cab of ILFD's fire engine.

"Do you know the difference between a fire engine and a fire truck?" Rand asked Eli.

"Uh." He looked across the enormous garage. "No. They're both red."

"I do," Chris chimed in. "A fire truck has the ladder and hydraulics. The fire engine carries the hoses."

"Like a pumper." Eli beamed.

"That's right." Rand smiled at Eli and picked up a fiberglass helmet with face shield and yellow helmet band, putting it on his head. "Now, that helmet really is too big. And they don't come in kids' sizes."

"That's okay, Mr. Nelson," Chris said with growing respect. "We have a lot to learn before we become firefighters."

Rand was surprised. "I didn't know you

were seriously thinking about becoming a firefighter. What about cooking?"

Chris leaned over. "That, too. We'll talk about it privately," he said seriously.

"Okay." Rand winked, then turned to pick Eli up and put him back on the garage floor. He looked out at the ten children that Beatrice, Maisie and Cindy had driven to the fire station for their field trip. He'd struggled to keep his focus on the kids, but each time he glanced over their heads and into her blue eyes, he felt something shift inside him.

He was a ball of want, desperation, guilt and hopelessness. They were at an impasse. She'd even rejected the idea of being friends. He'd never felt so alone or lonely in his life. She was afraid of his job. And she was afraid that in the end, he would hurt or disappoint the kids. It was a logical concern. But she was wrong.

If only there was a way to convince her that his risks weren't as frightening as she'd made them out to be in her mind. If only…

He reached behind him. "Kids. This is a Nomex suit. This is what protects firefighters when we go into a blaze. Our gloves are made of Kevlar and can withstand very intense temperatures. We wear face shields, special boots and Kevlar socks to protect our feet. Our pants are also made of Protera and Nomex. Come here, Chris." Rand wiggled his fingers at the boy. "Put this jacket on. I know it's too big, but check it out."

Then Rand outfitted Chris with gloves and had him stand in a pair of boots. Rand took out his cell phone and took a picture. "I'll send a copy of this photo to Miss Beatrice so that you can have it to remind you of this day."

Rand walked the kids through the station, showing them the dining room, the television-and-game room. And the barracks.

After each room, Chris hung back and asked more questions.

Rand noticed that Beatrice watched them both with interest. He hoped he wasn't spending too much time with Chris and not the others, but Chris was keenly interested.

When the tour was over, Beatrice said, "Cindy will take the younger children in her SUV. Chris and Eli, you help me with the kids in my SUV."

"Yes, ma'am," Eli said.

But Chris hesitated.

He turned to Rand. "Sir, I was wondering. In the break room there's a magazine about firefighting. Could I borrow it? I promise I'll give it back."

"Sure, Chris. Go get it. And by the way, you can have it."

Chris took off.

Beatrice came over to Rand. "That was very nice. Thank you. But I'll get the magazine back to the station when he's finished with it."

"Beatrice, it's just a magazine."

Chris raced up. "So after I read this, would you teach me some firefighting skills?"

"You're a bit young right now. But how about this? In the future, I promise I'll do just that."

"And I promise to learn all I can 'til then. Miss Beatrice will tell you. I've been doing a lot of reading lately. I think I like it."

"You didn't like to read before?" Rand asked.

Chris glanced away. "My parents... I mean, we didn't have any books and the schoolbooks were lame. Miss Beatrice takes us to the library and we can get all the books we want for free. Then we take them back and get new ones."

"That's good you enjoy learning," Rand said, looking up at Beatrice with admiration.

"Eli does, too."

"It's important to be a good model for younger brothers."

"I know what you mean," Chris agreed and suddenly thrust his arms around Rand's middle. "Thank you for the magazine. And especially the promise."

Rand was bolted to the spot. It was a simple thing. A hug. His mother had hugged him a thousand times. His brothers, sister, friends. But it had never moved him like this.

Rand smoothed Chris's hair and pressed the boy to his middle.

His eyes met Beatrice's hard gaze. She'd been right. Chris and Eli were pinning far too many hopes on him.

Rand didn't know from one day to the next where his next call would come from. He'd have to make explanations to them. He would leave.

And a child would be hurt.

She was right. Had been right all this time.

"Thank you" was all he said. Too much emotion cut off his voice.

THE CALL CAME the next morning.

"Rand. Jim Osborn here." Rand recognized the voice immediately. The man's gruff tone was one Rand would never forget. "McCall Smoke Jumper Base in Idaho."

"I remember, sir. How's everything at Payette Lake?"

"Placid. For the moment. But I'm not calling you for a fire gig. I have an opening for a trainer. I thought of you immediately. I wanted to offer you the job first."

"Trainer?" Rand felt his windpipe close. The image of Perry's burned body fluttered in front of him like a demon mirage. "I'm honored, sir."

"That's nice. And thanks. The thing is I've got recruits galore and my trainer had to quit suddenly for medical reasons. You've done the job, so you can jump right in."

"I'm not quite ready to move at this point."

"Let me sweeten the deal. The job description here has been expanded, Rand. We're testing new technology quite a bit. Safety equipment, parachutes. New chemicals. You'd be in charge of leading those tests."

"I've petitioned hard for that kind of increased safety over the years, sir. Saving lives is supremely important."

"Glad to hear it. You'll take the job, then? It's full-time. All benefits. Bonus pay for actual firefighting."

"I'm...speechless."

And hesitant. This was the dream of all dream jobs for him. He'd be instrumental in rolling out cutting-edge firefighting technology. In a way, he could affect the future of every firefighter to follow him. Maybe affect Chris's life if the boy decided to become a firefighter.

But he was doing just what Beatrice had accused him of—jumping into the nearest danger zone to avoid making a change in his life here.

For the first time, he considered someone else's needs and wants more than his own. Beatrice had told him she didn't want to see him again.

But he also knew that no one had ever held him so tightly to her heart as Beatrice did. She cared for him. It was in her kiss. Yet, she'd sent him away. Would probably keep sending him away, no matter her true feelings.

And the boys? It was better to end things with them, too, before their hero worship went too far.

"Rand? Don't jack with me."

"I'll take the job, sir. I have to clear it with my captain here, but I don't think he'll have a problem with it. We have a couple new rookies who are very promising."

"If you gave them any training, I'm sure they're top-notch."

"Again, I'm honored you thought of me."

"You're one of the best. There's just one thing."

"Sir?"

"I need you out here in twenty-two hours."

Twenty-two hours?

It was enough time to make a clean break.

"Not a problem. I'll tie things up here and be on my way."

Rand hung up the phone.

His life had done another one-eighty.

He punched in Beatrice's number. After three rings she picked up.

"Rand?"

"Hi, Beatrice. Do you have a minute?"

"Just a minute."

"I've been offered a job training smoke jumpers. It's in Idaho."

"Idaho! That's…so far."

"I know. And I have to leave immediately."

"A trainer. Wow. Uh, well, I'm happy for you, Rand. You should be very proud."

Rand's stomach roiled. She spoke to him as informally as if he was the delivery boy dropping off the pizza. Thanks. See ya. She was true to her word. She didn't want an adrenaline junkie like Rand.

"Yeah. Proud. I was wondering, Beatrice, if I could say goodbye to the boys."

"They're in the middle of swim rescue lessons right now. I'll be happy to deliver the news to them."

"I wanted to talk to them."

"I understand. But my way would be best, Rand."

Ever their protector, he thought. "Sure. Okay. Well, you take care, Beatrice."

"You, too, Rand."

She hung up.

Rand stared blankly at the phone. It was as if their summer together had happened to someone else.

CHAPTER TWENTY-TWO

"I TRIED TO tell you," Beatrice said to Luke Bosworth as he stared at the area where he'd dug up the dirt to expose the pipe that Rand had expertly glued and laid.

Luke scratched his head. "This is really good pipe. I mean really good."

"Better than what you were going to use?"

"No." He shook his head. "It's the same, but seriously, he did a great job. There's nothing left for us to do but hook everything up to the hydrants."

"Which the city delivered this morning," Beatrice said.

"Right." He shoved his hands in his back pockets. "I wish he would have told me."

"I assumed he did."

"Nah. I haven't heard from him. Frankly, Beatrice, he's saved you nearly the entire cost of the construction."

"I'm sorry if this caused you a problem. I mean, you could have taken on another job."

"No worries. I was squeezing this job in to

help you out, actually. I can return the pipe for credit. So, all around it's no big deal."

"You're sure?" She felt suddenly quite bad. He'd been so kind as to sign his children up for camp.

"I'm sure." He smiled.

"You and Sarah are such good friends and I wouldn't do…"

Luke laughed. "Apparently, not as good of friends to you as Rand is."

She stared at the trenches as two of Luke's crew got out of their trucks and began running down pipe into the ground for the hook-ups. "Yes. He is."

"We better get this job wrapped up for you. This last tie-in has to be accomplished by a city-licensed plumber. That's Al over there."

She looked up at the burly middle-aged man in overalls who apparently hadn't shaved in several days. She waved. "Thanks so much."

Al waved back and went straight to work.

"I'll leave you all to it, then," she said and went up to her office.

Luke had spoken the truth as he saw it— and as it was. Rand had been a good friend to her. Maybe the best she'd ever had.

But now he'd gone to Idaho chasing his dream job. She'd known all along that he would never be happy in a youth camp, like she was. Lazy days and quiet winter nights were not Rand's style.

Tears welled in her eyes. Fear did that. Anger, too. Maybe a little shock in there for a true mix.

This was all her fault. She'd pushed him away with enough thrust to propel a 747.

This is what she wanted. Right? Distance from him. Well, halfway across the country would do. This way, he couldn't show up on a field trip. Couldn't come out to see Chris or Eli, even though this was their last week at camp.

She might never see the kids again, especially if they were adopted. And now that Rand had made such a positive impact on both the boys, giving them goals and guidance, parents would be happy to adopt those two lovable boys. They would make any mom and dad happy.

She dropped her face to her hands as tears spilled from her eyes with abandon.

"What's the matter with me?"

"I dunno," Amanda said, walking into the office with a glass of lemonade. "You listening to those sad songs again? I mean, who ever heard of anyone your age listening to Linda Ronstadt?"

Beatrice smiled and wiped her fingers under her eyes. "It's not the sad songs."

"Good. I always listen to rap. I hate it. It makes no sense to me so it can't affect me."

"That's a waste of time. And your life."

"You know—" Amanda pointed her index finger at her "—you're right. How about that?"

Beatrice stared at her. "Come to think of it, I've never heard rap coming out of that kitchen. Adele. Taylor Swift, maybe. A hoarse Paul McCartney."

"Don't knock Paul. He's old. What can I say?"

"So what are you really trying to say?"

Amanda's eyes narrowed in that way wise old owls observed their surroundings. "Don't waste your life, either, Beatrice."

"Goodness, that's the last thing I'm doing. Why I've spent every nickel on my dreams."

"I'm not talking about coins."

"What are you talking about?"

"Chances. The kind that come only once in a lifetime."

"Like this camp?"

"Yes, some chances you've done well with. No one in their right mind would have bought this run-down place and turned it into a summer palace for broken kids. But you did. No one with a whit of business sense would give jobs to interns and old women like me with no experience running a kitchen. But you did."

"Well, you are all very good at what you do."

"And so are you. But when was the last time you took a chance on love? On your future?"

Looking back, Beatrice realized she'd based all her decisions on her past. She hadn't had a real childhood, so she'd wanted to create one for herself by building the camp. As a kid, she'd wanted to learn to kayak, plant a pioneer garden and grow real vegetables. She had wanted to finger-paint and play Ping-Pong and badminton and chess. All the things that had been missing from her own childhood that she believed would be good for other children.

In the end, she'd been right. The camp kids had grown and unfolded petals of their own creativity when they were forced to live without electronics for a few days.

Maybe she had come at her life with the wrong motivations, but her actions had worked not only to her advantage, but also been a benefit to the camp kids.

Sometimes, she realized, fear, loss and

pain were put in one's life to make one grow. To search for other means of maturing. For Beatrice, her father had been taken to heaven. Her mother had been self-centered. Because of her past, Beatrice related to her kids perhaps more than anyone else could.

But she doubted Amanda was talking about the camp or her childhood.

"I'm guessing you're talking about Rand."

"I am. You've come to a fork in the road, Beatrice," Amanda replied with a motherly smile.

"I'm not at any fork. Making a decision implies there are choices." She lifted her shoulders in a half shrug. "That would imply that I had options to consider. Rand is all wrong for me. It would never work out. He chose a life of jumping into flames. Fire, Amanda. Fire!"

"Oh, for pity's sake. I drive into Chicago once a week and that's twice as dangerous. That's not really the reason."

"Yes, of course it is."

"No. It's not. You're just scared."

"Of course I am! That's what I'm trying to tell you. He could die and then leave me alone."

Amanda shrugged her shoulders. "You're already alone. You know what that's like."

"I do."

"Sweetie. You're afraid to love him."

"I—I... That's ridiculous. Why would I be afraid of that?"

"Do you know what it is?"

Moments, scenes, whispered words, the feel of his kisses, the anger in his eyes, the sight of him walking away—all of those things filled her brain. "He told me that the fears of my past didn't need to be my future. I had let my mother's fears become my own. Honestly, he's done the same. His own past experiences have caused him to make wrong decisions. We're both broken."

"Beatrice. What did I tell you about this camp? Every kid here comes to us broken. And you make them well again. You give them heart and hope. Because that's what you are. You just have to learn to do it for yourself."

CHAPTER TWENTY-THREE

BEATRICE TOOK THE check from Mr. Hamilton, her banker. His bushy gray eyebrows knit together in concern. "Are you sure you need this?"

"I am and I appreciate you doing this for me," she said, folding the check in half and putting it in her purse. "I have to pay someone back. Someone very, very kind."

"Apparently."

"He's generous to a fault," she said. "And courageous." She thought of Rand carrying her out of the fire. "I didn't see it at first, though."

"Well, I'm glad for you that you do now."

"I will pay you back. I have a new program for the fall and we're booked up nearly every weekend 'til Halloween."

"That's great news, Beatrice. Great news."

He shook her hand and walked her to his office door.

Beatrice left the bank and crossed the street to Scott Abbot's Book Stop and Java

Shop. She had a few extra dollars in her budget for spending.

"Hi, Scott!" She smiled as she walked in.

Scott was stocking children's books on a rack. In the far end of the store she could hear Isabelle's voice as she read a story to the preschool children gathered around her.

"Beatrice," Scott said and walked over to her. He hugged her. "How nice to see you. Isabelle is nearly finished with her story hour." He smiled toward his wife as Isabelle winked back at him.

"I don't wish to disturb. I was wondering if you got those books in for me that I ordered."

"I did. I have them behind the counter." Scott walked over to the coffee bar and bent down. "*Fly Guy Presents Firefighters* and *A Day with Firefighters*. Good selections. These are for the camp, right?"

"Actually, for two special boys." She pulled out a piece of paper from her purse. "Here's some other books I want to order for them."

"They like to read. That's good."

"It's a new adventure for them both," she replied, feeling quite proud of Chris and Eli.

She paid Scott, waved to Isabelle and left.

Back in her SUV, she headed north out of town.

As she passed Indian Lake she realized

that if she took the road to the right, only two blocks away was Rand's house. On a whim, she flipped her turn signal and drove to his house.

She parked in front.

The lawn had been mowed and edged. The flowers looked healthy. She guessed he must have hired someone to care for it while he was away. Her heart felt heavy. He was gone—maybe forever.

The thought that he might never come back turned her mind dark. Then black.

She couldn't and wouldn't allow herself to think such a thing. She remembered the Sunday when she and the boys had met his family. A collage of memories blurred her vision. She heard his voice, then his laughter. She pressed her fingers to the back of her neck, where he'd first kissed her.

Today, there was no family gathering. No smell of grilling food coming from the backyard. She realized she hadn't properly thanked him for the barbecue. And for other things.

Just then the front door opened and she saw Laura walk out onto the porch with a watering can. Flint followed her out.

"Laura!" Beatrice brightened and got out of her SUV. She walked up to the porch.

"Beatrice. Hello!" Laura opened her arms wide, waiting for a hug. "Oh, it's good to see you, dear."

Beatrice embraced her.

"What are you doing here?" Laura asked.

Beatrice leaned down and petted Flint, who wagged his tail.

"I, uh. Actually, I have something for Rand and I thought I'd drop it off. I didn't realize anyone would be here. I'm happy to run into you, though."

"Come, let's sit down," Laura said, pointing to the Adirondack chairs.

Beatrice noticed that the red-and-white-striped pillows were missing. Yet Laura was watering the ferns. Maybe Rand wasn't going away for good.

Laura followed Beatrice's eyes as she looked at the watering can. "Oh, I told Rand I'd take care of the ferns and the impatiens while he was gone. I did take Backdraft and Flint home with me, though. Today, Flint wanted to visit with me."

"Dogs love to ride in cars."

"I think Flint misses this house. And his daddy."

"I'm sure he does. So, er, is Rand planning to sell the house? Now that he's gone?"

"Sell? Goodness, this has all been so sudden. I don't think it's entered his mind." She looked around. "He's put his heart and soul into the remodeling. The new kitchen and bath. He built this porch nearly by himself. Of course, he did get some help from Luke Bosworth."

"Yes. Luke and Sarah are wonderful friends."

"Oh, good. You know them."

"I do. Rand and Luke have done so much to help the camp."

"How is everything at the camp?" Laura asked, smiling easily at Beatrice.

"It's fine. I mean, since Rand, well…"

Laura reached over and touched Beatrice's arm. "He told me what he did. Putting in those water lines for you. That's just like him."

"Is it?"

"Oh, yes. His father was the same way. God rest him." Laura beamed. "Did Rand tell you how I met his father?"

"Er, uh. No. He didn't tell me much about his father at all."

"Really? Rand is very proud of his dad, Admiral Malcolm Nelson. Of course, he wasn't an admiral when I met him. You see, I was a navy nurse, surgeon's assistant, and he was just a lieutenant, not long out of Annapolis, when he wound up in the naval hospital in San Diego, where I was stationed."

"Was he injured?"

"Yes. But not from wartime activity. He'd been on the sidelines, so he said, of a pool-hall brawl. I was working the night shift, ER, actually, and they brought him and his buddy in. One of the pool-hall gang had pulled a blade and knifed him in the ribs. It barely missed his heart. The surgeon on duty was excellent. Malcolm was a lucky man."

"I'll say."

Laura's eyes held a wistful gleam as she reminisced. "Rand is almost the spitting image of his father, you know. Anyway, that night, as I prepped Malcom for surgery, I asked him if he was all right. And he said, 'I will be if you hold my hand until they put me under.' I told him I would. But what stayed with me was that this very strong man, who looked like he could lift a battleship single-handed, gave me the most gentle smile and said, 'I want yours to be the first face I see when I wake up.'

"I told him I didn't work in the recovery room. He promised he wouldn't wake up until he felt my presence next to him. Naturally, I thought he was kidding until my shift was over and I went down to the recovery room. The nurse on duty mentioned that Malcolm had not woken up and they were getting concerned. So I went to his side and put my hand over his. In seconds, his fingers wrapped around mine, he opened his eyes and said, 'Don't leave me again.' And I never did."

Beatrice couldn't stop the welling tears in her eyes if she tried. She lifted her fingertips to her cheeks and swiped them away. "I'm so sorry he's gone."

"So am I. There will never be another man for me." She looked back at Beatrice. "The boys are all splinters of Malcolm and so is Cassie. She wants everyone to think she's as rough as her brothers, but she's not. Rand is like that, too. But I suppose you noticed."

Oh, she'd noticed a great deal. "Yes."

"You know, Beatrice, before we met you, he talked about you all the time."

Beatrice's eyes flew open. "He did?"

"He admires you tremendously. He's always talking about everything you do for those kids. Of course, at first he thought you were more a daredevil than he, running into that forest so recklessly."

"Uh, well. He was right. I didn't think and that was really stupid of me. But I'm glad

I did it—saving Eli and Chris was all that mattered."

Laura nodded. "Yes. You are two peas in a pod."

Beatrice looked down at the envelope sticking out of the top of her purse. "Actually, we aren't. Apparently, we are very much the opposite. Rand and I are friends. Good ones, I hope. Maybe not. But I don't want you or the family to think that there's anything romantic going on between us. Certainly not as romantic as what passed between you and your husband."

Laura was silent as her green eyes observed Beatrice. "You're in love with my son. I'd bet the bank on that."

Beatrice felt her heart heave in her chest. She was in love with him, but his heart was lodged in his career. As it should be. He was a man of conviction and passion. She had her own commitments as well. What did it matter that she loved him?

Rand wasn't ever going to be the guy who would ask her to stay with him forever.

And even if he did, she would have to turn him down.

Wouldn't she?

"You see, my father was a Chicago detective and he was shot in the line of duty when

I was young. Rand is a lot like my dad. He wants to protect people, but in the end, he hurts the ones he loves. Maybe not today, but eventually. A person can tempt fate only so often."

"And you believe Rand will die on you like your father did?"

"I do."

Laura shot Beatrice a piercing look. "Did Rand ever tell you how his father died?"

"No."

"The flu."

"What?"

Laura shrugged her shoulders. "All those years at sea. Gale-force Arctic winds. Hurricanes. Sitting in the Persian Gulf with missiles aimed at him. He walked away from every near-death experience a navy man could imagine. And what takes him down? A microscopic virus."

Beatrice was astonished. She didn't know which was more frightening: the fact that Rand put himself in harm's way on purpose, or the realization that he could be taken from her at any given moment by something as common as the flu.

Beatrice had spent a great deal of her life under the wing of fear, she realized. She'd been looking for stability and security and every day, life reminded her that there was no such thing.

One minute her finances were in the black and the next she owed the bank again. From one day to the next, she couldn't be sure what was solid...except for the friends who showed up at her camp to help her.

She could count on them.

And in that group, she had to include Rand. He'd not only saved her the labor on the water lines, but he'd also bought and paid for the pipe. He'd shown caring and interest in two young boys who'd completely turned themselves around, thanks a great deal to him. He might even have saved them from following in their drug-addicted parents' life-style. Only the future would tell about that, but she believed that because of who he was, Rand had given the boys an ideal to emulate.

And she'd pushed him away.

"So if you love him, why not take what time you have together?"

"I don't have to love him. I'll get over it," Beatrice said.

Laura slapped her palm over her mouth as she broke out in a chuckle. Then she laughed. Both palms went over her mouth as her laughter increased. "Oh. Ho. I'm sorry." She kept laughing. Then she reached over and put her hands on Beatrice's arm. "Dear sweet girl. You don't get over love."

"Of course you do. People do it all the time. They fall in love. They fall out."

Laura pursed her lips and shook her head. "No, they don't. Not real love. I'm not saying it isn't hard and there aren't times when you'd like to slap them silly, but anger is a fleeting thing. Love endures. Believe me. Even after death."

It was Beatrice's turn to touch Laura. "It must be so hard to have loved your husband so much and then be without him."

"Just as hard as it is for you having this situation with Rand go unresolved."

"He's in Idaho. I think he resolved it." She pursed her lips tightly to beat back a sob that ached for escape.

"I see. And you came here today because…"

She pulled out the envelope. "I'll always be grateful to him for what he did for me and the camp. I want to pay him back. This should cover his expenses, and someday, I'll save up enough to repay him for his labor, too."

"You should say all this to Rand," Laura said.

"I tried to send him a text but my phone said the message was undelivered. When I dialed his number, I was told it was no longer in service."

"Wait here a minute." Laura got up and went into the house. She returned in a few seconds with a folded piece of paper. "Here. It's Rand's new private cell-phone number. He was issued a new phone out in Idaho. You call him."

Beatrice shoved the paper and the envelope back in her purse and rose. "Thank you for taking this time with me, Laura."

Laura hugged Beatrice and then held Beatrice's chin between her thumb and forefinger. "Rand can be stubborn and rigid sometimes. But he always does the right thing. What I want you to ask yourself is why you'd give up on him."

Beatrice's eyes stung as she looked into Laura's caring eyes. "I wish I'd had a mother like you. I—I think things would have been different. I...would be different."

"Maybe. Maybe not. All those things and situations you thought were wrong were just lessons. That's all. They made you the person you are and that's a good thing." Laura released Beatrice and then halted. "I believe Rand is in love with you, Beatrice. Whatever obstacles you believe are between you can be melted faster than butter under a blowtorch, but that's up to you two." She glanced at the note she'd given Beatrice. "I'm betting he's there. On the other end of that line, waiting."

Beatrice bit her bottom lip to keep from sobbing all over Laura's shoulder. She had never been this prone to tears and certainly never to outbursts. She could control her emotions.

She always had before.

"Thanks for this, Laura."

"You're welcome. And, Beatrice, if you want to talk about anything, I bought a new cell phone that doesn't eat my voice mails. I'm here. Drive safely," Laura said with a wave and picked up her watering can.

BEATRICE WAITED UNTIL she was back at camp, her chores finished and the children in bed for the night before she took out Rand's new cell-phone number.

She sat on the edge of her bed and punched in the numbers, but she didn't hit Send. She stared at the phone.

She had no idea what she should say other than to thank him for his help. That's really all she'd wanted to do.

She wanted to get his new address in Idaho so she could send the check. Being a cashier's check, he would have to cash it since the money had already been withdrawn. He'd be forced to accept her payback.

And then what?

They were even?

Is that what she wanted? Or was it more?

"More," she said aloud as tears rose unbidden to her eyes. She kept swiping them away, but it was no use. They fell like a river. In all her life, she'd never cried so much and for no good reason as she had since she'd met Rand.

She hit Send. She sniffed as the phone rang. She wiped away a palm full of tears.

"McCall Smoke Jumper Base. This is Rand Nelson. I'm not available at the moment. Please leave a brief message and I'll get back to you."

Two days. It had been two days since she'd heard his voice and it felt like it had been forever. A lifetime of forevers. The pinch in her chest twisted and the pain sharpened.

If it was this difficult after only two days, how long would it take to get over him?

She heard a beep.

"Rand…" she said. Then another onslaught of tears broke through. She ended the call and fell face-first into her pillow.

CHAPTER TWENTY-FOUR

RAND HELD A copy of the "Decision Memorandum for the Director, Fire and Aviation Management" in his hand as he addressed the room full of rookies. There were sixteen eager-faced men listening to his every word. He'd only been on the job two days, but he knew a third would not make the grade. They would fail the rigorous drills or the tests, or find the work unglamorous and backbreaking.

In the United States there were currently 320 smoke jumpers. McCall Smoke Jumper Base was one of two base camps in Idaho, the other located in Grangeville. There were two Bureau of Land Management smoke-jumper bases, one in Boise and the other in Fairbanks, Alaska. Rand had been to both.

In his years as a smoke jumper, there had been changes, but the one he was about to speak to the recruits about, the Ram-Air Parachute Delivery System, was the most needed change he'd seen come through in a long time.

"The US Forest Service intends to replace all the FS-14 round parachutes we've been using with the new Ram-Air System. We've received a new shipment today. And we're going to learn how to pack 'em, fold 'em and jump with 'em."

A round of "hurrahs" nearly rattled the windows as the men shouted their approval.

Once they settled down, Rand continued. "We all know the stats, or you should. We've had too many injuries and even fatalities that were directly linked to the FS-14s. The ram-air will enable smoke jumpers to deploy in higher winds, allow slower vertical and horizontal speeds, which, in my opinion, is critical. This will help minimize impact-landing injuries. No more slamming into trees or onto rock, or granite-hard dirt. We want to glide onto the earth and that's exactly what we'll do with the ram-air. In addition, the ram-air is equipped with a reserve static line, which automatically opens the reserve container when the main parachute is cut away due to malfunction. It's also got an activation device that automatically opens the reserve container if the jumper is unable to open the primary chute. In other words, men, this puppy is expensive."

Rand put the document on the desk. "Today, we're going to test-drive these ram-air parachutes. You will all suit up and I'll time you. Yesterday, it took us nine and a half minutes to suit up. Today I want to cut thirty seconds off that record. Remember, every second at base is another acre that can go up in flames. The Twin Otters can only take eight to ten of us. Therefore, we'll make two trips today. Also, we will have a spotter up with us, just as if we'd gotten the call."

He continued. "Critical to the ongoing research and technology the US Forest Service has committed to, you all will make observations about the parachutes. I want you taking notes. Video. Anything you can. I'll track velocity and winds on my end. So will the pilot. Every bit of data we can provide will not only help you and your fellow smoke jumpers, but it will help those who follow in our footsteps."

He pulled out his stopwatch and looked around the room. They knew what was coming and were ready to spring into action. "Suit up!" he shouted and started his stopwatch.

Sixteen guys raced through the door to their gear.

Rand felt that familiar rush of adrenaline he always experienced whenever the call to action came. It didn't matter if it was a forest fire, a warehouse fire or…a fire at a kid's camp.

He rushed out of the room. "Get moving," he shouted as he hit the door to the outside to check on the pilot and plane.

Revving up on the tarmac was the US Forest Service red-and-white-painted twin-engine plane. He waved to Cary Springer, the pilot. Cary was getting to be an old-timer, but no one could fly in and out of flames like Cary. Some said his plane and the man himself were immune to flames. Rand always joked that it had been fire that had seared off Cary's hair and left him bald. Cary never disputed the claim.

Rand rushed into his office, where he stowed all his gear. He suited up in his regulation beige jumpsuit and timed himself. Eight minutes and two seconds. He was slowing down. His personal best had been seven minutes and forty-nine seconds.

"Maybe Cary isn't the only old-timer around here." He grabbed his red helmet and shot out of the office. He darted across the tarmac. An assistant held the straps of his parachute for him as he buckled into the chute. Ordinarily, he would have put his chute on himself, but this was a trial run. Everyone on base was watching him.

Rand was the first on the plane. He clocked the men as they hit the door. They were only three seconds behind him. Satisfied, he stowed his stopwatch in his pocket. He checked with Cary and got a thumbs-up.

The men scrambled onto the plane, sat in a straight line on the bench seat and strapped in. The plane taxied to the end of the runway.

The liftoff was smooth as glass, Rand thought, as he turned to address the men. "Remember, once on the ground, communication is key. We're nothing if we don't all work together. Every jumper depends on his team. Ordinarily, we would be jumping in pairs. After I jump and we test this ram-air, we will go back up and every one of you will test your own ram-air."

"Sir? You mean today?" Willie Herod asked. Willie was the youngest recruit in the group. His father had been in the forestry service all his life. Willie had smoke jumping in his blood.

"Yes, Herod. Today."

"Well, wahoo!" he hollered.

The group broke out in yells and high-fived each other.

Cary's voice announced the drop was imminent. Rand rose and went to the side door. It was a crystal clear summer day. The area had been dry for over six weeks. In another two weeks it would be Labor Day. As far as Rand was concerned, the end of summer brought the next season. Fire season.

From California through Oregon to Idaho and across the country, wildfires would burst into life. Some man-made, most not. Rand was well aware that the environment in which the US Forest Service operated grew more complex each year. Hazardous fuel build-ups. Insect and disease infestations, nonnative species invasions and drought topped the list before even addressing climate changes. Scientists had confirmed that the number, size, intensity and duration of wildfires had increased, and if anything, fire seasons were longer. He'd read that some scientists predicted that by 2050 the number of acres burned would double and possibly triple by then. Due to another seventeen million housing units being built within 30 miles of national forests, which had proven to increase fires and dangers to those living near the trees, by the year 2030 that encroachment would make fighting those fires even more difficult.

This parachute drop today might seem like an infinitesimal punch at the huge wave of dire predictions for the future, but it was significant to Rand and every smoke jumper. If they could do just as Rand had said—glide down to earth without injury—precious minutes would be saved. The smoke jumper's life would be saved. All would benefit.

"Go!" the spotter yelled.

Rand didn't hesitate. He was out the door and sailing through the air before the spotter finished his command.

The ram-air performed as well as his superiors claimed it would. Rand easily directed his fall to the exact narrow clearing the spotter had chosen. There was a clump of tall pines to his right, a group of wide-limbed sycamores to the left. Rand was able to maneuver the chute first right and then left. He picked up a wind gust that normally would have blown him smack into the trees. But the chute obeyed his strong arms. His transit was swift. Just what the US Forest Service wanted.

He slowed the vertical slide to the ground when he was only twenty-five feet above the earth. The slower descent promised easy contact.

He hit the ground with a light thud, barely jarring his ankles, knees or hips as he often did with the traditional parachutes.

Carefully he folded his parachute and shoved it into the pack.

Using a recorder, he gave his data and began his "walk out" to the main road, where a fellow jumper was waiting in a truck to drive him back to camp. He shielded his eyes with his palm as he watched Cary dip his wing and fly back to McCall, where each of the rookies would test their parachutes in a controlled jump.

In a few hours, Rand would repeat his jump for the last group of recruits. Tomorrow, all the men would execute a second jump into the forest using their new ram-air parachutes and each would record their data.

As he hiked through the forest, smelling the dry pine nettles and hearing his boots crunch against already fallen golden leaves, he thought of Eli and Chris.

It was nearly summer's end. The kids would be leaving camp and going home.

But where was home for Chris and Eli?

Strange. All these weeks he'd thought

of them as part of the camp. As Beatrice's "charges." Her kids.

But they weren't hers. Right now, they weren't anybody's. He didn't understand parents who abandoned children. He didn't understand Beatrice's own mother, for that matter. Beatrice was the kindest, most open-hearted, giving person he'd met. She was impossible not to love.

"Love?" He halted and nearly ran into a tree branch. He pushed aside the branch.

Had he thought that?

"I'm not in love with Bee." He started walking again. "I'm not."

For one thing, it was impossible. Their lives were incompatible.

He loved being a firefighter. And he believed what he was doing here in Idaho was important. Meanwhile, his first assessment of Beatrice had been dead-on. She was all about planting roots and watching them grow. Her camp alone proved that. She would wither and die if she didn't have all those kids to watch out for. She adored them and they loved her in return. From what he could tell, most of the kids would be returning next summer just to be with her and learn from her.

He wondered if Eli and Chris would come back. Would Zoey Phillips make that happen for them? And what about those week-end botany field trips Beatrice had talked about? He'd bet both boys would have liked that. Though Eli more than Chris.

Chris.

He wanted to be a firefighter. After their trip to the station, Chris had caught the bug. He understood the feeling. He'd been like that when he was Chris's age. He'd known exactly how he wanted to spend his adult life. The kid even showed an interest in cooking. Chris couldn't be more like Rand if—

"If he was my own."

He rubbed his eyes and then realized the burn in his eyes was a slow well of tears.

"Stop it, Rand," he admonished himself.

He peered through the cluster of trees.

The scent of the forest reminded Rand of camping trips with his dad and siblings in his youth.

On those trips, Rand had fallen in love with the towering dense forests, crystal icy Michigan rivers and the wildlife that roamed free in them. His father had taught the boys to respect every shrub and pine tree, every brown squirrel and majestic elk they saw in Pigeon River Country State Forest, four hours north of Detroit.

It had taken only one camping trip with his

family for Rand to figure out that he could never spend his life sitting behind a desk. He had to live outdoors.

But it was at the age of twelve, when a bolt of lightning started a forest fire barely a half mile from their rustic campsite in Sleeping Bear Dunes park, that his fate was inked. The fire had frightened his brothers and Cassie and, for the first time, he'd seen fear in his stalwart navy admiral father. His father had been afraid for his family. Rand knew then he never wanted to see that look again. Though it made no sense and he wasn't even a teenager yet, Rand was sure he had it in him to keep that kind of fear at bay for other people. That day, as they hustled to break camp, pack their truck and head away from the fire, Rand made a vow to become a firefighter.

He'd come to respect fire, even appreciate its power and beauty. Even the way a blaze altered the light in the forest was like a magical siren. The glow would change from amber to crimson, sometimes to charcoal and then to gray blue. He would stop and hear the crackling flames and the crunch of his boot on a wasted stick or branch and the sound of his own breath inside a mask.

He was a firefighter through and through.

He had a feeling that Chris would someday find that same sense of awe. At least he hoped so.

If Chris did become a smoke jumper, these tests Rand was conducting now might save the kid's life. Rand was excited about the new equipment. Technology changes like this had to happen, and swiftly.

Of all the statistics that Rand had pointed out to the men there was one he withheld.

With the increase in the length of the fire season and the number of forest acres burned, the number of smoke jumper and wildland firefighter deaths had increased.

When Beatrice said she worried about Rand in Copper Country, she had good reason. Until these recent changes in the parachutes and some other equipment, the US Forest Service had been relying on hand tools and strong backs for too long.

Rand hoped this change was rolled out quickly because a high-tech parachute could save a life. His life.

Rand wasn't a religious man, but he was a spiritual one. He believed that every person was put on the earth with a purpose. For most of his life, he'd told himself he was strong and fit because he was destined to fight fires. Save lives. Carry Beatrice and Eli out of danger.

Since knowing Beatrice, he wasn't quite so certain about his purpose.

A lot of things had become jumbled in his mind since he'd met her.

And he hadn't the first clue how to unravel that jumble.

"Trainer Nelson!" A voice called to him from a US Forest Service truck that rolled across the dry grassy terrain.

Rand waved. The truck stopped.

The sandy-haired, green-eyed young man could only have been twenty-one at the most, Rand thought as the guy shoved his hand at Rand. "Clint McGowan," he said proudly.

Rand eyed him. "Do I know you?"

"We haven't met. I was at a family funeral when you came back to base. I was instructed to come get you."

Rand's eyebrows knitted. "And you were told to drive out to meet me or to stay up at the road?"

"Aw—" he put the truck into gear "—I saw you jump, sir. And I couldn't wait to meet you. I'm sure you'll agree it's a small change to my orders."

Rand shoved his parachute into the back

seat. "Disobeying orders is never a good choice."

"Well." Clint winked. "I'll remember that next time."

"McGowan, do you know why you were instructed to stay on the road?"

"Just regulations?"

Rand got into the truck and shut the door. "No. There's a reason for every rule. This area out here is rocky. Some of these rocks are sharp enough to split a tire. A tire that you'd have to change. On a truck. Which would take time. And what if there was a fire? Every second is valuable to a smoke jumper, McGowan."

"Sure, but..." He kept driving toward the road.

"As a trainer the first thing I look for in a recruit is obedience."

"Sir?"

Rand scrutinized the kid more carefully. He was a bit on the puny side as firefighters went. And he smiled too much, as if he was hiding something. "Why did you decide to become a smoke jumper?"

"My dad's in Redmond, Oregon."

"He's a jumper?"

"Yes, sir. He's the best."

Rand lifted his chin and narrowed his

eyes. There was something about this kid that reminded him of Perry Shoal. This time he wasn't going to be duped. "Let me guess. He wanted you to become a firefighter."

"Sure does. My granddaddy was a firefighter, too. I come from a long line of 'em."

Rand kept his eyes on Clint. He noticed the guy had dropped his smile. "What do you like most about firefighting?"

"The trees. The flowers and the foliage. All of it."

"Yeah. I know that feeling."

"You do?"

"Uh-huh," Rand agreed. "But there are other ways to appreciate the trees and the flowers."

Clint draped his wrist over the steering wheel now that they were on the smooth road. "Now that you mention it, if I had my way, I'd be a landscaper. I love working with all kinds of shrubbery and flowers. Back home, I laid out a circular patio for my mom and then I surrounded it with five varieties of lavender and purple impatiens and deep purple irises. She couldn't believe it. I designed and built it with my own hands. Paid for it, too, from my summer job."

"Where was that?"

"At a local nursery. They had six massive

greenhouses. All built right after World War Two. Glass ceilings. Glass walls. At Christmas we imported a thousand poinsettias. Red ones, pink, white, speckled and striped. Man, I loved that place."

"You should go back there," Rand said firmly.

"Sorry?"

"Take my advice. Don't do this job just to please your father or your grandfather. My dad was an admiral in the navy. I always knew he dreamed of me becoming a navy man like him. But that's not what I wanted. He died when I was young. He wasn't around when I made my choice to become a firefighter. But you know what? I'm sure he would have been proud of me."

"Really? How?" Clint glanced at him seriously and then turned his eyes back to the road.

"He loved me. Does your father love you?"

"Oh, yes, sir. He does."

"Well, that's more than a lot of people have in their lives, isn't it?"

"I suppose so."

Rand rubbed his cheek. "I knew a guy like you once. He was my rookie. Maybe if I'd had this conversation with him back when he first started training, he'd be alive today."

"He's dead?"

Rand nodded. "He wasn't cut out to be a firefighter. I don't want that to happen to you. It takes a special kind of heart and will to do what we do. I'm not saying we're special, but we are different. Just like what you love to do is different from the guy who wants to be a banker. It's important to follow your heart." Rand paused.

Who was he talking to just now? Clint or himself? Had he been following his heart when he'd dropped everything in Indian Lake and flown to Idaho? Yeah, he'd answered the call to fulfill his innate sense of duty. But had it been what his heart wanted?

Rand's eyes slipped to Clint. "You understand what I'm saying?"

Clint was silent for a long moment. "Yes. I do."

"Good. Then I'll expect your resignation in the morning."

Clint smiled slowly, but it eventually filled his face as he beamed at Rand. "How about tonight?"

RAND FINISHED HIS second jump, handed in his data to the director and went to his bunk. He'd left his cell phone with the ringer off under his pillow, as he always did.

He'd spoken to his mother the day before and he hadn't been expecting any calls.

So when he punched in his code he was surprised to find that he had a voice mail.

He read the number of the caller and stared at the phone for a long moment.

Inexplicably, his hand trembled as he pressed the screen to listen to her message.

"Rand…"

That was it. The call ended.

He touched the screen again and listened. "Rand…"

She hadn't left him a message. But she *had* called him, and on his new government-issued cell phone, which could only mean that she'd gotten the number from his mother.

Beatrice had talked to his mother. Why?

If Beatrice truly didn't want anything to do with him, then why had she sought out his mother? Or had they simply run into each other at the grocery or pharmacy?

Did it matter? Beatrice had his new number.

And she'd attempted to call him.

Her impulse had been to connect with him, something he wanted as well.

He flopped back on the cot and put his arm under his head. He stared at the ceiling. The tiles were stained and needed replacing.

Just like the ceiling over his bed at the last base camp.

Was that what the future held for him? Being alone? Going from one training facility to another? Sure, he was making a mark on the future for others, but what did he want? What was best for *him*?

He'd believed Beatrice when she'd said she didn't want to see him again. He'd retaliated by telling her to leave him, because he didn't want to admit how painful those words were to him.

They'd agreed they were incompatible, and after that he'd thought there'd been no more to say to each other.

He'd been wrong.

CHAPTER TWENTY-FIVE

"WHO'S GOING TO water the trees when we're gone?" Eli asked Beatrice as she poured a stream of water from an old watering can she'd bought at the Goodwill store several years ago.

"Yeah," Chris said, dousing the tallest sapling they'd planted. "You're going to be all alone out here and there's a lot to do to run a place like this."

"You're right, Chris. It's almost like taking care of a farm, though without the animals. It would be very hard on me if I had to milk cows every morning."

"Every morning? Even Saturdays and Sundays?" Eli rolled his eyes. "No way do I want to be a farmer."

"Well, now, Eli, don't be too hasty. There's all kinds of farmers. I was talking about dairy cows. You could be a farmer who grows only herbs. That's getting to be a big industry in America."

"What kind of burbs?"

"No," Chris corrected. "Herbs. Like basil and thyme." He lifted his eyes to Beatrice. "I like those ones."

"Really?" Beatrice watered another sapling. "Did Amanda show you those herbs?"

"Yes, but I also read about them in one of the firefighter magazines that Mr. Nelson gave me. They have recipes in the back." He dug a little moat around one of the droopier saplings then filled it with water.

"Where did you learn that trick?" she asked, kneeling next to him.

"Mr. Nelson." Chris lifted his face to look at her. "Why didn't he come say goodbye? I know you said he's got an important job now, but I thought he liked us." Chris kicked the dirt and a clod shot behind him. "I miss him."

Beatrice understood Chris's disappointment and loss. Rand was probably the first adult male Chris had ever come to trust. Rand's leaving had caused both boys to withdraw. She reached out to Chris and caressed his arm. "Chris, I told you, there wasn't enough time."

"Yeah, I miss him, too," Eli said, slipping his arm around Beatrice's shoulder and leaning his head down to her cheek.

"So do you think he'll ever come back?"

"I suppose he'd come to town to see

his family. His mother would miss him at Thanksgiving if he didn't."

"Thanksgiving?" the boys chorused.

"That's a long, long way off." Eli frowned.

"I was hoping he'd come home for Labor Day. This is a holiday," Chris offered. "Some of the other kids said they go to picnics and watch fireworks."

"I never celebrated a Labor Day like that," Eli said sadly.

Beatrice placed her palm on Eli's cheek. "This year you will. I have it all arranged with Miss Phillips for you both to go with me to Mrs. Beabots's Labor Day party."

"Why would you do that?" Chris asked, his eyes filled with surprise.

"I didn't want you to be alone for the holiday. And besides, I'd kinda be by myself if you didn't go with me. Did you ever think about that?"

"But you have the counselors and Miss Amanda."

"They'll be leaving this afternoon with the rest of the kids. Only Amanda will stay here overnight with us. Then she'll leave in the morning. Of course, Amanda and the counselors will all come back every weekend for the field trips and the day campers. But they have other weekly jobs and homes during the school year."

"Oh." Eli stared down at the saplings. "I didn't know that." He reached over and took her hand. "Then, really, you need us around here more than you thought."

Beatrice put the watering can down on the ground and pulled him into her arms. She reached over for Chris to join her. "Group hug," she said.

She knew exactly what the boys were asking. They wanted her to be their mother. She felt as if she already *was* their mother. Her eyes spilled with tears and a lump burned in her throat.

"Boys, I can't promise you the world, but what I will do is talk to Miss Phillips and see what we can do about you both coming out here on weekends through the fall. Though it will depend upon where they place you, of course."

"What if we have to move out of Indian Lake?" Chris asked, his voice cold and edgy.

That was a real possibility. How could she have allowed herself to fabricate daydreams of the boys being around through the fall? And the holidays? She'd gone so far as to think of the jackets and hats they'd need by Christmas. She'd bought puzzles and games, envisioned taking them ice-skating and sledding when the snow came.

She'd known she was setting herself up for heartbreak by including them in her daydreams. She'd never done that before with any of the other kids. Until these boys, she'd been so concentrated on the camp finances, the repairs and construction improvements, that she hadn't allowed herself to dream about personal happiness.

But something had happened to her the night of the fire. She'd been tested and she'd tested herself. She'd never had a brother or sister to look after or…to love. With no children of her own, she'd simply figured her maternal instincts were on hold.

But they'd come blasting out of her like the inferno that had raged around them that night. She hadn't thought about her personal safety when she'd charged into the fire. All she'd known was that Eli was in danger and she wanted to save him.

When she'd realized that Chris was somewhere in the burning forest, those instincts had gone into overdrive. She'd vowed not to rest, not to feel her own pain, until she'd been sure Chris was alive and unharmed.

In the midst of it all was Rand. Despite the

protective shields he erected around his own heart, she respected him and she loved him.

But she had no ties on him. They'd both agreed that was best.

He still harbored bone-deep grief over Perry Shoal's death. One of the traits she admired about Rand was that he took his responsibilities seriously. She did the same. Just as she did with Eli and Chris.

And she was guilty of manufacturing impossible fantasies that included these boys.

They were guilty of doing the same.

"Oh, Miss Beatrice," Eli cried and hugged her tight. "If we have to move, I'll miss you so much."

"I don't want to go, either," Chris said with a halting voice. He was struggling not to cry.

Beatrice felt painful fissures splinter across her heart.

She was well aware of the crisis that Zoey Phillips and other administrators in the Indiana foster care system were facing on a daily basis. There weren't enough homes for the nine thousand children already in foster care, let alone the newcomers. Zoey was barely able to keep up with the flow.

Siblings often had to be broken up in order to place them, but now they were also often parted by hundreds of miles.

Some parents worked diligently to prove to the courts they were fit parents and take their children back home with them. That would not be the case with Eli and Chris. Zoey said their father had indicated he'd relinquish his rights and the mother had vanished.

Beatrice had enlisted Trent Davis's help to locate the boys' mother, but even Trent, with all the resources of a detective, hadn't had any luck. Trent had said, "We've exhausted our attempts. This woman doesn't want to be found. She may not even be in the United States any longer."

Beatrice's heart went out to the woman who must have truly been in a dark place in order to feel that she had no other choice but to throw her children away.

But with both parents out of the picture and the incident with the fire, Zoey was having trouble placing them. Zoey had told Beatrice that as of this very morning, they still didn't have a foster family to take Eli and Chris. The summer was over and they would be expected to start school on Tuesday. They needed school supplies and new sneakers.

Mostly, they needed stability, love and safety. They needed a real home, not just a summer camp with games and kayaking.

They needed more than what Beatrice could give them.

"Boys," she said with as much assurance as she could muster. "I talk to Miss Phillips all the time. I'm hoping we can work something out with your new foster family. Maybe you'll be able to come out here on the weekends when I'm holding the botany field trips."

She held Eli's little hand. Funny. Over the weeks in camp, she'd thought he'd grown up so much. Matured. But now she realized how very young and vulnerable he was. Though his skin glowed with a bit of a tan, at this moment he looked pale and wan, as if he hadn't slept for several nights. Maybe he hadn't.

Chris, always his brother's protector, was looking at Eli, eyes older than they should be. What had the boy seen with those long-lashed deep violet eyes? Had he been watching when the police arrested his father? What had he been thinking during those traumatic moments? How many addicts had come and gone from his parents' apartment buying drugs? Had Chris seen his mother high? Eli had told Beatrice that their mother was always in bed and that she slept a lot. Chris was too street-smart not to realize the truth.

Chris was the kind of older brother who

would do everything in his power to keep the dark reality from Eli. The icy arrogance Chris displayed when they'd first come to camp was understandable. But once Rand had hacked through Chris's facade, the boy had revealed his true self. Though he carried his own code of honor, he was a loving boy, protective of anyone younger or weaker than he. With Rand's encouragement, Chris had already revealed the kind of noble attitude that befitted a firefighter—like Rand.

"Did Miss Phillips say she has a family for us?" Chris asked.

"Well, not quite yet," Beatrice admitted, pushing his dark hair off his forehead. Chris was going to be a very handsome man someday. Strangely, he seemed like a man in a boy's suit to her. Whereas Eli was all little boy, still filled with wonder and anticipation about life, Chris was already displaying his maturity. He'd seen the dark underbelly of life and, fortunately, he'd chosen to learn what not to do with his own life.

Chris had come to Beatrice's camp at just the right moment, when he'd needed to see another kind of life. She, Rand and the counselors had shown Chris that neglect, drugs and danger were his parents' choice. There was another way to live.

Beatrice had always envisioned the camp being more than simply games and water-safety classes. She'd wanted the kids to find friendship and guidance. To experience attention and affection. And most important, to discover their own value.

Though Chris and Eli had endured the harrowing experience of the fire and its aftermath, they had also grown in wisdom and experience.

And a good deal of that growth was due to Rand and his outpouring of generosity toward her, the boys and the camp.

Every kid had seen him working on the water lines.

They knew he didn't have to help, but he'd done it all willingly, and he'd even gone so far as to donate the cost of the pipe. The children saw a heart full of charity in action.

For the rest of their lives, they might not witness that kind of love again.

Beatrice felt guilt grow into a whirling gale inside her. She hadn't done enough to thank Rand. Sure, she'd tried to pay him back, and sure, she'd attempted to phone him.

But she'd restrained herself each time she'd felt the need to text him.

She told herself she was honoring their

decision to not pursue a relationship. She wanted him to be happy.

But she was miserable.

She couldn't make herself stop loving him. It was just there. Everywhere. Rand was on the other side of the country, and yet, she felt his presence smack-dab in the midst of her camp.

The boys admired him. They looked to him for guidance. She recognized now exactly what Rand had seen when he'd argued with Beatrice about what the wayward children needed.

The kind of guidance Rand had envisioned wasn't strictly discipline. It was loving guidance. It was a ball cap for a kid who didn't have one to shade his face from the sun. It was respect for a little sapling tree that required watering and a moat around it to grow. It was the satisfaction you got when you've accomplished a task and done it well.

She and Rand were so similar.

"What if Miss Zoey can't find us a home?" Chris asked. "Where will we live?" Eli's face contorted as he fought tears.

"Eli." She held his chin between her thumb and forefinger. "Listen to me. Miss Phillips is one of the best in the state. She's got all kinds of resources. You'd be amazed at what can happen between now and Tuesday morning."

Chris put his hand on her shoulder. "Miss Beatrice. She's had weeks to find us a home. We're not stupid. Nobody wants us. It's because of the fire."

She narrowed her eyes. "Don't you ever say that again, Chris." She knew her tone was scolding. "It's not you. And it has nothing to do with the fire. Don't take that guilt on yourself. The fire was an accident. You understand?"

"I shouldn't have gone to the woods to make the s'mores."

"No, you shouldn't. But that was misjudgment. I don't blame you for the fire. Mr. Nelson doesn't blame you, and neither does the entire Indian Lake Fire Department."

Chris shook his head. "Mr. Nelson said we had to make restitution."

"Yes, well, I talked to him about that. He admitted that he was too hard on you boys."

Eli touched Chris's arm. "He said we did make restitution by helping with the trenches. I believe Miss Beatrice." He looked at her. "Mr. Nelson felt bad for yelling at us, didn't he?"

"How did you know that?"

"Because he gave us the ball caps. And he

let me wear his own hat. And, Chris, he let you wear his gear. Remember?"

"Yeah."

"See? Mr. Nelson was showing us he was sorry."

"But he didn't *say* he was sorry," Chris muttered.

Beatrice touched Chris's cheek. "Your brother is very smart—and he's right. Rand is like my father was. A man of action. He doesn't say much, but he feels things deeply. He might not have said he was sorry, but he showed you instead. He showed you that he loved you."

"You think so?" Chris asked, his eyes growing wide.

She saw wonder shining in Chris's eyes. "I do."

"I want to thank him. I wish I could talk to him." A smile bloomed over his face. "I know! I could write him a letter."

Eli's face filled with discouragement. "I can't write a letter. I've never written a letter."

Beatrice smiled at them both. "A letter is a fine idea. A thank-you note. That's what we could do. Eli, you could paint a picture and that could be the front of the card. Then

I'll help you compose what you want to say for the inside."

"Awesome," Chris said and high-fived his brother.

"Yes." She smiled and stood up. "A fine idea." *I just might do the same thing myself.* She picked up the watering can. "Come on. We need to fill these cans back up and get the rest of the saplings watered before we start that thank-you note."

As they walked across the road and toward the camp, Eli said, "We should help with your chores, Miss Beatrice. You still walk kinda wobbly."

"It's only been one day since the doctor took this new boot off. It feels lighter not having anything on my leg. Kinda funny, actually."

"But you're all healed, right?"

"The doctor says I am."

"I'm sorry you got hurt," Chris said lowly, not raising his head to look at her.

She put her arm over his shoulder. "It was an accident, Chris. Accidents happen to people. Part of it was my own fault."

"How do you figure?"

"Rand said that if I'd stayed away from the fire and let the professionals do their job, I wouldn't have been injured. I'm afraid I'm the guilty party here, Chris."

"Still…"

"Stop. Okay? Let's forget it and put it behind us. Besides, I'm doing just fine now. And who knows? In a couple weeks, I could be running sprints."

"Sure, you will," Eli chuckled.

"I can run very fast when I want to, Eli. I ran like the wind when I saw you in that fire."

"Yeah. You did. And I'm glad." He lifted his hand and slipped it in hers as they walked. "Real glad."

"So am I, Eli. So am I."

CHAPTER TWENTY-SIX

LATE AFTERNOON ON the Friday before the Labor Day weekend brought a bank of rain clouds over the camp as the Kettering sisters waved goodbye to Beatrice and Maisie.

"That's the last of them," Maisie said. "Except for Eli and Chris, of course."

Beatrice watched the Ketterings' black Mercedes disappear down the country road. She glanced up to the sky. "I can't believe it. We've needed rain all summer and now it looks like it's going to pour."

"But if we'd had a rainy summer, the kids would have been stuck in their cabins or in the dining room begging for activities and complaining they were bored. We were fortunate that they all had a summer to remember."

"They did, didn't they?" Beatrice sighed.

"And so did you, I'm thinking." Maisie winked. "You hear from Rand?"

"Uh, no."

"Why not?"

She shrugged her shoulders and hugged her arms around her middle. "Dunno."

Maisie lifted her chin and frowned. "I'm not buying it. I figured he would have been on the phone texting you every day."

"Why on earth would you say that?"

"Aw," she snorted. "Who could miss those looks he gave you."

"What looks?" She dropped her arms.

"Seriously?" Maisie's eyebrows rose. "How could you not notice? Were you too absorbed with the accounting books? The number of jars of peanut butter we ordered?"

Beatrice lowered her eyes.

Maisie slapped her clipboard to her right thigh. "I have to pack my gear. I have orientation at my new job in a couple hours."

"What new job? I thought you were teaching this semester."

"I am. But this is a second job."

"Maisie, the camp is your second job. Weekends this fall, remember."

"I know that. This is, er, uh, for after school. Sorta."

Maisie blushed and glanced back at her clipboard.

"You're helping out that wholesaler. Whazzis name again?" she asked jokingly. "You're not talking about a job, are you?"

"Hey! You tell me what guy isn't work?" Maisie giggled and jogged in reverse toward the women's counselor cabin. "I'll email you a report."

The Labor Day holiday brought the closing of the camp for the summer. The kids had been picked up by their parents earlier in the afternoon. The counselors would leave that evening. Only Beatrice, Amanda, Eli and Chris would remain over the weekend. Beatrice hoped by Tuesday, they'd have word from Zoey Phillips about a foster home for the boys.

Beatrice walked around the back of the dining hall to check on Bruce, who was securing the kayaks on stainless-steel racks. She walked up to him as he adjusted a red strap with the ratchet. "Next summer, I'd love to have a little boathouse to protect the kayaks from the weather instead of just tarps and straps."

"We move them into the dining hall, and they do all right. But I get what you mean. It's never-ending, isn't it?" he asked.

"What?"

"The improvements."

"I know. The minute I think I'm ahead, something else pops up or becomes a necessity. But the kids deserve the best."

"And you'll make sure they get it." He smiled.

"I'm trying. Once you get this done, you can head on out as well."

"Cindy's gone?"

"Yes. She left an hour ago. Maisie is about packed."

"All right, then. I'll see you next weekend." He glanced across the little lake. "It was a good summer. Fire and all."

"It was."

She walked away.

It had been a wonderful summer. It was the summer she'd fallen in love.

She started up the steps of her cabin when she heard the roar of a truck's tires against the gravel in the camp drive. Glancing over her shoulder, she saw Rand's monster black Toyota Tundra.

She grasped the railing for support, her hand trembling. Her heart froze.

I should drop dead right now. Maybe I'm already dead. I'm seeing things. Mirages. Illusions.

He got out of the truck. He was wearing black slacks, black boots and a black short-sleeved knit shirt with a banded collar as he stomped across the gravel, the stones spitting out from under the heels of his boots as he strode purposefully toward her.

What was he doing here? She thought he'd moved away forever.

"Beatrice!" he called.

Her mouth was dry. She could barely speak. "Y-yes?"

"You called me and you didn't leave a message," he said.

"Oh, that…"

"Didn't you want to talk to me?"

"It was a butt dial."

"Was not," he retorted. He came to a stop on the step below hers. "You meant to call me. You said my name. Then you hung up."

"It was a mistake."

"Why?" He moved even closer, and as he did she noticed his eyes twinkled with merriment, as if he had a secret he was dying to share.

And was that a glimmer of a smile on his lips?

"Because—"

Stop, Beatrice! she scolded herself. *Don't tell him how much you miss him. How much you love him.*

He'd only tell her again that they were better off being apart. She stared at him. But then, if he thought that, why was he here?

Besides, she knew now she had to take the risk. She lifted her chin. "Because I wanted to tell you…"

He reached out and gently took her hand. His eyes gleamed with a soft light that gave her hope.

"Tell me what, Bee?" he asked in that velvet tone she remembered he'd used right before he'd kissed her.

She blinked and tried to put her thoughts in order again.

"How—how much I appreciated everything you did for me. That I want to pay you back. I went to the bank and I got a check. I'll make good on the rest—in time."

The lights in his eyes danced with a bit of delight. "I heard all about that. I talked to my mother."

"She told you about our visit?"

"She did. She also told me what a dolt I've been. But by the time I talked to Mom, I already knew I'd made the wrong decision."

"Wrong?"

"Everything about it was wrong. First of all, I made it too quickly. You scared the living daylights out of me, Bee."

Her lips parted as she started to speak, but he put his fingers over her lips.

"Don't say anything. I need to apologize

to you, probably every day for the rest of my life. I should never have left. You had to feel abandoned. Betrayed. Here I was telling you that I would never hurt my family because they mean so much to me. But I treated you abominably and you're the one I love with all my heart. I don't blame you if you hate me forever." He lowered his hand but his eyes still probed her face, her every flinch and blink as if trying to read her mind. "But I hope you don't."

She was in shock. Disbelief.

"What did you just say?" She felt a lightness fly through her being.

"You have every right to hate me."

"No, the other thing. The loving me thing." She felt giddy, as if she'd spun around and around with her arms spread out like the kids did on the grass before they all fell down laughing.

"I love you, Bee. I think I fell in love with you when I saw you run into that fire."

"You said I was foolish and rash to do that."

"I said a lot of things because I didn't or couldn't face the truth. I was afraid. I've been smoke jumping from one end of the country to the other because I've been scared."

"Because of what happened with Perry."

"Yes. Because of my guilt. My past. That's what I told you I was doing. But the real truth was that I was running away from loving you." He moved up the step and put his arms around her. "I can be that guy you want. I don't have to fight fires. I'd rather change my lifestyle, Bee, than be without you. These past two weeks apart from you was just about more than I could stand. I want you to be happy. I want to be the guy who makes you happier than you've ever been."

"Rand, I can't do that."

He stiffened. "You can't love me or you won't love me?"

She held her palm on his strong jaw and rubbed the faint stubble on his cheek with her thumb. "Silly. I'll love you 'til the day I die. I can't not love you—I realized that these few weeks without *you*. What I meant was that I don't want you to change anything for me. You are the most unique individual I've ever met. Without you and people like you, this camp, people's homes and businesses wouldn't exist. Folks in this town need you to protect them and look out for their welfare. I wouldn't dream of taking you away from that calling. If anyone needs to change around here, it's me. I've come to that revelation. I meant it when I said you remind me of my father, and I was proud of his courage and commitment to others. For a while, I forgot how proud I was of him. You were right, I took on my mother's fears. But I can't live in fear anymore. A person can die from the flu. A car accident. It's all a matter of fate. I want to live every day I have with you."

"You mean that, sweetheart?"

"I do," she assured him. Her thumb touched the edge of his lips. "But I have to say, I don't like the idea of you being gone so much. I missed you these past few weeks. A lot, really. Even when I thought you never wanted to see me again."

He lowered his face toward hers until their noses touched. "I've been an idiot. And you can tell me so anytime you want. I deserve it."

"Idiot."

"Thanks."

His lips pressed against hers, tentatively at first, as if he was testing the truth of her words. But when she put her arms around his neck and leaned into him, he deepened the kiss. The thrill of his mouth against her lips and the remembered taste of him ignited a warmth inside her that burst through her body like a bolt of lightning striking dry kindling. This kiss might end, but her love for him was everlasting.

Rand might have jumped from a plane into life-threatening fires, but Beatrice jumped into Rand's love with her body, mind and soul. There was nothing she wouldn't give him. Nothing she wouldn't do for him.

When he tore his lips from hers, she grabbed his face with both palms and pulled him to her for another kiss. She would never tire of being in his arms and she wanted him to know it.

When she pulled away, Rand rested his forehead against hers. "There's only one thing, Bee."

"Name it," she whispered, wondering if she'd ever catch her breath again, and at the same time she couldn't wait for him to take her breath away once more.

"Promise you'll marry me?"

"Oh, Rand. Are you sure? Very sure?"

"As sure as the sun burns and the moon glows."

"Yes!" She kissed him again as he put his hands on her face. "I will."

"You've made me so happy," he laughed. "I didn't believe I could feel this kind of joy."

"I think we'll always bring each other joy," she said.

"I believe you," he replied.

"Good. Because I have an idea." She smiled at him, love and joy bursting inside her like fireworks.

CHAPTER TWENTY-SEVEN

Labor Day

MRS. BEABOTS'S 130-YEAR-OLD Victorian house was decorated with pots of red geraniums, white impatiens and blue salvia. Tiny American flags had also been planted throughout the front gardens. She'd draped red-and-white-striped festoons along the white railings on the front porch. The wind caught an enormous American flag and blew it out from an extended pole attached to the third-floor gable.

Cars not only filled the driveway all the way back to the "carriage house"—which Luke Bosworth had converted into a garage—but were also along both sides of Maple Boulevard. A line of couples and families walked toward the house carrying food to share, children's toys and gifts for the hostess.

As promised, Beatrice had checked with Mrs. Beabots and made certain Eli and Chris were invited as well. Since the boys had become friends with Annie and Timmy Bos-worth, as well as Danny Sullivan, who was the first to sign up for her new fall day-camp weekends, both Beatrice and Rand knew the boys would have a good time.

From the back seat of Rand's truck, Chris was staring out the window at all the cars. Eli, in a car seat that Rand had installed, took one look at the police station that was across the street from Mrs. Beabots's house and whistled. "Wow. She lives close to the cops!"

"That's right," Rand said. "Better be on your best behavior today."

Beatrice turned to face Eli. "Don't let him tease you. Honestly, Rand." She clucked her tongue. "Besides, the boys already know Danny Sullivan's father, Trent Davis, and he's a cop."

"Detective," Rand corrected.

"And he's famous," Chris added. "Every-body knows he arrested the entire Le Grande drug gang."

Beatrice laid her hand over the seat and rested her chin on it. "And how did you hear about that?"

"Danny showed us the article that ap-peared in the newspaper about him last sum-mer."

"Is that right?" Rand asked.

"It is. And the article was written by Mr. Abbot. He's married to Isabelle, and her sister, Violet, is a cop, too. She's going to be at the party," Chris informed them.

"You sure know a lot more about this party than I do," Beatrice remarked.

Eli put his fingers over his mouth and giggled. "And we know something else you don't."

"Hey!" Rand said, quite gruffly, glancing in the rearview mirror and shaking his head at the boys. Then he quickly smiled at Beatrice.

"We're here!" He pulled the truck into an open parking place a block away.

Eli whistled again. "Wow. Look at all these cars! Mrs. Beabots sure has a lot of friends."

Rand unbuckled his seat belt. "Any woman who bakes as well as she does would absolutely have lots of friends," he joked.

Beatrice playfully punched him in the shoulder. "I brought a basket of blondies. I bake pretty well myself."

"Blondies?" Rand asked. "To match your pretty hair?"

"No, they're salted caramel brownies."

"No kidding. Well, I'm all over that," he said and leaned over to kiss her.

Eli and Chris made smooching sounds to each other.

"All right, enough." Rand got out of the truck. "Bee, I'll get the roaster of pulled pork if you get the kids." He hoisted the roaster with both hands and piled the blondies on the roaster lid.

Beatrice helped Eli out of his car seat. She walked with the boys over to Rand and together they went up to the Victorian house.

"One person lives in this huge house? By *herself*?" Eli asked.

"Yes," Beatrice said, turning the tinny bell in the middle of the beveled glass and walnut wood door. "Though she does rent the third-floor apartment out from time to time."

"Wow." Chris took in the abundant gardens, the wide screened-in porch and the Boston ferns with wide eyes. "I've never seen anything like this before."

"Is this how really old people live?" Eli asked.

"Not many people live like Mrs. Beabots," Beatrice answered.

"But like most people, she loves my pulled pork," Rand said.

"Of course she does."

Beatrice heard the sound of footsteps— quite a few footsteps—coming to the door.

"She brings pies to the firefighter fund-raisers and I make the pulled pork. It's my secret recipe."

"What's the secret?" Beatrice asked.

He grinned. "Love."

Eli and Chris made smooching sounds again. They smiled at Rand.

Rand glared at them as the door opened.

"Hello!" Mrs. Beabots said, flinging back the door. She was dressed in navy slacks and a red-and-white-striped silk blouse with a big navy bow at the neck. She wore blue sapphires in her ears. "Welcome!"

Behind her were Annie, Timmy, Danny, and three other children around the same age. Luke and Sarah's toddler, Charlotte, came up, too, and behind her was another baby just about a year old holding a very stylishly dressed blonde woman's hand. "We all came to greet you to your first Labor Day party at my house!" Mrs. Beabots said happily as she reached out to hug Beatrice.

The kids rushed to greet Eli and Chris, dragging them inside to show them around.

Mrs. Beabots turned and put out her hand to the pretty blonde woman. "Beatrice Wilcox and Rand Nelson, this is Grace Barzonni. This is her son, Jules. They just flew in all the way from Paris with Jules's daddy,

Mica. Just for my party! Isn't that wonderful?" Mrs. Beabots clapped her hands and kissed Grace's cheek.

"I'm so happy to meet you." Grace smiled and shook Beatrice's hand. "Mrs. Beabots, if you'll take Jules, I'll help Rand with this roaster."

"No way," Rand said. "I'll take it to the kitchen. Just straight down the hall, as I remember."

"It is, Rand." Mrs. Beabots shut the door behind Beatrice.

"He knows his way around, huh?" Beatrice asked.

"Good heavens, yes. Rand was kind enough to drive me to a couple fund-raisers for the firefighters last spring." She put her arm around Beatrice's waist. "Come in and meet everyone you don't know, Beatrice."

Grace picked up Jules. "He's just learning to walk," Grace said. "I'm afraid if he takes to it as fast as he took to crawling, he'll be running across our apartment in no time."

Beatrice couldn't take her eyes off the beautiful dark-haired baby boy with the Mediterranean blue eyes. He wore a navy-and-white suit that reminded her of a Victorian sailor suit from over a hundred years ago. "Children dress differently in Paris, huh?"

"Actually, they do. But this is from my new children's clothes line I'm designing."

"It's fantastic. And the detail," Beatrice said, pointing to the red piping around the middy collar. "You're so talented. Gosh. Paris! I've always wanted to see it."

Grace beamed brightly. "I'd love for you to come and visit. Truthfully, Mica and I are trying to get the whole family to come for Christmas."

Beatrice dropped her smile in surprise. "The entire Barzonni family?"

"Sure. Why not? And I'm serious about you visiting. I would be thrilled to have a friend from Indian Lake come to see us. There's so much history. So much fun!" she gushed.

"I—I never thought about traveling to Europe." Beatrice looked at Jules, who had placed an openmouthed kiss on Grace's cheek. Grace kissed him back twice. He giggled and kissed her again. "I should think about it."

"You should," Grace said as she walked with Beatrice into the dining room.

The dining table was decorated in silver candlesticks, red, white and blue candles and a huge crystal vase of white hydrangeas. On top of a white linen tablecloth was just about every summer food she could have imagined. Hamburgers and hot dogs, a spiral ham, all kinds of salad, mounds of pickles, stuffed peppers, sliced beefsteak tomatoes, watermelon wedges, a crystal bowl of summer fruit and four pies.

"There's more food in the kitchen, if you can believe it," Rand said, coming up to Beatrice.

Just then Zoey Phillips walked up to Rand and Beatrice. She handed Beatrice three folded sheets of paper. "It's done."

Beatrice looked at Rand, who grabbed her and pulled her close. "I told you. Believe in me."

"I do. I will. Always."

Gabe Barzonni came out of the living room. Spotting Rand, he walked up to him and slapped him on the back. "Rand! Glad to see you. I'm going out to the kitchen for a bottle of a new pinot noir we corked last fall. Care to try it?"

"Love to."

Gabe leaned over to Beatrice. "Liz is excited about your weekend day camp for Zeke. During harvest we have zero time for him."

Beatrice smiled. "I'm going to love having him with us."

"Aw." Gabe swatted the air with his palm. "I bet you say that about all the kids."

Rand smiled at Beatrice. "Actually, Gabe, you're right. She loves kids. But there are some that are very special."

"No wine for me. I'm driving back. I'll have tea," Beatrice said. "But we have something we want to celebrate with everyone."

The doorbell rang again. Mrs. Beabots placed a casserole dish of macaroni and cheese on the table on her way to the door. She winked at Rand. "I'll get it."

Rand winked back.

She scurried away.

"I'll help her." Rand followed Mrs. Beabots, leaving Beatrice wondering why Mrs. Beabots and Rand were acting strangely.

Then she heard more familiar voices coming from the foyer.

"We're so happy you invited us, Mrs. Beabots," Laura said. "My crew is all here. Even Cassie. She's the one on the motorcycle."

Beatrice excused herself from Grace and Gabe and went to the foyer. Rand's entire family filled the entrance.

"Laura." Beatrice went to her and hugged her. "I didn't know you were coming."

"It's a surprise." Mrs. Beabots smiled as

she took a coconut cake from Laura. "This looks yummy. I'll just put it in the kitchen."

"We brought sodas and beer," David and Ed chorused.

"I've got chips and salsa," Jonas added. "I stopped at the marina mini-mart."

"All good." Rand leaned over to kiss his mother's cheek. "Come on in, Mom. I want to introduce you to everybody. And with this crowd, that's going to take some time."

Beatrice hugged Cassie and Rand's brothers, who then went to the kitchen to deposit their drinks.

Rand introduced Laura to Grace, Jules and Zoey. Together they walked to the entrance of the living room. Grace took Jules and sat next to Mica, who had saved her a space on an enormous beige, bullion-fringed ottoman.

All the children were in the middle of the living-room floor playing with hand puppets. Beatrice noticed that Chris was patiently demonstrating to Timmy how to work the delicate paddles and strings of what looked like an antique French harlequin puppet on his right hand.

"Chris? How do you know so much about how to work that puppet?"

"There was a book in the library at the

camp." He went back to working with Timmy.

Once again, Beatrice was hit with gratitude for the experiences her camp offered to kids—the experiences all camps offered to kids. Who knew how many children across the country would have their perspectives enhanced by a book they read, a game they played or a skill they'd learned at a summer camp? Those idyllic days when a person was removed from their normal habitat were very important.

While Rand introduced his mother, brothers and sister to everyone, Beatrice gazed around the room at all the familiar faces. Sarah and Luke, of course. Liz and Gabe Barzonni. Nate and Maddie Barzonni. Louise Railton, who owned the Louise House Ice Cream Shop. Olivia and Rafe Barzonni. Chloe Knowland, who worked for Maddie and lived with her aunt and uncle in the house behind Mrs. Beabots. Gina Barzonni Crenshaw and her new husband, Sam, Liz's father, sat next to Katia and Austin McCreary. The entire Hawks family—Connie, Sadie, Violet, Christopher, Dylan and Ross—stood together behind Isabelle Hawks Abbot, her husband, Scott, and their adopted children, Michael and Bella. Cate Sullivan Davis sat on her husband's lap as space was getting tight, though the room was very large, as they watched the kids with the puppets.

"That old puppet is older than I am," Mrs. Beabots said. "I found it in a flea market near Les Halles."

"Really?" Grace asked. "I wonder if it's still there. Honey, we should go look. Jules would love to play with a puppet like that."

"Absolutely," Mica replied and kissed her temple. "Anything you want."

He mouthed, *I love you*.

Grace kissed him.

Beatrice felt her heart leap due to all the love and friendship in this house.

"I love you," Rand said, slipping his hand around her waist and pulling her into his side.

She dropped her head back, hoping the smile in her heart shone through in her eyes. "I love you, too. More than you know."

"That's really good, because..."

He slipped his hand off her waist and down to her hand as he pulled her to the middle of the room. "Everybody, may I have your attention."

"Rand, what are you doing?"

"Shh." He lifted his wineglass. "I don't mean to break up the puppet show, but, kids, we'll get back to you in a minute."

"Rand?" she asked, feeling a bit uncomfortable with everyone in the room watching them.

He turned to her and kissed her quickly. Without another word he handed his wineglass to Gabe, who winked at Rand and grinned broadly.

"What's going on?" she asked.

Rand stuck his hand in his pocket as he sank to one knee. She leaned down a bit and whispered, "You've already proposed."

He whispered back, "Yeah, but now I have witnesses." He grinned.

He withdrew a diamond ring and held it out to her. "Beatrice, no one could love you more than I do. Marry me. Be my wife. Always and forever."

"Yes. Yes!"

The room burst into laughter, with the Barzonni family making the most noise.

"See, Mica?" Gabe said. "You gotta have the ring. No question."

Rafe hugged Olivia. "I got that part."

Beatrice leaned down and took Rand's strong face in her hands, "I love you to the ends of the earth, my hero. Yes. I will be your wife. I can't wait to be your wife."

Rand shot to his feet and kissed her.

"Give her the ring!" Nate urged.

"Oh, the ring!" Rand slid the ring on her finger. It was a perfect fit. "I hope you like it."

Beatrice looked down at the round cut antique ring. "It's so beautiful and very unique."

"Rand had help with that one," Mrs. Beabots said, coming over to kiss them both on the cheek. "It had to be something very, very special for such an extraordinary lady." She smiled.

Beatrice's eyes flew to Rand. "This looks..." She lowered her voice to a whisper. "Really old." Her eyes slid to Mrs. Beabots, who was smiling far too broadly.

Had Mrs. Beabots given Rand this antique ring?

"Shh," Rand whispered. "We'll talk about it later."

Mrs. Beabots winked at Beatrice. "Thank you for all you do for the children, Beatrice. You have an abundant heart. And it has not gone unnoticed."

Rand kissed Beatrice and the room exploded into applause and whistles.

"I love you, Rand."

He leaned forward and whispered, "Tonight too soon to get married? Maybe Mrs. Beabots could arrange that if we asked her."

"Good thinking."

Out of the corner of her eye, Beatrice

saw Zoey as she went over to Eli and Chris, who had been clapping as hard as any of the adults.

Beatrice nodded to Zoey and the other woman nodded back.

"I can't thank you all enough for sharing in our joy," Beatrice said, squeezing Rand's hand.

"But," Rand said, "we have another announcement to make. Though the ring makes it official about our engagement, Zoey was the first in town to know about our plans to marry. And the reason she was the first was because…"

Beatrice looked at Eli and Chris and realized their smiles held anxiety. They loved Rand and they loved her. Rand had obviously told the boys about his plan to present her with a ring that night. But their future was still a mystery to them. She wanted to rectify that.

"Not only will Beatrice and I become foster parents for Eli and Chris, but we are petitioning for adoption."

Beatrice held up the papers that Zoey had given her. "Our papers were officially filed on Saturday. We aren't wasting any time to be a real family."

The room exploded into more applause.

Each of the Barzonni brothers bounded forward and slapped Rand on the back, then he hugged and kissed Beatrice. Rand's brothers were next in line, whooping even louder. Half the women burst into tears. Mrs. Beabots went to the bathroom to get boxes of tissues. The first box was for herself.

Rand gazed down at Eli and Chris.

The poor kids looked shell-shocked.

"If you adopt us, does that mean we stay with you forever?" Eli asked.

"Well, until you're all grown up. And then you'll want to have your own home."

"No, I won't," Eli replied and rushed to them both, throwing his arms around them and crushing his head into Beatrice's stomach.

Chris was slower to approach. "And this is legal?"

"It will be," Rand replied. "We have a great deal of paperwork to do. We have to get permission from your father. Jail or no jail."

"I understand," Chris said hesitantly. He looked up. "But you want us?"

Rand put his hand on Chris's head and pulled him into an embrace. "More than you know."

"Me, too," Chris replied and stretched his arms around Rand.

Beatrice glanced down at the boys and then up at Rand. Tears rolled down her cheeks, but they were happy tears. "I've always said, group hugs are the best."

"I have to agree, my love." Rand kissed her forehead and pulled both boys in tighter. "They are the best."

* * * * *

Get 4 FREE REWARDS!

We'll send you 2 FREE Books plus 2 FREE Mystery Gifts.

Love Inspired® books feature contemporary inspirational romances with Christian characters facing the challenges of life and love.

FREE
Value Over
$20

Get 4 FREE REWARDS!

We'll send you 2 FREE Books plus 2 FREE Mystery Gifts.

Love Inspired® Suspense books feature Christian characters facing challenges to their faith... and lives.

FREE Value Over $20

HOME on the RANCH

YES! Please send me the **Home on the Ranch Collection** in Larger Print. This collection begins with 3 FREE books and 2 FREE gifts in the first shipment. Along with my 3 free books, I'll also get the next 4 books from the Home on the Ranch Collection, in LARGER PRINT, which I may either return and owe nothing, or keep for the low price of $5.24 U.S./ $5.89 CDN each plus $2.99 for shipping and handling per shipment*. If I decide to continue, about once a month for 8 months I will get 6 or 7 more books, but will only need to pay for 4. That means 2 or 3 books in every shipment will be FREE! If I decide to keep the entire collection, I'll have paid for only 32 books because 19 books are FREE! I understand that accepting the 3 free books and gifts places me under no obligation to buy anything. I can always return a shipment and cancel at any time. My free books and gifts are mine to keep no matter what I decide.

268 HCN 3760 468 HCN 3760

Name	(PLEASE PRINT)

Address	Apt. #

City	State/Prov.	Zip/Postal Code

Signature (if under 18, a parent or guardian must sign)

Mail to the **Reader Service**:

IN U.S.A.: P.O. Box 1341, Buffalo, New York 14240-8531
IN CANADA: P.O. Box 603, Fort Erie, Ontario L2A 5X3

Get 4 FREE REWARDS!

We'll send you 2 FREE Books plus 2 FREE Mystery Gifts.

Harlequin® Special Edition books feature heroines finding the balance between their work life and personal life on the way to finding true love.

FREE
Value Over
$20